THE TRAIN

SARAH BOURNE

BLOODHOUND
— BOOKS —

Copyright © 2021 Sarah Bourne
The right of Sarah Bourne to be identified as the Author of the Work has been
asserted by her in accordance to the Copyright, Designs and Patents Act 1988.
First published in 2021 by Bloodhound Books.
Apart from any use permitted under UK copyright law, this publication may
only be reproduced, stored, or transmitted, in any form, or by any means, with
prior permission in writing of the publisher or, in the case of reprographic
production, in accordance with the terms of licences issued by the Copyright
Licensing Agency.
All characters in this publication are fictitious and any resemblance to real
persons, living or dead, is purely coincidental.
www.bloodhoundbooks.com

Print ISBN 978-1-913942-42-7

1

JUDITH

She hadn't told anyone about Lawrence leaving her. Who would she tell? Her mother would only say that all men were the same, selfish and uncaring. And she certainly couldn't tell her friend, Deidra, given that she was married to him.

'I shouldn't have done that to my friend,' she said out loud to the bathroom mirror. She shrugged. 'But I wanted him. I couldn't help myself.' She sighed. 'He said it was the same for him.' She gave a strangled laugh. 'What a load of shit.'

He was a bastard and a liar.

She took a deep breath and looked at herself. She didn't like what she saw; frown lines beginning to crease her forehead, mouth downturned, sadness – no, yearning – in her red-rimmed eyes. A sob rose from deep in her belly. She tried to quash it but it rolled up and out in a series of gasping breaths making her double over, hugging herself tight.

Finally, she stood upright again, pulled her shoulders back and lifted her chin. Only days ago that would have made her feel stronger, able to face the world, but who was she kidding? She had no energy anymore for pretence. She'd been trying so hard for so long.

She'd spent her school years trying to recede into the background and shut her ears to the taunts. Even though no one could call her overweight these days she had never been able to drown out the voice in her head that told her she was fundamentally unacceptable.

In some ways, that was no bad thing. It had motivated her to work hard at university and she got a good degree. She tended to develop interests that had nothing to do with how she looked or whether other people approved of her. She was an accomplished ukulele player, for example, even before the recent craze for the instrument. And she had been fostering injured animals and nursing them back to health for years. Needing to get fit, she'd signed up to the local cycle club and had enjoyed the evening rides in the summer but they only met at weekends during the winter and she worked Saturdays and Sundays.

On bad days the negative commentary in her head made her hide from the world and doubt her abilities and even whether she deserved to be alive.

'Depression's in our family,' her mother used to say when she was having one of her low periods. The message being, *'just get over it.'* And Judith did, usually. Eventually. She had become adept at chasing her bleak thoughts away and distracting herself with work. Now she was so tired of it all. Of having to constantly battle her feelings of inadequacy. She felt herself sinking into the murky pit of despair.

At four thirty in the morning, she rang and left a message to say she had a cold and wouldn't be in. Her job wasn't important. No one would die if she wasn't there. Most people wouldn't even notice. She felt another sob rising and gulped it down. When had self-pity ever made anything better?

Her thoughts turned to Lawrence again. And from him to all the other men who had let her down. Her father, who had walked out when she was three and whom she'd never seen again. Steve, the boy she had a crush on when she was thirteen, who never noticed her. Fergal, to whom she'd lost her virginity at sixteen in a squalid squat with his friends shooting up in the next room. In her twenties there had been a couple of relationships. She'd gone out with Wayne for three years. He managed a local café and talked about wanting to have a family, but when Judith suggested moving in together he ran a mile. Several miles. He moved to Cheshire. After him there was Keith. He might have stuck around if he hadn't died of a massive heart attack when he was out running one day. Since him there had been no one until Lawrence. She'd met him through his wife.

She'd first spoken to Deidra at the hairdresser's in town one day. Judith didn't usually spend a lot of money on her hair, but she'd had a few good weeks at Brook's Property where she worked, including selling the dilapidated Bramley House for the full asking price, so she decided to splurge. She and Deidra got talking and became so engrossed in a conversation about the local animal sanctuary that they continued on for coffee at a nearby café. Since that day they'd met there regularly, always just the two of them. Over the weeks, Deidra had persuaded her to take more care of her appearance as if she was ashamed of being seen with someone as dowdy as Judith. So she'd become a regular at A Cut Above and at the neighbouring nail salon. She enjoyed her new-found glamour. It gave her a confidence she hadn't felt before.

And then one day, a man was waiting when they left the café.

'Oh, Lawrence, I didn't know you were coming into town.' She turned to Judith. 'This is my husband, Lawrence.'

Lawrence smiled tightly and took Deidra by the elbow.

'I wasn't going to, but you're later than you said you'd be so I thought I'd pick you up on the way. Don't want to keep the old boy waiting, do we?'

Deidra looked at her watch. 'We've got plenty of time. This is Judith Strasser. We both support the sanctuary. Judith actually volunteers there, caring for the animals.'

Lawrence swung his gaze to Judith.

'Just a day here and there.' She felt herself blush under his appraising gaze.

He had grey eyes, a healthy glow to his skin – probably from time spent on the golf course. 'How altruistic of you.' He shook her hand.

Afterwards, Judith couldn't stop thinking about Lawrence holding her hand just a moment longer than necessary. A strong hand. A firm grasp.

Two days later, she got a call, at home, late.

'Judith, Lawrence Kelly here.'

'Hello. Is everything all right? Nothing wrong with Deidra?'

'No, nothing like that. I just wanted to apologise – I was rather short when we met the other day. Other things on my mind. How about I take you out for a drink to apologise for it?'

'No need. Apology accepted.' She kicked herself. That's not what she meant at all.

Fortunately, there was a pause, and then, 'I know a quiet little pub off the Northampton Road that boasts a number of very nice boutique gins. How about I pick you up tomorrow at seven?'

And that was how it began. Lawrence not taking no for an answer and Judith flattered that anyone, particularly a good-looking man like Lawrence, would want to take her out. At first she was troubled by the fact that he was married to her friend, but were they really that close? It hadn't escaped Judith's notice that Deidra had introduced her as someone who worked at the shelter, not as a friend. Judith knew Deidra was the type of person who had two tiers of friendship; those acquaintances she saw during the day and those friends who got invited to the dinner parties she hosted, or the weekend gatherings she was always talking about. There was now no doubt where Judith stood in Deidra's system.

She sighed and headed down the stairs. Had a part of her always known Lawrence was using her, that she was one of his 'serial affairs' Deidra hinted at but seemed to have resigned herself to? No, Judith knew this was different. Not a sordid affair, although perhaps not love either. When they were together he was relaxed, entertaining, attentive. And even though the sex was average, he could give her what she wanted most in the world – a baby. She wanted a child to love and care for, who would love her back and make her feel needed. No one had ever needed her. Certainly no one had ever wanted her for very long. Not long enough for marriage and babies. She'd persuaded herself that if she got pregnant Lawrence would do the honourable thing – if not leave Deidra, at least be there when he could and support her and the baby financially.

All had gone well for a few months. They saw each other a couple of times a week, had dinner, sex, spoke a bit about his work, rarely hers.

Then last Friday he texted. Didn't even come and talk to her face to face.

I've enjoyed our meetings but all good things must come to an end, don't you think?

Judith stared at the text on the screen, mouth agape, all warmth seeping from her body.

Meetings? He'd enjoyed their meetings? What a cold-hearted prick. And to phrase it as a question, as if he actually cared about her thoughts on the matter. When she tried to call him his phone was turned off. His decision wasn't open for discussion.

Judith had spent the weekend in bed with a bottle of Scotch and the Leonard Cohen mix she always played when life turned to shit.

He'd tired of her. No doubt moved on to a younger, prettier object for his urges.

Opening the garden door, she called for Gertie, making mewing noises. But even her blind old cat had left her. She hadn't been home for days. Judith suspected she'd gone away somewhere quiet to die. A tear slid down her cheek.

Back in the kitchen she stared at the fridge. There was a magnet at eye level urging her not to worry, to be happy. She tore it off and threw it across the room. Then she sank into a chair, head in hands. She couldn't be happy, not anymore. Lawrence was gone and had taken with him her last chance to be a mother. She was forty-three and wasn't about to find another man to father her child any day soon. She had once thought about going it alone with IVF, but at the time she couldn't afford either the treatment or long-term single parenthood. And now... now she'd sell her soul to get IVF, but it was too late. No, Lawrence, with all his faults, had been her last hope and now the bastard was gone.

She lifted her head. Out the window the first rays of the sun were visible in the cloudy sky. There was a heaviness in the air. No birds were pecking at the feeders she'd hung in the garden. The trees were still.

She jumped as a peal of thunder cracked overhead. Large

raindrops started falling and soon she couldn't see out for the sheets of water pouring down the glass. Lightning lit the room briefly followed almost immediately by another crash of thunder. The storm was right overhead but Judith felt strangely calm. She experienced a sense of peace, a kind of clarity, release. She wanted to feel it again, to shut out the pain and despair that accompanied her every breath. She went out into the rain, looking into the sky, arms wide, begging the lightning to strike her, the thunder to crush her. Instead, the storm passed as suddenly as it had come and left her drenched, by the bird table, tears mixing with the rain on her face.

Going back into the house, she went upstairs, dried herself off and dressed carefully, choosing the dress Lawrence had always liked. Liked taking off her, at least. She felt peaceful, even hummed a little as she applied eyeshadow and mascara. She didn't eat breakfast – it was too early.

She wrote a note and left it on the kitchen table. It was an apology to those who were affected by her death, that was all.

She'd considered giving Lawrence a piece of her mind, letting him know what a total shit he'd been, but that would make it look like it was his fault, and although being dumped by him had been devastating, it was merely a last straw. A final reminder that she could see nothing but loneliness in her future.

So now she was making the choice to end her suffering. She suspected people would think of her as a coward, unable to face life as a middle-aged spinster. Let them think what they liked. Perhaps they were right, although she thought of her decision as an act of courage.

Judith took a final look around her house. It had never felt like a home however hard she'd tried to make it so.

She closed the door behind her and started towards the railway line that passed through the fields nearby. She thought about Harvey, the donkey at the sanctuary, his warm breath and soft lips as he snuffled for the bits of carrot she offered. He'd love all this luscious grass. Then she glanced at her watch and quickened her step.

She had a date with Lawrence's commuter train.

2

CLARE

The brakes screeched and the train shuddered to a halt. Stressed commuters glanced out the window and then broke the unwritten rule of maintaining privacy long enough to roll their eyes at each other. Soon, however, it was back to eyes on phone screens, noses in books or newspapers, fingers on keypads, working again already or readying their excuses for lateness, should they need them. Clare looked around the carriage. No one seemed curious as to what had happened. Staring out the window she saw only that they had stopped in a field with a large milking shed at the far end. Maybe a cow had wandered onto the line. It had happened before. Why weren't farmers more careful with their stock?

Closing her eyes, she took a few deep breaths and let her mind wander.

She wriggled her toes in her shoes and thought about the red stilettos she'd seen in the shop. There was something about red shoes. She'd even gone in and tried them on but they pinched a bit. The saleswoman tried to convince her they'd give, as leather always did, but Clare hadn't been taken in. Now she wished she'd been more daring.

With the train sitting on the tracks like it was worn out from carrying all these passengers to and fro, day in, day out, she smiled at the idea of trying to walk to and from the station in heels four inches high. It made her feet ache just to think of it. At forty-four she was too old to wear uncomfortable shoes. And old enough to know better than to spend so much on something as frivolous as red stilettos.

The ticket collector passed through the carriage avoiding eye contact but still several people asked him what had happened.

'I don't know,' he said to the man sitting over the aisle from her. 'I'm going to find out, then I'll make an announcement if necessary.'

He was young and pretty rather than handsome. But there was something about him. She couldn't help herself.

Running her tongue over her lips, she blinked slowly once or twice.

'I'm just going to go along to the bathroom. The one at the end of the next carriage,' she breathed, then picked up her handbag and, resisting the temptation to look back, she sauntered along the compartment.

In the cramped toilet she took out her hand mirror and checked her lipstick. There was a knock on the door and she took a deep breath before opening it.

The ticket collector was standing in the doorway, a smile on his face.

'So,' he said. 'There's you and there's me and this train ain't going nowhere fast. Some sort of object on the line. Could take ages to clear.'

'Oh, how awful,' said Clare. 'Better come in then.'

'I should be finding out what's happened and making an announcement to the passengers about the delay.'

'Plenty of time for that after,' said Clare, pulling him into the loo and locking the door behind him.

There's an art to having sex in a train toilet. Or a plane toilet. Or any tiny space. Clare pushed the guard against the wall and started unbuttoning his shirt.

'I'm–'

'Let's not talk, eh?' Clare unbuttoned her own shirt, revealing her red lace bra. She liked red.

He breathed hard, his eyes slid from hers down to her breasts and he smiled. Clare pulled her shoulders back and enjoyed his gaze. She had a good body and she was aroused by his admiration. The heat spread between her thighs. She took his hands and placed them on her breasts and closed her eyes for a moment to savour the sensation. This was always the moment she knew whether it'd be any good or not. Sometimes she stopped it right there because a man didn't know how to address a woman's breasts. There were the squeezers, the strokers, the suckers and the lookers. He took her breasts and eased them out of her bra and held them firmly, rolling the nipples with his thumbs before taking one in his mouth, licking and tugging gently with his lips. Clare lifted her chin, closed her eyes, and sighed.

The train juddered just long enough to make them stop and listen but, as the guard had said, it wasn't going anywhere.

Clare pushed him onto the toilet and unzipped his Virgin issue trousers. He was a surprisingly big boy for his slender frame, standing proud already. He wanted her as much as she wanted him. He tried to pull her towards him, but she took control; she wouldn't be rushed. Easing herself onto him, she rolled her hips, watched his face flush and heard his breath quicken. He slipped his hands round her back, but she placed them on her breasts again, gasped as he squeezed hard and buried his face in them, groaning as she thrust her hips harder and harder, letting out a long sigh as he came. She lifted herself off him and started rubbing herself, staring at him from under heavy lids as she did. It didn't take him long to take over; he licked his finger and started circling her clitoris and sucking on her nipples. The heat grew and Clare gasped. He knew what he was doing, bringing her to a high and backing off again and then bringing her to the edge again until she also came with a long, shuddering breath, riding the waves of pleasure.

She pulled her panties back up, smoothed her skirt over her hips and checked her hair.

'See you,' she said as she opened the door.

Clare opened her eyes and fanned herself with her notebook. Then she took out her Kindle. *Fifty Shades of Grey* wasn't the kind of book she wanted people to know she was enjoying. Thousands of women were reading it, but she hadn't seen too many of them reading it in public. It was like their guilty secret. She smiled to herself at the idea of a covert greeting shared only between the initiated. A wink, a knowing nod. A sisterhood of sexually-empowered women.

She laughed at herself. No one would call her empowered in any way.

Looking around, she wondered what the other people in her carriage did in their lives. It was one of her favourite things to do. She called it research.

That teenager over there with the eyeliner and upright – no, statuesque – posture sitting across the aisle, she was a dancer, going to an audition at the Royal Ballet School. Clare knew it was all rubbish, of course, but it was nice to imagine, to give people histories they might have enjoyed. More likely she was on holiday from Sweden, judging by the attractive Scandinavian woman (blonde hair and long legs) next to her who was probably her mother, although they didn't talk to each other.

The older woman couldn't stop fiddling with the buckle of her bag and Clare noticed that the polish on one of her thumbnails was badly chipped. Maybe she was a corporate mother who thought the best way to bond with her daughter was a day out in the city but, now they were together, they had nothing to say to each other. She certainly looked smart with her pearl earrings and nine nail-polished fingers. She had a hard face, though, as if she'd had to fight for everything she had.

Clare sucked in her lips. They were dry so she dabbed some lip balm on. Travelling on trains always dried her out so.

The black man opposite her was a drug dealer. No, that was a cliché. He was the head of a charity for homeless people on his way to deliver a conference paper on funding alternatives for homeless youth in the South of England.

Clare smiled to herself. She was good at this. And so she should be after all the time she spent on the train making up lives for people. Sometimes she considered actually engaging with people and finding out what they really did but always talked herself out of it, preferring to imagine – it did away with the tedium of hearing about their empty lives, or the envy she might feel if she discovered they had more than her. She put her Kindle away unopened and reached for her notebook again to jot down her ideas, and add a few more details for each person, trying not to stare at any one of them too obviously as she searched their faces for clues. Of course, she never knew if she was right about people, but it didn't matter; it was the creativity that was important. Like the sex-on-a-train scene she'd just written. She felt herself reddening again just thinking about it.

She looked up from her writing to see that the Scandinavian woman was now talking to the girl. They seemed to be sharing a joke. She edged closer to the aisle, hoping to hear what they were talking about but they were leaning into each other and speaking in low voices so she only heard snippets; something about a driver winning a cup, singing a song to someone and making toast. Or a roast. It was all rather odd. Clare shifted to the very edge of her seat, but to her frustration, they leant closer to one another and lowered their voices even further. Clare sat back again and pretended to look past them out of the window on their side of the train. It didn't really matter what they were talking about, but she did like to listen in to other peoples' conversations. More research.

The black man opposite shifted in his seat, drawing her gaze. He was reading *The Sun*. Or rather, the newspaper was in his hands, but his gaze was roaming around the carriage and he sighed from time to time, closing his eyes momentarily, as if he was in pain. Perhaps he was a drug dealer after all, or a junkie needing a fix. People who read *The Sun* were, in her opinion, the sort who would go in for that sort of thing.

Clare sat back, notebook in hand. It had started raining, blurring the scene outside as fat raindrops streaked the grimy glass. She sighed and closed her eyes, waiting for her imagination to project its images onto her eyelids, but for once, nothing happened. Instead, she heard someone in the seats behind her wondering if the stoppage was because of a suicide on the line. Alarmed, she opened her eyes again and caught the black man looking at her. She smiled but looked away again, reaching into her bag for her phone. She had to let work know she'd be late in.

Of course, no one answered – that was her job, and she was stuck on the train. She left a message.

'Sorry, Dr Moncrieff, I'm stuck on the train. There's been a suicide on the line, I think. I'm not sure when I'll be in.'

Was it really a suicide? Suddenly there could be no other explanation for the stop. A death. It knocked the wind out of her.

She threw her phone back into her bag and sat, head resting, eyes closed, breathing in, out, in, out to a slow count of four, like her counsellor had told her to do when she felt a panic attack coming on.

I focus on my breath. I am not panic. I am not anxiety. I am bigger than them, I can contain them. I focus on my breath, in, out, in, out.

It wasn't working. Her breaths were shorter, her heart thumping painfully against her ribs. She was having a heart attack this time, she was sure of it. All the breathing exercises in the world weren't going to help now. She bit her lip to stop herself from screaming. A tear squeezed out from between her tightly closed eyelids.

She was going to die on a train to London surrounded by people who didn't care.

She didn't die. The black man sitting opposite her reached over and offered a crisp white hanky. She looked at it, at the man, and in the absence of any other choice, took it and wiped the sweat off her face and held the damp cotton over her mouth, forcing herself to take long, deep breaths. Eventually she was able to look around and name some objects in her vicinity to anchor herself to the present – a jacket lying on the floor, the dirt-smudged window. She felt the seat beneath her thighs, wriggled her toes in her sensible brown shoes. Finally, she lowered the hanky and thanked the man who was leaning towards her, concerned.

'Keep it,' he said, nodding towards the hanky scrunched in her hand.

Embarrassed, she thanked him again and got her Kindle out. She didn't want to talk, to explain to this man that she was barely managing to breathe, to sit upright, to prevent herself from running, screaming from the train and her life. She could so easily have been the person on the track. Perhaps not this morning, but there were other mornings when she had to drag herself from her bed, force herself to wash, dress, drink a cup of tea. When she had to paint on a face she could show the world, build herself up in order to get out of the house. There were days when even her minimal contact with Dr Moncrieff's patients required superhuman effort, when she had to remind herself to talk and smile, when she crept into the kitchenette or the bathroom and curled herself into a ball to stop herself shaking, or just to feel safe.

The rain stopped. The train shuddered and started moving again. She let her head rest against the back of the seat and took deep breaths, eyes closed, feeling the watery sun trying to warm her cheek through the window. She repeated her mantra, *I focus on my breath*, and finally she felt calm enough to turn her Kindle on and start reading.

Clare rushed through the ticket barrier at Euston and plunged into the underground, stepping onto a Victoria line train as the doors were closing. Being later than usual, commuters had been replaced by tourists with maps out or suitcases parked in front of them, talking in loud voices in a dozen languages. Clare recognised Italian, Spanish, German, Swedish, Arabic and Dutch. Or imagined she did. Some, she had to admit, she guessed from the look of the person or the little flag stitched on a backpack. She wished, as she always did when confronted by foreigners, that she had travelled more, that the parameters of her life were not confined to home, London and the occasional holiday in the Lake District or Cornwall. Although she hadn't even been to either of those places recently. She thought about exotic-sounding places like Marrakesh or Timbuktu, though she had to admit she would probably hate the realities of them – the dirt, the heat, the insects.

At Oxford Circus she took a deep breath as she reached street level. It was a primitive response to being outside again, and entirely beyond her control. She knew the air was not fresh, that it was filled with exhaust fumes and sweat, the cast-off cells of the people shoving their way past her in their hurry to get wherever it was they had to be. Drawing in lungfuls of this pollution was not particularly healthy, but she couldn't help herself. Shaking her head, she set her course along Regent Street, Margaret Street, into Cavendish Square which was hosting a picnic for a group of young language students all glued to their phones, and on into Harley Street.

In the plush reception area of Dr Moncrieff's private consulting rooms, sound muted by triple-glazed windows and deep-pile carpet, Clare hung her jacket in the cupboard, stowed her bag under her desk and took her seat. There were files scattered across the desk in what she interpreted as the doctor's annoyance at her tardy arrival. He was a man who liked routine, for whom the late arrival of his secretary-receptionist was an inconvenience almost too great to bear. She thought once again how she would happily resign if it weren't for the money. Dr Moncrieff paid generously.

She tidied the notes into a pile and opened the first one to find a note written in his precise handwriting. Logging on to the computer, she typed it into the electronic records and filed the hard copy, wondering for the thousandth time why the doctor insisted on hard copies as well as the digital files. Maybe it was his age, she thought. He belonged to a generation for which computers and storage clouds were newfangled and therefore untrustworthy. It didn't matter how often she explained it all to him, Dr Moncrieff wanted things done his way.

A man entered reception and approached the desk, the worried look of a recent diagnosis on his face.

'Good morning, sir. Can I help you?' He looked vaguely familiar but he hadn't seen the doctor before.

He smiled the thin smile of one condemned and said, 'I hope so. I have an appointment at ten thirty.' He pulled an envelope out of his jacket pocket. 'Here's my referral. Ray Dreyfus for Dr Moncrieff.'

He looked a little ruffled, as if he'd been rushing, and the referral letter he passed to her was creased and had a coffee stain on it.

'Sorry,' he said, looking at it in her hands. 'I hope it's still all right.'

Clare smiled one of her real smiles; not the encouraging smile, the comforting smile, or the smile saved for the dying which was a smile that at the same time creased the area between her eyebrows.

'Not a problem,' she said. 'Coffee cups have a way of leaving their mark.'

Ray laughed. It was a nervous chuckle rather than a full-throated laugh and Clare felt sorry for him.

'Dr Moncrieff is the best there is,' she heard herself saying, although in reality she had no idea if she was right; he might have a higher mortality rate than others for all she knew, but she wanted to believe she worked for one of the best and so she sounded confident when she said it.

'Yes. He comes highly recommended,' said Ray before lapsing into silence. It was as if mentioning the doctor's name had reminded him of why he was there. Clare was pleased to see that at least he allowed himself the comfort of a sofa rather than one of the hard chairs to fill in his paperwork.

'I thought I was going to be late,' he said as he stood and handed it back to her. 'My train was delayed, and I had no idea how long it would take to get here from the station.' He ran a hand through his hair and then patted it down as he spoke, as if expecting it to be sticking out at odd angles from the stress of the journey.

'My train was delayed too.'

Ray looked at her, wide-eyed. 'A Milton Keynes train?'

'Yes. Same one?'

'Yes. A suicide on the line. Terrible thing to happen.'

Clare noticed the patient had started sweating.

'Take a seat, Mr Dreyfus. Can I get you a glass of water?'

'No, thank you. I'll be fine.' He sat and took a few deep breaths, his head resting against the back of the sofa.

The intercom buzzed and Dr Moncrieff asked her to step into his room.

He was a good-looking man, even though he was well into his sixties. Tall, upright, his grey hair neatly cut, his tie always matched by the handkerchief in his top pocket. He inspired trust and confidence in his patients, even though Clare knew he couldn't save them all.

'Ah, Clare. Finally.'

'Yes, doctor. Sorry. As I said in my message, there was a delay on the line this morning.'

'Very unfortunate.' He handed her the file he'd been writing in. 'I haven't had my coffee yet.'

And thank you for your concern over the incident on the train, she thought to herself.

'I'll make it now. And your next appointment is here. Mr Dreyfus.'

She swept out, hands clenched. How was it that he was such a competent doctor and yet he couldn't work the coffee machine? Or wouldn't. She put in more sugar than the half teaspoon he liked and took it in to him with the new patient's file, pausing long enough to see him take his first sip and grimace slightly before asking her to send the patient in.

'You can go in now, Mr Dreyfus.' She watched him walk, stiff-backed, through the door to the executioner. Or his saviour. They could never be sure before the first appointment. His referral suggested prostate cancer. There had been tests. Now a second opinion was sought as to whether surgery was an option. Clare sighed. Cancer was such a terrible disease, eating away at you sometimes for years before it offered up any symptoms, before it alerted you to its deadly presence. She herself had regular mammograms and Pap smears, and visited her GP for blood tests designed to discover minute changes in her blood that might be due to some silent danger.

She hadn't always been so cautious, but since working for a urologist, she knew life was delicate, that you could be struck down at any moment. It had caused many of her panic attacks. She had learned with the help of her therapist to manage them, by and large, but the anxiety still lurked. She and the counsellor had discussed many a time her determination to face her death anxiety by working for a doctor. She said she felt somehow inoculated from her own fate if she faced it in others day in, day out. If she could make the last weeks or months of others' lives even a little bit more pleasant by way of an encouraging smile or a kind word, perhaps death would leave her alone.

A suicide. She'd known it, of course, but Mr Dreyfus said it so nonchalantly as if these things happened every day, and of course they did, but not to her. Not in front of the train she took to work. Someone had actually died not far from where she'd been sitting. Her hands started shaking and she couldn't breathe properly. She tugged at her collar to loosen it and tried to suck in air, but her chest seemed to have solidified, her diaphragm suddenly immobile. She darted into the kitchenette and ran the cold water. Sometimes letting it run over her wrists soothed her.

Not today. She doubled over, sliding her bottom down the cupboard to the floor and started repeating her mantra: 'I focus on my breath. I am not panic. I am not anxiety. I am bigger than them, I can contain them. I focus on my breath, in, out, in, out.'

When she was able to go back to her desk, Mr Dreyfus was coming out of the doctor's consulting room.

'All done?' The last traces of the panic attack caused her voice to tremble.

He turned. His cheeks were wet. 'All done,' he said.

She hated it when they cried, especially the men. And most of Dr Moncrieff's patients were men. She felt impotent in the face of their pain, unable to alleviate it. She never had an adequate response, even though she practised phrases in private; 'I hope you have good support around you at this difficult time,' or, 'there's great benefit in looking after your general well-being with a good diet and plenty of sleep.' Neither were appropriate really, just things to say because she couldn't say nothing, and she certainly couldn't take them in her arms and let them weep while she quietly had a panic attack as, together, they faced their mortality.

'Can I get you anything?' she managed.

His features were mask-like – set into a look of terror. 'No. Thank you.' He walked out the door, his arms tight to his sides.

When he'd gone she sat at her desk going through the mail. She frowned when she came across a letter addressed to Pauline de Winter. There was a Post-it note stuck to the front and a message in Dr Moncrieff's neat writing: *You promised this would stop.* She could almost hear the implied, *'Please see me.'*

Two more patients arrived, one extremely early for his appointment. Neither acknowledged the other, each submerged under the weight of their diagnosis, the hope that their faith in the doctor hadn't been misplaced, the fear of 'what next'.

Clare tapped away on the computer, followed up on the

results of tests ordered, offered teas and coffees, looked compassionate. There was, she had learned, a fine line between professional compassion in which a patient may be reassured by a 'there, there' or comforted by a cup of tea, and the compassion that invited an unburdening. Clare was not interested in listening to details of symptoms and tumours, surgery and drugs. Not at all. So she'd learned to apply just the right amount of sympathy to her features and the timbre of her voice. These days, a patient had to be really desperate to try to talk to her.

At one o'clock, Dr Moncrieff emerged from his office and announced he was going for lunch and straight on to the private hospital where he performed his life-saving, or maybe life-prolonging, surgery. Clare nodded seriously, and said, 'Yes, doctor', as if this was in any way unusual when, in fact, he always operated on Monday afternoons.

'And the letter for Pauline – I thought you said you'd stop receiving mail for her here – didn't you say she'd got herself a post-office box? I don't like the idea of being the *poste restante* for someone like that even if she is your cousin.'

Clare bit her bottom lip to prevent herself from responding. After a deep breath she said, 'Sorry, doctor. I'm not sure why it came here. I'll make sure it doesn't happen again.'

'Well, speak to her would you – make sure it doesn't.'

'Of course.'

He gathered his coat and umbrella and left.

Clare slumped onto one of the sofas and let out a sigh. She'd worked for Dr Moncrieff for over five years and he was still so stiff and formal. What would it take to crack him? She thought back to the first time she'd seen him, at her interview.

She'd arrived in plenty of time and sat waiting nervously, eyeing the other candidate who was waiting – a woman in her fifties, Clare reckoned, with varicose veins and wispy permed hair. Not the right sort to front a private doctor's rooms. Clare had checked her own nail varnish, tucked a strand of her blonde hair behind her ear, and taken some deep breaths.

The doctor had asked a colleague's receptionist to help with the interviews, an officious-looking woman with thin lips. Clare knew immediately it was her she had to impress, but that she must address all her comments to the doctor or his ego would be bruised. The interview had gone well and on the train on the way home she'd celebrated with a cup of tea and an iced bun. She hadn't been at all surprised when three days later, a formal offer of appointment arrived but only then did she do the maths; working out whether, even with the generous salary offered, it was worth accepting a job in London given the hefty train fares. She'd always known really she would have taken the job even if the numbers didn't stack up; she wanted to work in London, whatever the cost. Surely, she'd thought to herself, she had a better chance of finding love in a bigger city?

She shrugged and raised her eyebrows, a short sharp breath escaping her nostrils; how naïve she'd been. London was so anonymous. People walked past day after day without glancing at each other; either they were on their phones or their gaze slid over their fellow men – and women – without registering them.

She shook her head and settled back into the sofa. With the doctor gone for the day, all she had to do was finish typing the notes, file the clinical records and answer the phone if it rang. Plenty of time for Pauline de Winter before her therapy appointment later.

When all her work was done Clare settled herself on one of the sofas in Dr Moncrieff's reception area and took out the letter addressed to Pauline de Winter. Such a fine name. Elegant, sophisticated. Hers. She'd fabricated the cousin.

When she began writing as a hobby she had no idea she was going to write books. She thought she might bash out a couple of short stories and send them off to a magazine to see if she could get them published. She discovered the short form wasn't for her though. She couldn't tell a decent story in so few words. She had an idea to tell a modern-day tale of an independent middle-aged woman looking for love, but she found it so depressing that she started adding in the woman's fantasies and found she had a flair for writing hot romance. Tasteful books, not even erotica really. Definitely not porn, as Dr Moncrieff had called it. More sensual. That's how she thought of it. And therefore she needed a name to write under. She didn't want people to know it was her who wrote those bodice-rippers. She had no idea how he knew what Pauline de Winter wrote, as he had surely never read any of her books. Maybe his wife had, or one of his clever daughters who looked down their noses at her when they occasionally came in to meet their father for lunch.

She turned the envelope over in her hands. She knew who it was from. Clare and Nadia, her agent, had talked about letters once early on, bemoaning the fact that email had taken over. So unromantic. They both loved a good letter and had sworn to communicate as far as possible by snail mail. It had been good enough for the likes of Dickens and the Brontë sisters. And Clare loved the fact that Nadia wrote to her as Pauline, as if she were a real person.

Clare had had no choice but to give Nadia an alternative address when she found her mother throwing one of the letters out.

'I don't know who this is, but she doesn't live here and there's no return address. Anyway, she's got a harlot's name,' her mother had said, and torn it in two. Clare had been too shocked and embarrassed to admit it was her. She really should get a post-office box.

Now she felt the texture of the envelope, the weight of the paper. Handmade. Expensive. Typical of Nadia. And the name and address written in purple ink with a fountain pen. Clare looked at the handwriting – round, sweeping letters, long, bold tails. A fair hand. She noticed her heartbeat speeding with anticipation. She was almost as excited as she had been when she received her first response from a publisher. It had been an email, and she'd looked at the subject line for fully five minutes, heart pounding, only to open it and read that her submission wasn't of interest to them. Since then, she'd learned that the minutes before opening any correspondence were often the most fulfilling.

Finally, though, she could wait no longer. She slid a finger along the lip of the envelope and took the letter out. Two sheets of paper.

Dear Pauline,
I am writing to let you know your sales figures for September to March are exceptional. You are a sensation with the ladies! The monies will be sent to your account within the day.
Well done! You will see that your popularity is growing exponentially in the United States, Canada, the Antipodes and South Africa where they seem to love sex in a stately home!
I have also negotiated contracts in other territories – South America mainly – for your first two books.

Clare pulled the second piece of paper forward and scanned the lines of the spreadsheet for the amount. Nadia had mentioned the last time they spoke that the books were selling well, but Clare stared at the numbers her agent had underlined for her and felt her heart skip a beat. Then she realised that was just the British sales. The knuckle of her left index finger made its way into her mouth. There was another amount from South

Africa. And another from Australia and New Zealand. More from the States and Canada. She felt giddy. Her eyes could take in no more. She leant back into the sofa, taking deep breaths. She wasn't great at mental arithmetic, but she reckoned it all to add up to almost £80,000. She put her hand on her chest to make sure her breathing stayed calm. In six months she had made more from her writing than she'd make in years working for the good doctor. The phone rang. She let it go to the answering machine and read the letter again.

On the strength of these figures, I have negotiated a three-book deal for you with your current publisher. There was a bit of a bidding war, to tell the truth – you are hot property these days. The advance will be £250,000. I'll take you out to lunch next week and if you agree to the terms – very standard apart from the large amount of money – you can sign the contract.

Clare gasped and her hands covered her face – was this a joke? Things like this didn't happen to her. She lowered her hands to her lap and her eyes to the letter lying there, waiting for the punchline.

I will, of course, call you to discuss it, but knew you would appreciate seeing the amount written down first. It's a big number to take in! I'm so sorry about all the exclamation marks, but I am very excited for you, and hope you will be too – how could you not? All the very best. Keep writing! Nadia.

Clare stared at the piece of paper in her hand. Had she read it correctly? A quarter of a million pounds? Excitement laced her body. A little squeak erupted from her throat. Her legs felt like jumping and a smile stretched her face. It was a life-changing amount of money. She looked at the spreadsheet again, at the total of her royalties at the bottom of the page: another hundred thousand pounds, give or take. She could afford to stop working, spend all her time writing. Travel. Buy a flat. Buy a dog. Have her hair done – every day if she wanted. Get that pair of red shoes she'd left in the shop.

She put the letter back in the envelope carefully, ready to be taken out again whenever she needed to be reminded of her fortune. Whenever she needed to read again the fantastic amount of money she was worth.

It was difficult to concentrate but she tidied away the files, closed her computer and washed the cups she and Dr Moncrieff had used.

Then she thought of the money and felt faint and had to sit again for a few moments.

When she'd collected herself, she shut the door behind her and put the keys in her bag. Taking a deep breath, she descended to the street and walked south, towards Cavendish Square and beyond. Not even the crowds in Oxford Street annoyed her. She swung her hips this way and that to avoid people, stepped into the gutter when necessary without so much as a grimace. The sky was blue, the sun was shining, the air tasted sweet.

She reached Fortnum and Mason in Piccadilly, and the noises of London – the laughter and voices raised over the traffic, the tooting of horns, the high-pitched buzz of mopeds – receded as she stepped across the hallowed portal into the understated elegance of her favourite shop.

She stood, inhaling the smells; chocolate, cinnamon, sugar, coffee. Subtle. No competition between them, each scent complementing the others. She made her way to the lift and got out at the fourth floor; the Diamond Jubilee Tea Salon. Her little piece of luxury.

At a corner table, away from the piano, but still able to hear the pianist playing his repertoire of classics, she took her time over the menu. So many treats to choose from, so many teas. In the end, she ordered the afternoon tea selection and lapsang souchong. She had considered an oolong, but why celebrate with anything but her favourite?

As she waited for her food to arrive she looked around at the other customers. Being a Monday, there weren't very many. A mother and daughter who Clare decided were wedding shopping, as they put their heads together and seemed to be writing a list. An elderly couple who hardly spoke to one another, a group of women in the uniform of the rich – Prada handbags, Versace, Johnny Was and Camilla clothing. Oh yes, she knew all about designer labels – her heroines wore them all. These women occupied the space with the easy confidence of the wealthy, as if this very tea salon had been built for their pleasure. Until now, on the rare occasions Clare had visited, she'd felt out of place and had shrunk into her corner hoping that no one would notice she didn't belong there. Today, however, she sat tall, looked around with a different eye. A wealthy independent woman's eye. She doubted if anyone else in the room had her personal wealth; the women had rich husbands, the elderly couple were giving themselves a rare treat. But she was her own person. She took the letter out and read it again, a flutter of joy tripping her heart.

She savoured her finger sandwiches, took a little clotted cream and raspberry jam on her scone, and chose a macaron from the cake carriage. Her lapsang souchong was perfect, just the right amount of smokiness. She dabbed at the corners of her mouth with her napkin, even though she knew she had made no mess, and asked for the bill. Leaving a generous tip, she made her way back down to the street and stepped out of her sanctuary.

Usually, walking in London wound her up. Today, it was as if she was in a bubble, protected from the noise and the fumes, the dirt and the busyness. She floated along Piccadilly looking in exclusive shop windows. She had no desire to enter any of them. Just knowing she could afford anything she wanted gave her a satisfaction, a confidence she hadn't felt before. She'd often wondered how the wealthy behaved as they did, and now she knew; the knowledge you had money, that you could have whatever you desired, bolstered your self-esteem, gave you an air of self-importance, smugness. She wore it like a cloak, aware of the weight of it, the texture, enjoying her new mantle and at the same time, marvelling at it. How quickly she'd made the transition from working woman to wealthy woman. Of course, she'd still be working, but at something she loved, and she wouldn't have to worry about the bills, the cost of repairing the roof. She noticed she was humming, and laughed.

Looking at her watch, her twenty-year-old Timex, she realised she would be late for her therapy appointment. She broke into a trot, and her mood sank a little with every person she had to dodge, each tourist who stopped just in front of her to take a selfie, every car, bus and taxi preventing her from crossing the road. Sweating and out of breath, she arrived at May's office five minutes late, and knocked on the door.

'Clare – you look different,' said her therapist as she entered.

'Sorry – I had to rush,' she said, dabbing at her forehead with a tissue and slipping out of her jacket.

'No, I mean different, not just hot and bothered.'

'I know. Strange, isn't it?'

May looked at her, waiting for more.

Clare took her seat, taking her time to get comfortable. Finally, she raised her eyes to May's and folded her hands in her lap. 'This morning, I was a struggling forty-four-year-old woman who fantasised about having sex with strangers on the train.

This afternoon, I am a wealthy forty-four-year-old woman who fantasises about having sex with strangers on the train. That's the only difference.'

May raised an eyebrow and tilted her head to one side slightly. She was economical in her movements as well as her words. Clare had once counted the words May spoke in a session and worked out she paid one pound twenty-five for each one. Still, they were worth it. May was worth it. She was the only person in the world who listened to Clare with all her attention and no judgement. Or at least, she suspended her judgement and didn't let Clare know what she really thought.

'It turns out the hours I spend imagining sex in toilets or in fields, with rich men or paupers, can be turned into cash. Lots of cash.'

May nodded. 'You've turned your fantasies into money?'

Clare sat back, crossed her legs and smiled. 'Yes. Pauline de Winter has been paid a very large advance for three books. Apparently she – I – am a big hit all over the English-speaking world.' Clare looked at her therapist's face. It gave nothing away. 'Aren't you pleased for me?'

'Of course,' said May. 'But I'm more interested in how this affects you, and whether it's the money or the recognition that pleases you?'

Clare looked at the plant in the corner – a tall Swiss cheese plant in a glazed ceramic pot – and sighed. 'Both?' she said but it came out as a question, as if she didn't want to admit to feeling proud or greedy.

'I ask because previously you've described yourself as feeling stifled, of having a sense you're not living a full or fulfilling life and that your fear of death stems from the idea of a life unlived, that you will never experience life's riches, before you are plunged into – in your words – eternal nothingness.'

May was earning her fee today, thought Clare. Words at two a penny.

And there were more. 'You never rated wealth as one of those experiences.'

'Maybe not, but there are so many things one can do if one has money.'

May nodded and waited.

'Travel, for example.' She thought of her earlier ideas of Marrakesh or Timbuktu, but knew they weren't really her sort of places. 'I've always wanted to go to Prague.' She hadn't, but it sounded like the sort of place one should want to go. 'And the Greek islands.' She'd never wanted to go to the Greek islands either. She wasn't a beachy sort of person. Was money making a liar of her?

'Travel,' said May, encouraging her to continue.

Clare sank into her seat. She wanted to cry. 'I don't know.' Her chest tightened. She put a hand on her stomach and tried to breathe into it.

'Okay, Clare. Press your feet firmly into the floor and name five things you can see around you.'

Clare tried to do as she was told but the panic rose within her, her whole body feeling as if it was alternately compressed and released. Her vision went fuzzy and her head spun. She was dimly aware of May's voice somewhere in the far distance.

'Long, slow breaths, focusing on the exhalation, in... and out... in... and out... And now look at me.'

Clare's gaze met May's. 'Good, and now notice what you can hear. Keep breathing. Keep pressing your feet into the floor.'

It seemed like hours, but when Clare looked at the clock, only minutes had passed. She slumped into her seat, exhausted. May sat quietly waiting.

'I'm terrified. I've never had money before. What if it changes everything?'

'What might it change?'

'What if I can't write anymore – what if I can't fulfil the deal but I've spent all the advance already and they sue me and I end my days in prison?'

'Clare, breathe, and consider what you've just said.'

Clare closed her eyes and slowed her breathing down again. May wanted her to realise she was catastrophising, that there was no basis for any of her irrational thinking. But what did she know? For the first time since she'd started seeing her, Clare questioned her therapist's competency. She felt a sinking in her stomach. What if May couldn't help her?

'What's going on?' asked May.

Clare said nothing.

'You're wondering if I can help you – if anyone can help you, is that it?'

How did she know that? She was a mind reader. Clare was ashamed of her doubts, and simultaneously worried that with this woman there was no hiding, no cover.

'It's common to question your therapist's ability when you're triggered. Part of you wants desperately to be understood and helped, another part is terrified of the same thing because "being helped" means making changes, and change is frightening.'

Clare had heard that before. She'd also read it in several self-help books, but it suddenly made absolute, spine-chilling sense. She had to change and she was scared, but if she wanted to do anything she had to step into her life and make it happen, whatever 'it' was.

She smiled. 'Maybe I do catastrophise sometimes, and I worry I'll die without achieving anything. But right now I'm alive. Maybe I should focus on that.'

'How does it feel?'

Clare thought for a moment, waiting for all her negative self-talk to kick in and tell her she was delusional. There was none. 'It feels good.' She felt light. Unused to such a sensation, she carried on. 'I should probably talk about the journey into work this morning. There was a suicide on the line.' She stopped and waited for her reaction. Nothing. No shortening of breath, constriction of chest, fluttering of heart. What had happened? Surely having money hadn't cured her. She wasn't that shallow. It wasn't that easy. She looked at her therapist, confused.

'Go on,' said May.

'I don't know any more about the person who died.' She paused, again waiting to see if the panic would start. 'I had a bit of a panic attack on the train, and again when I got to work, but I don't feel anything now. Well, I am sorry for the person and their family, but I'm not anxious.'

'And?'

Clare frowned. 'I feel guilty.'

'Guilty?'

'Yes, guilty that I don't feel more. I know panicking doesn't help anybody, but it proves that I feel. Now nobody will know I have feelings.'

'So panicking proves you feel love, happiness, sadness, concern, joy, empathy, anger?'

Clare looked at May as if she was mad. And then realised that was exactly what she'd thought. She had been afraid all her life to express her feelings; panic was her alternative. 'Oh, shit,' she said.

May smiled. 'Indeed.'

As she walked back to the station to get the train home, she considered how she might do things differently. Her breath quickened and her heart flip-flopped in her chest. She clutched herself, waiting for the panic to start, but nothing more happened. Maybe, she realised, she wasn't feeling anxious. Maybe this was what excitement felt like.

She wasn't naïve enough to believe that all her troubles were behind her, but she vowed to herself she would enjoy this new-found feeling while it lasted, and do whatever she could to make it stay.

For the last few minutes of her session, Clare had explored how her panic was a way of not allowing her feelings. Of not engaging with people. She caught the eye of a woman walking towards her, and smiled.

Clare didn't have to fantasise in the train on the way home. She had enough real-life excitement to keep her occupied. She did notice passing the field where the suicide had taken place earlier, however. Just another field full of cows again, but she'd always remember staring out at the cowshed and feeling for the poor person who'd died. And her panic attack. She wondered whether she should have asked for the name of the man who gave her his handkerchief; she could have laundered it and sent it back to him with a thank-you note. In fact, now she could send him a whole drawerful of new hankies!

Was it really only that morning, a mere ten hours ago? One life had been lost, but hers was about to begin.

She pulled out her notebook and started jotting down her wish list:

Pay off mortgage
Go on holiday – overseas somewhere –

She stopped. Where did she want to go? She'd said Prague

and the Greek islands to May, but she'd just plucked them out of the air. Now she sat, tapping the end of her pen against her lips, thinking of all the places she could visit. Iceland to see the geysers, Australia to see a kangaroo bounding through the outback. Norway to see the aurora borealis. She'd written a book in which the protagonist, Lady Sybil Fraser, had an erotic fling with a reindeer herder in an igloo under the Northern Lights. She really should go and see them for herself. Who knew what might happen?

She looked at her list. Two items. How pathetic, but she couldn't think of anything else she wanted. Not that money could buy, anyway.

No good going down that path, she said to herself, and did what she always did when she felt lonely. She started writing.

Mr Kenneth Gresham had eyes the colour of a thundercloud and a gaze that smouldered from beneath dark eyebrows. He wasn't traditionally handsome; his nose was slightly too long, his cheekbones too wide. But those eyes, oh, those eyes. Arabella couldn't resist them.

She crossed the room to get closer to him. He was talking to Lord Finlay – or rather, Lord Finlay was talking to him. Mr Gresham was listening politely, one elbow resting on the mantel. Arabella sat on the love seat and opened her book, but really she was watching his every move. She adored the way he stood so erect, the proud tilt of his head, the sound of his laughter when Lord Finlay uttered an amusing comment.

The room seemed too warm around her as she continued to gaze at him. She wanted to loosen her bodice which felt suddenly too tight.

'Are you all right, Arabella?' her mother asked, carefully lowering herself onto the seat beside her.

Arabella started. 'Yes, Mother. Very well, thank you.'

'You look a little flushed, my dear. I hope you are not coming down with a chill.'

'No, Mother, I assure you, I am in the peak of health.'

Lady Donnington nodded. 'If you say so, my dear. But perhaps you should not go on the hunt tomorrow, just in case.'

Arabella's heart sank within her tightly bound chest. Not go on the hunt? That would be too cruel. She knew she held her seat well, and in her new riding habit, her figure was shown off to full advantage. If Kenneth Gresham didn't notice her tonight, surely he would tomorrow.

'I will be quite well enough, Mother. I am looking forward to it.'

'There will be other hunts,' said her mother, and rising again, she brushed an imaginary crease from her dress and swished away.

Arabella knew her mother would not change her mind. Instead, she must ensure that Mr Gresham noticed her this evening. She lifted her eyes to him and met the full force of his gaze.

She reddened, her hand going to her bosom. His eyes followed.

Clare put her pen down. Her heart was beating faster as it always did when she wrote. She got so carried away with the scenes she created, living the lives of her characters. Of course, the heroine always got her man, there was sex and lots of it, sometimes with a happily ever after, but often not. Her women didn't need men to make them happy except in the bedroom – or the library, the forest, the yacht. Clare lured the reader in with lavish or exotic surroundings, handsome men, beautiful women – all the trappings of a romance. But she liked to think her plots were a little out of the ordinary, that she wasn't just trotting out your typical romance. Who else would have thought of a reindeer herder having his way with a British lady in Lapland, for example?

Two hundred and fifty thousand pounds. She smiled at her reflection in the train window, the scenery behind blurred into lines – green, brown, grey. She tried to focus on herself, but her eyes kept tracking the lines. Soon she felt sick with all the movement and had to stop. She took a peppermint out of her bag and sucked on it to stop the queasiness. With her eyes now closed, she thought of all that money. Would that many twenty-pound notes fill a wheelbarrow?

Suddenly she sat bolt upright. It was a three-book deal; what if she couldn't write three more books? What had May said about it in their session? What had she said? She couldn't remember. Her breathing began to speed up, her heart rate too. She pushed her feet into the floor and clasped her hands together. Forcing herself not to think about anything but to concentrate on the pattern of the seat fabric, she calmed down.

I always think each book is the last, but the reality is I keep creating other plots and new characters, she reminded herself. Long breath in, long breath out. She repeated this comforting phrase to herself for the rest of the journey.

As the train approached Milton Keynes she made sure she had her possessions, shouldered her bag and was waiting at the door when the train stopped. She flashed her season ticket at the barrier although the ticket collector wasn't there, and pulled her scarf tighter round her neck as she left the station. A man in a cashmere coat and in a hurry bumped into her, making her stumble as he headed off towards the car park.

'No, that's okay. Don't bother apologising,' she said to his retreating back. She watched him go, briefcase in one hand while the other fished in his pocket for his car keys. She wondered what kind of car he drove, where he lived, if he had a wife waiting for him at home making dinner, ready to pour him a drink as soon as he walked through the door. He walked tall, his long legs striding fast. Rude though he'd been, she liked watching attractive men and couldn't tear her eyes away. She imagined him getting home to a kiss, a smile, small talk over dinner. They'd watch the ten o'clock news together, he'd say, 'time for bed?' and hold a hand out to her. And she'd smile a knowing smile and lead him upstairs.

Clare sighed. She had to stop these fantasies. Or try to channel them into her writing rather than get enveloped in them outside the station at half past six in the evening with commuters spilling out into the night all around her, pushing her this way and that, tutting as she stood lost in thought.

She decided to walk home rather than catch the bus. It only took a few minutes longer and she wanted to enjoy these last few moments of peace. As she walked, she allowed herself to think more about how she'd spend her new-found wealth. A donation to the local animal sanctuary – she'd call Judith about it. New clothes. Nadia hadn't mentioned it, but maybe there would be a book tour and she'd need to look her best. A personal trainer might be a good idea too. She always meant to exercise and never got round to it. Paying someone to make her do it would be a good investment. The house needed repainting inside and out. And maybe she could add another room, a study. Or build one in the garden with a bathroom and kitchenette. *A Room of One's Own* where she could write and dream. It would be an extravagance, certainly, but why not? Didn't she deserve it?

Too soon she arrived at her front door. As she was trying to find her key, it opened.

'Evening, Clare.'

'Hello, Marion. How were they today?'

'Your mother's been quite upset. She kept asking when her mummy was coming to see her and wouldn't be fobbed off with my usual "tomorrow". I had to ring my sister and ask her to pretend to be her mother so they could talk. It cheered her for a few minutes, until she forgot it had happened and asked again when she'd be seeing her mother.' Clare suddenly felt deflated.

Dream had collided head-on with reality. She took a deep breath.

'That was creative of you, Marion. What about Dad?' She didn't really want to hear any more, but Marion prided herself on her ability to look after them both and provide a detailed report at the end of the day. Clare couldn't afford to piss her off by not letting her present it.

'He's been quite chirpy. Took his medication, ate his lunch, watched a bit of TV, had a sleep this afternoon. He says his left arm is sore, but I'm not sure it really is – he hasn't been able to feel it properly since the last stroke, has he? It might be he's getting some feeling back, but unlikely. Anyway, he asked me to make him an appointment to see the doctor, so I have. And I've ordered the taxi to take him.'

'Thank you. You're a star, you really are. I don't know what I'd do without you.'

Marion smiled. 'Well, I'll be off then,' she said, and put her bag over her shoulder. She always had it ready and waiting in the hall when Clare got home.

'Wait a moment, Marion.' Clare fished out her phone and transferred a hundred pounds to Marion's account. 'I had some good news today. Here's a little bonus for you. Give yourself a treat.'

Marion looked at the screen Clare was showing her and a smile lit up her face. 'Thank you, Clare. Very generous of you.' She called goodnight to Clare's parents, and left.

Clare hung up her coat and scarf thinking how nice it was to make someone happy, how easy to make them feel appreciated. She took a deep breath and opened the sitting-room door. Her father turned to her and gave her his lopsided smile. He'd been a good-looking man until he started having strokes. Now one side of his face was frozen, forever unlined, and the other, by comparison, looked like it had aged twice as fast as normal as the skin slid towards his jaw and sagged there, empty, useless flesh. A thin line of saliva dribbled from his mouth but he seemed unaware of it. Her mother sat in her chair, a table clipped in front of it so she couldn't wander. She had a pack of cards in her hands and was shuffling them over and over again. She had loved card games. Not the highfalutin bridge, but whist and canasta. No one could beat her until she started getting forgetful, couldn't remember what cards she'd played. It used to frustrate her, and she'd throw the cards in the air with a scream of anger. Now she was content just endlessly shuffling them.

Clare watched her for a moment, this shell of a woman who had once been funny, intelligent, caring. She was the kind of mother who still sent Easter cards when no one sent them anymore and remembered birthdays and anniversaries. Clare had taken it all for granted at the time, but in the last few years she'd missed them.

'Did you have a good day?' Her question was for both of them, though she didn't expect an answer.

'What's for tea, Mummy?' asked her mother.

'I'm not your mother, I'm your daughter,' said Clare.

Her mother straightened, sitting taller and put the cards down. 'No one told me. I think I'd know if I had a daughter.'

Clare sighed. Her father closed his eyes. The left one drooped and didn't close completely. It looked red and sore and Clare reached for his eye drops.

'Here, Dad, let me put these in for you.'

'Oh, Clare, you're good to me.' Tears welled in his eyes making the drops redundant.

'I had good news today,' she said.

Her mother started shuffling the cards again, her father wiped at the tears running down his cheek. 'I have earned a bit of money from my writing.'

She looked at her parents, neither of whom had responded.

She tried again, louder. 'I said, I have received money from selling my books.'

'That's good, dear,' said her father. 'What are you going to do with it? You deserve a holiday, that's what. You've always wanted to go to Scotland, haven't you? Why not go there for a day or two?' He started crying again and wiped angrily at the tears falling down his left cheek. He'd been labile since the last stroke, crying at the drop of a hat, getting angry over nothing. There was no telling what he'd do next.

'No need to cry, Dad.'

'I'll miss you, though, you know that. You're all we've got.' He put a hand out to grasp hers, and she squeezed it gently.

'I'm hungry,' said her mother.

Clare felt a lump in her throat and a vice around her ribs. She stood holding her father's hand, counting her breaths until she'd managed to subdue both sensations.

'I'll start dinner.' She sighed and went into the kitchen.

Marion had left a pot of soup on the stove and there was a loaf of bread on the side. Clare heated the soup, cut the bread and buttered it, got out the plates, bowls, spoons, served up and put it all on trays. All the while pushing away any thoughts other than what she was doing. She focused entirely on organising dinner, noticing that one bowl was chipped (*I'll have that one*), and one of the spoons hadn't been washed properly (she rewashed it and dried it on a clean tea towel).

She went back into the sitting room and put her father's table in front of him, tucked a napkin into his collar and brought him his dinner, making sure the spoon and the bread were on the right side for him to feed himself. Then she went back to get her mother's.

'I don't want it,' she said as Clare put it down in front of her.

'Come on, it's lovely lentil soup.' Clare's voice was bright, encouraging as she offered her mother a spoonful. Her father slurped his slowly.

'I want my birthday cake,' said her mother. 'It's my birthday, you know.'

Clare tried to smile at her mother, but her jaw was tight. 'Cake after soup. You know the rules.'

Her mother shut her mouth and turned her head away.

Clare let out a long, slow breath. She was exhausted, her earlier elation spent.

'Just one mouthful,' she tried to cajole her mother, but she wasn't having it. Quick as a flash, she upended the bowl on the table. Clare had to clench her fists and bite her tongue so as not to lash out.

Hot tears of frustration ran down her cheeks.

'It's burning me,' shrieked her mother, lifting one leg after the other as if she was trying to run.

Clare mopped up as much as she could with paper napkins and went into the kitchen to get a cloth. She knew it wasn't burning her mother, it was only tepid, but she couldn't be bothered arguing.

'Are you okay for the moment, Dad? I need to get Mum changed.'

'I'll be all right,' he said.

Clare pulled the table away from her mother's chair and held out her hands. 'Up you get, Mum, let's get you into dry clothes.'

'I'm not going anywhere with you. You want all my possessions and you're not getting your hands on any of it, I can tell you that for nothing.' She clutched the sides of her chair with bony fingers. 'And tell the ugly old man there to get out of my house. My husband will be home soon for his dinner and he won't want that goblin here.'

By nine o'clock, Clare had managed to get both of them into

bed. The stairlift they'd got for her father was a blessing. Her mother loved it, going up and down two or three times every night before she'd go to bed, laughing as she waved her hands in the air with the excitement of it all.

Clare flopped down on the sofa and stretched her legs out. She wasn't sure how much longer she could go on like this. Marion was fantastic, but she didn't want to work more hours. Nursing homes were expensive, and her father had always said he wanted to die at home, not in a urine-smelling, plastic-chaired facility people went into to wait for death to take them. She had money now, it was true, but how long would it last if she had to pay for a home for her mother and twenty-four-hour care for her father? Not long. A lifetime of having to be careful, of scrimping and saving had made her wary of spending. She wasn't going to squander it on things she could manage herself.

She laughed at the idea she could go off on a holiday, leaving her parents at home. It wasn't going to happen. A sob choked her. Nothing was going to be different. She had been wrong earlier when she thought this was the day her life changed. The reality was she was going to spend the next however many years looking after her demented mother and her frail father, wishing their lives away so hers could begin, hoping that by then she wasn't too old to enjoy it.

She sucked in her lips, took a deep breath and heard May's voice in her head telling her to put her feelings into a strong box and slam the lid on them. Of course, May only meant her to put her panicky feelings in a box, but Clare found it a useful exercise for any emotions she didn't want to feel. It took a while to stuff them all in, but she was well practised. In her mind's eye, she put the box of feelings in a safe and locked it away.

She got out her notebook and pen and started writing.

3

TIM

Tim was tired. He'd worked overtime for the last two weeks, what with Danny being off with one complaint or another. Danny was often off. Tim and the boys wondered if he was moonlighting somewhere, working on the trains not being enough.

'Wouldn't put it past him,' Tim had said last time they talked about him. 'He's a sly one that Danny. Notice the way he's never there when it's time to buy a round? Always there to drink it though. Tight-arse. Wouldn't surprise me if he was a millionaire on the quiet. Cash-in-the-mattress type. Not one to trust a bank.'

Frank had laughed. 'Yer probably right there,' he'd said, and scratched his excuse for a beard.

Frank was proud of his bumfluff. Tim had once laughed at him as he groomed it with a special brush in the Men's. Frank had called him a worthless bastard and Tim hadn't mentioned it again.

Tim hated the early trains. Too many wankers and uppity country types who were outraged in their uptight, going-puce-but-saying-nothing way if someone sat in their seat. As if it was their seat.

He rolled his shoulders to relax them a bit. They'd just left Milton Keynes, it was still before eight and he was doing a double shift. Wouldn't be home till gone nine this evening. Three trips. At least he'd be sleeping in his own bed, not like last night when he got stranded in Manchester and had to kip at a mate's place. What a dosshouse. He shuddered at the memory. Wouldn't be surprised if he got fleas, and he scratched at an imagined bite. Still, at least it was free.

He made his way to the on-board food shop and got Sandra to make him a cup of tea the way he liked it – two teabags and a breath of milk. His mum used to say it'd put hairs on his chest. What did she know – when was the last time she'd seen his chest, or any of the rest of him for that matter? Must be more than fourteen years – he'd been about nine. They used to drink tea together in the evenings while she watched *Coronation Street* and he pretended to do his homework, in the peaceful time before his dad got home. He spent the first few months after she left believing she'd come back and the time since wondering whether there was anything he could have done to make her stay.

He downed the tea, thanked Sandra and headed off down the train. Ticket time.

Suddenly the brakes squealed and the train started slowing down fast. Either a twat had pulled on the emergency brake, or there was a problem. He braced himself against the wall just inside the first-class coach, closed his eyes and took several deep breaths. The screech of the brakes was like a knife in his head, and the air smelled of burning metal. Eventually the train stopped and Tim opened his eyes. The passengers were looking out the windows to see what had happened. There were paper cups and sandwich wrappers all over the floor, and spilt tea running across the aisles, but everyone stayed in their seats and quickly got back to their phones or laptops.

As he tried to make a quiet exit to find out what had happened, some pillock in a suit caught him by the sleeve, wanting to know how long it would be until they got going again.

'I have a very important meeting. I can't be late.'

'I understand, sir,' Tim said, in his most soothing voice, pulling his arm away from the man's grasp, 'and I'll look into it, but right now I need to find out what's happened and make an announcement for all the passengers.' He emphasised the 'all the passengers', so this twat knew he was being an arsehole.

The man followed him along the carriage, badgering him. As they passed the toilet, Tim heard a thud and a groan from inside and knocked on the door. The Suit tried to push him forward, insisting that he find out what had stopped the train. Tim turned and glared at him. He wanted to punch him in the head and tell him to stop being such a tosspot, but he'd lose his job if he did. He sighed and shook his head. Then he heard a grating sound, like someone clearing their throat, and the door opened.

'Are you okay, sir?'

'What happened?' The man leant against the sink. He had a cut on his head and blood was oozing down his cheek. Tim rolled off a wad of toilet paper and handed it to him.

'Emergency stop, sir. You must've got thrown around a bit.'

He nodded. Blood was beginning to seep through the toilet paper.

Tim looked at the Suit again. 'Please go back to your seat while I look after this gentleman.'

The Suit looked him up and down, a sneer on his face, but retreated back to first class.

What a tosser. Some people thought they were so important. He glowered and watched him go. He walked like he had a poker up his arse.

'Better come along with me, sir,' he said to the man in the toilet. 'We'll get you cleaned up.'

He wished the day was over. In fact, he wished he could get another job altogether. Trouble was, this one paid all right and at least it was inside. He'd done his time labouring, breaking his back for eight quid an hour, being told to stay at home when it was raining and they couldn't do anything. You can't plan for things when you don't know how much'll be in your pay packet each week. Nah, this was better, for now. And although sometimes it was challenging, dealing with the passengers, at least every day was different. He nodded to himself and made his way towards the front of the train to find out what was going on, keeping his head down and trying to be invisible so no one stopped him to ask any questions.

As if that'd work.

An elderly woman grabbed his jacket as he went past. 'Excuse me, young man, but how long do you think we'll be here?'

He gently pulled his arm away and put on his apologetic, representative-of-the-company smile. 'Can't say, I'm afraid. I'm on my way to find out more right now. We really are sorry for any inconvenience.' Train conductor speak.

The old lady sighed and slumped back into her seat. She reminded Tim of his grandma; white hair, soft, creased skin, too much blue eyeshadow. But his grandma had never had a bruise like that on her jawline, all purple and swollen. He felt sorry for her. She must be shaky on her pins and taken a fall. His grandma had been healthy until the day she died. One massive stroke and off she went. Just the way she would've wanted, his dad said, but Tim knew she didn't want to die at all. She had more living to do. He shook his head and carried on towards the engine.

It seemed to take hours to make it to the front of the train.

Tim had to fend off inquiry after inquiry until he wanted to scream he'd never know what had happened unless they let him go and find out. As he neared the front of the train he saw the flashing blue-and-red lights of police cars pulling into the field. A few minutes later he made it to the engine and saw Brian sitting on the engine step, the door wide open, talking to a policewoman and he knew there'd been a jumper on the line. Brian was wrapped in a silver blanket. He mumbled something and the policewoman wrote it down in her notebook. Why didn't they record the shit people said instead of jotting it all down? Maybe it was about tradition. He was always hearing about 'traditional policing methods' on the news, like they were something to be proud of rather than outdated and cheap.

'You okay, man?' he asked when there was a break in the mumbling.

Brian turned to him and Tim suddenly realised what ashen-faced meant. Brian's skin had turned grey and he looked ten years older than he had half an hour ago.

'Shit, man–' Tim didn't know what to say so he sank onto his haunches and put his hand on Brian's shoulder only to pull away when Brian let out a sob and crumpled in a heap.

'I didn't see her, honest, I didn't see her. She was suddenly just there.' He started rocking.

Tim put his hand back on Brian's shoulder, feeling bad he'd taken it away in the first place. People in shock needed support – the comfort of a familiar face, the weight of a friendly hand. He'd needed those things when his mum left and when his grandma died. And when Tess dumped him. He took a deep breath. He didn't want to remember any of those things.

'It's all right, man, no one thinks you did it on purpose.'

The policewoman was still standing around and he looked to her for support. He nodded at her, eyes wide, and then cocked his head at Brian, dragging a few words of comfort out of her. Stiff bitch.

'Yes, that's right. No one thinks that,' she said with about as much warmth in her voice as yesterday's tea.

'Fuck,' said Brian. 'Fuck.'

'You'll be all right, man,' said Tim because once again, he didn't know what else to say and thought the words probably didn't matter but the hand on the shoulder did. Brian had stopped rocking at least.

Tim peered out the door to see what was going on outside. Several men in disposable white overalls knelt at the front of the train. Scraping blood and guts off the engine, he thought, and imagined he could hear the scrape of spatulas and the pluck, pluck of tweezers. He wondered what happened to all the bits – did they pack them all up and give them to the family to be buried?

He also saw the police cars and vans parked untidily in the field next to the train. The policewoman was asking Brian if he was able to stand up.

Tim helped him, one hand under his armpit, the other round his shoulder. He could feel Brian shaking and struggled with the weight of him. He wasn't a small man. Six foot four and liked his food. Tim wondered if he'd be able to hold him if he had to but once Brian was on his feet he leant against the door frame.

'We'll take you to the station to make a statement and drop you home after,' she said, taking his arm.

'What about the train – who's going to drive it?' he asked.

'They'll get a relief driver.' She pulled on his arm to get him moving.

'Off you go, man. Look after yourself, all right?' said Tim and gave him a farewell pat on the back. He felt sick. Thinking about scraping the guts off the train had done it. And he felt angry.

How fucking dare someone do that and make his mate blame himself. Brian would have to live with the vision and the memory of the woman's last seconds on this planet for the rest of his days, wondering if he could've stopped if he'd seen her sooner. Course he couldn't – it takes hundreds of yards to stop a train going at eighty or ninety miles an hour, and Brian would know that, but still... that's a cruel thing to do to a man. And somehow it made it worse that it was a woman. Such a violent death.

Tim made his way slowly back towards the passengers. He didn't want to talk to anyone but he knew they'd ask questions, and they had a right to know something.

An Indian man with glasses and a sharp parting in his hair was the first to stop him. His glasses made his eyes look bigger and Tim noticed he had the longest eyelashes he'd ever seen. They sort of curled away from his eyes, framing them darkly. Tess would kill for eyelashes like that, he thought, before he could stop himself.

'What's the problem?' asked the Indian with the faintest hint of foreign, musical tones behind his polished English accent.

'Unfortunately there's been an accident,' said Tim. 'I'm going to make an announcement.'

'Oh my Lord,' said the Indian, and slumped into his seat, closing his eyes.

The woman next to him looked out the window, craning her neck to see if she could get a glimpse of the mess.

'Best not to look,' said Tim, disturbed by her eagerness to see, even though he'd done the same only minutes ago. It was human nature, wasn't it, to be fascinated by blood and gore, to be interested in bad things happening to people? As long as they weren't people you knew and liked. It was why horror movies so often did well at the box office and people slowed down to look at accidents.

Tim made his announcement about the accident and asked everyone to stay in their seats. He apologised on behalf of the railway for the inconvenience, then made his way towards first class murmuring responses to the passengers who asked questions, but kept moving so as not to get caught in long explanations. He wished he could take his uniform off and sit quietly in a corner seat. He was suddenly so tired, so heavy-limbed that he could barely make it to first class. Is this shock? he wondered. Or the effort of not telling the passengers to get stuffed. All they could talk about was how the delay would affect them. Not one of them had asked how the driver was, whether he would ever get over it.

'Tickets, please,' he said as he entered the carriage.

They were all there, in their usual places, copies of *The Telegraph* on their laps. The first man lifted his head as Tim reached him, sighed and pulled his wallet out of his inside jacket pocket as if it was the greatest inconvenience he could imagine. Tim glanced at the season ticket and nodded.

He moved on to the next person, the man he thought of as Mr Self-Important. 'Thanks,' he said when he flashed his ticket. He was turning away when he felt a hand on his arm. Here we go, thought Tim. Sir's going to complain about the delay and tell me how important he is and how it's vital to world peace or European security that he gets to London NOW.

'Is the driver all right?' he asked.

Tim wondered if he'd heard right. He turned, stared at the suited man with the polished shoes and said, 'He's gone to give his statement to the police.'

'Yes, but is he all right? I mean it must have been one hell of a shock, poor man.'

Tim blinked. Once. Twice. He couldn't form a sentence. The man cleared his throat and waited.

'He's – he's very upset,' said Tim.

The man nodded. 'My grandfather drove a train. It happened to him once too. It really shook him. Will the company look after him? Is there a fund or something, to help him out until he can work again?'

Tim hadn't thought of that, and didn't know. 'There's sick leave.'

'Yes. Of course. Well, I hope he recovers quickly.'

Tim felt guilty. This man may be an upper-class twat and wear a cashmere coat and scarf, but he was a decent sort after all. He thought about giving him back the expensive pen he'd left on the seat a few weeks back but decided not to. His gran had always said, 'God helps those who help themselves'. And anyway, just because he'd been sympathetic today didn't mean he was actually nice. And Tim liked that pen. It felt just right in his hand and although he didn't write very much, preferring to make notes on his phone when necessary, that pen made him think about writing. What he'd say about things and how he'd say it. Maybe one day he'd start a diary or something. He gave a little laugh. All because of a pen.

And why not? He'd always been all right at English. His mum, and later his gran, had read to him and then, when he could read himself, made sure he always had books. He looked at his hand, imagining the pen in it, then he looked at the other man's hands – soft and white, tapered fingers, buffed nails. And small. Almost a child's hands. They didn't deserve to hold a pen like that. Tim's own hands may be rough, but he always kept them clean and the nails short. Art was his great love though. His fantasies about the future always centred on having a solo exhibition of his works. Or being asked to paint a huge mural somewhere prominent. His art teacher had said he had talent. Maybe he'd use the pen to sign copies for his fans.

'Are you all right?' asked the man, and Tim realised he was

still standing beside him, daydreaming and probably smiling like a loony.

'Yeah,' he said, and moved on.

Half an hour later, Tim was ready to quit his job and walk away. It didn't seem to matter how many announcements he made, or how often he apologised, the passengers were getting antsy. He'd rung head office to find out what else he could do and even when he announced a discounted train journey for every passenger, there were still complaints. He felt like telling them all to take a flying jump but knew it would cost him his job which, much as he hated it right now, he needed to keep a bit longer. So he glued an apologetic smile onto his face and walked the length of the train again, listening to people go on about their important jobs, appointments, meetings, shopping, family reunions and God knows what else until he wanted to ask if any of them actually did anything that was a matter of life and death – did it really matter one tiny rat's arse if they were late – would people die?

He tucked himself away in one of the loos for a few minutes and called Brian to see how he was.

'I'm still at the police station, man,' he said, sounding agitated. 'I've given my statement, but they want me to see a counsellor before I go. I don't want to talk about it anymore, you know? What damn use is a counsellor gonna be? I just want to go home.'

'Not long now, I'm sure. You'll have to see the company counsellor – tell them that and they might let you go. After that you can get home and take a bit of time for yourself. If you need anything, call me, okay?'

'Yeah. Ta, man.'

Tim leant against the hand basin and sighed. He knew all about counsellors. When he'd let slip to one of the teachers at school that his mum had left after one too many bashings, they'd hauled him in to see a psychologist. He hadn't wanted to. Only pussies saw people like her, but over time it had helped. Gran had been great at the day-to-day stuff, but the psychologist was the only person who actually listened to what he said and helped him make sense of what he was feeling. Which was sad and empty, angry and confused, and then just angry and in the end sad again, but not the bone-shattering sadness he'd started with, more a dull ache that increased to an acute pain every now and then – birthdays, Christmases, school events where parents went along. All those times when he realised afterwards he'd been holding his breath, hoping this time she'd come. She never did. He wondered where she was, what had happened to her. His father had banned any mention of her and Tim remembered all too clearly what had happened last time he'd asked. The knuckles of his left hand were still stiff and two of his fingers misshapen from the pounding he'd got.

They'd been sitting in front of the telly, the dinner trays still on their laps. *EastEnders* had just finished and his dad was going on about how in TV shows everything got sorted out in the end, everyone knew what was happening, as if it was a bad thing. It was the day after Tim's twenty-first and he still had the knot of pain in his stomach from yet another birthday passing without his mum so he asked, without thinking, why she'd gone.

As soon as he said it the sadness was replaced by anxiety. He wanted to eat his words, swallow and silence them.

'Sorry, Dad, I didn't mean it.'

But it was too late. His father was on his feet and coming at him, steak knife in hand. He'd had a few drinks before he got home and several more since, but his hand was steady, his eyes fixed on his son. Tim felt a shiver of fear but stood to face him, still holding his tray. Tim didn't know whether to brace for a punch or watch the knife. Not that his father had ever done more than threaten when he had something in his hand but this time felt different. He took a step back, his calves hitting the chair.

His father never said a word. When he thought about it afterwards that was what stuck with Tim. The quiet. The only sounds came from the falling of crockery and cutlery and the thwack of fist into flesh and Tim's groan. He reeled but remained standing, dazed. The next punch doubled him over and he fell to the floor and drew into a foetal curl. He saw his father's heavy work boot swim into view and heard the crunch of his hand underneath it before he felt the pain.

He'd taken himself to the hospital, his hand wrapped in a tea towel. After the surgeon had put several metal plates in to hold the bones together, Tim asked to see a social worker. She'd found him temporary accommodation. He hadn't seen his father since.

No wonder his mother had left.

The door handle rattled and Tim heard an impatient hrmph from the other side. He ran the tap, slicked down the bit of hair that always seemed to stick out no matter how much product he put in it, took a deep breath and opened the door.

'Sorry, sir. All yours,' he said.

His phone vibrated in his pocket.

'Hey, Timmy – Gavin. I'll be taking this blood-soaked bucket to Euston for you.'

Tim's heart sank. Gavin may drive a train okay but he was the last person Tim wanted to see right now. He'd never heard a serious word come out of his mouth, and today was obviously going to be no exception. He was the kind of bloke who, when someone was going through shit, would make jokes about refugees or people shagging sheep. A class act.

'Hi, Gav. Glad to be in your capable hands,' he said. 'Are we clear to go? Shall I let the passengers know?'

''Nother few minutes. Boiler suits are still scrubbing the train down. Trust Brian to flatten a girl. I've only had men.'

'What's that meant to mean?' asked Tim, bristling on behalf of his friend. 'He'd never willingly hurt anyone and you know it.'

Gavin laughed down the phone. 'All right, keep your hair on. Didn't mean anything by it, just making conversation.'

'Yeah, well, it was a bloody stupid thing to say, okay?'

Gavin was known to have been back at work the day after he'd hit someone, making jokes and laying bets on who'd be next to slam on the emergency brakes.

Tim sighed, rolled his shoulders a few times and made his way to the intercom to update the passengers.

Twenty minutes later they were on their way again, the rain-sodden fields blurring as they gathered speed. Tim started down the train checking tickets, making small talk with the passengers so they didn't get a chance to ask any more about the suicide. He found it repugnant that people wanted the facts in all their gory detail. *Repugnant*. What a good word. Someone had told him the other day he thought President Trump was repugnant, so he'd looked it up, wondering if he'd ever use it. And here he was.

When, finally, they pulled into Euston, Tim let out a sigh of relief. The cleaners boarded the train but not before he'd done a quick check to make sure there was no lost property. As he walked the length of the platform towards the station staffroom, he avoided looking at the front of the train. It was probably clean as the proverbial whistle and he didn't need to check.

It was only just past ten but he could have killed for an ice-cold, numbing shot of vodka.

~

Tim started shaking when he got to the staffroom at Euston, nearly two hours later than usual. His boss had been called and he'd been given the rest of the day off but only so long as he agreed to see the staff counsellor the next day. Sandra from the food shop and Brian the driver would have to go, too, it was company policy that all staff on the train were debriefed and counselled in the event of a suicide or other incident. No ifs, buts or maybes.

He decided to go and see Brian, who had been dropped home by the police after giving his statement. At East Acton Station he looked along the road. The day had turned out warm. Tim unzipped his jacket and wondered if he should buy Brian something. He didn't know what people did in these situations; Brian wasn't ill, but he'd had a shock. Fags? A car magazine?

In the end he bought nothing and thrust his hands deep into his pockets as he walked through the housing estate, trying to remember which block Brian's flat was in. There were too many kids around for a school day and Tim wondered why no one cared, why there weren't adults out there herding them to school, reminding them they'd never get anywhere without an education. His gran had made him go to school. She'd also made him join the local youth club run by the church. He'd protested at first, but made new friends and enjoyed the activities. He'd never thanked her for it at the time but later, when he saw his schoolmates begin to drift away and get into trouble, or start on drugs, he knew she'd been right. Not that he'd done too well, except in English, art and woodwork, but at least he'd finished.

Rounding a corner, he recognised Brian's block. Red brick, graffiti tags all over it, paint peeling from the wooden window frames, outer door splintered. Tim was dismayed the council did so little for its tenants. Couldn't they imagine what it would be like to live in a place so run-down and depressing? No wonder the kids didn't bother going to school, their whole lives were lived in this shitty place where nothing made them feel worthwhile or valued. They grew to match their environment, their horizons as limited as the boundaries of the housing estate. You could grow up to become a drug dealer, a teenage mum or a car thief. They should pay him to do a mural on the walls, cover over the mindless graffiti and paint something inspiring. Although he couldn't think what that might be in a place like this. He'd hunt for Banksy images when he had time. Or Warhol.

He took the stairs to Brian's door two at a time and knocked.

'I don't want to see anyone, go away.'

'Brian, it's me. Tim. Just came to see how you are.'

He heard shuffling and a lock being pulled back. Brian had changed into a grey tracksuit, old and shapeless. The knees bagged and made it look as if his legs were bent, and the bum hung down. The curtains were drawn, making the flat gloomy and uninviting. Tim wanted to pull them back and open the windows, let the light and warmth in but it wasn't his place. Brian led him into the kitchen and slumped into a chair.

'Want tea?' he asked as an afterthought.

Tim realised that if he did, he'd be making it. He filled the kettle and plugged it in, went through the cupboards to find tea, sugar, mugs. Brian stared into space, not caring or perhaps not even registering what was going on around him.

Tim put a mug of strong sweet tea in front of him.

'Get that down you,' he said.

Brian lifted his head and looked at him and Tim saw the shock still in his eyes, the disbelief. And something else – an edginess, fear, as if he'd been caught doing something bad and didn't know how to make it right.

They sat in silence for a while. Now he was here, Tim didn't know what to do.

Slowly, Brian seemed to relax. He pulled his tobacco and papers out of his pocket and took his time to roll himself a cigarette. His hand shook as he struck a match to light it and he inhaled deeply, closing his eyes. 'What am I going to do?'

Tim shifted in his seat, unsure how to answer. Unsure exactly what the question meant. He sat, waiting.

Brian opened his eyes again. 'I can't drive a train again, not after that.'

Tim nodded. Not because he agreed, but because he understood that was how Brian felt right then.

'I mean, shit – I killed a woman. It could happen again.'

'You didn't kill her, she killed herself. You just happened to–'

'I saw her too late. She looked right at me. Right in the eye. And then she stepped onto the rails.' He shuddered and closed his eyes again as if it would stop him seeing her, stop him reliving the moment when the woman took that fatal step.

They lapsed into silence again, occasionally lifting their mugs to their mouths, placing them down again quietly. Outside, a car screeched to a halt, a man shouted, a woman responded. The car drove off. Tim looked towards the sounds but Brian seemed not to hear them, caught in his own drama.

The clock ticked loudly. Tim washed the mugs, running the water for longer than necessary. When he turned round, Brian was standing.

'Thanks for coming,' he said. 'It was good to talk.'

'Sure,' said Tim, feeling guilty he was so ready to leave, that Brian felt so bad and he couldn't make it better for him.

At the door, Tim squeezed Brian's shoulder and was surprised when Brian pulled him into a hug. Tim felt the shuddering of his friend's body as he wept and held on to him. When Brian stepped away he couldn't look Tim in the eye.

'Thanks again,' he muttered, opening the door.

~

On the Tube Tim sat picking at the skin around his thumb. He'd become a nail-biter after his mother left, a difficult habit to break but he'd managed to get it down to this one finger. He was proud of his willpower. His gran had always said he should count not only his blessings but also his good points, because no one else would count them for him. Sometimes it made him feel big-headed and other times he was hard-pressed to find anything positive about himself at all, but he thought that overall it was a good thing to do.

He was worried about Brian but didn't know what more he could do. He felt unsettled and wasn't ready to go home and be on his own with all the thoughts whizzing through his head. He'd moved out of the boarding house the hospital social worker had found for him into a bedsit. He liked having his own place, not having to answer to anyone, but it was lonely. At the boarding house there'd always been someone to talk to, even if half of them were mad and the other half hardly spoke any English. Never a dull moment, he'd thought when he counted his blessings there. He changed onto the Circle line at Notting Hill Gate and sat in a corner going round and round the loop, trying not to think, until his stomach rumbled and reminded him he hadn't eaten since five in the morning. He waited until the train got to Euston again and took the escalator to the concourse.

Euston was familiar. He knew the cafés and pubs, the hum of the station, the lay of the land. He could have gone to the staffroom to hang out but he didn't want to talk to anyone. So he stood and watched the indicator board announcing the train departures for a few minutes, soothed by the normality of it, then got himself a coffee and a sandwich and sat watching the people going about their lives. He found himself wondering about the woman who had killed herself. What did she look like, how did she spend her time, did somebody love her? What would make someone feel so bad they wanted to be dead? Tim had had his share of difficulties but he had never wanted to top himself. He'd always believed that problems could be worked out, and even though he'd lost the two people in his life who'd meant the most, he thanked them daily for the influence they'd had on his life. He felt lucky to have known them. Of course, he'd prefer it if they were still around, but there was nothing he could do about it. He wondered if clever people were more likely to kill themselves because they tortured themselves with options and possibilities. Perhaps people like him saw things more simply and were happier for it. Or not. He liked the fact he had thoughts like that. Big Ideas his gran had called them and called him her clever boy. But they could be frustrating because too often there were no answers.

He got his notebook out and started sketching. He drew a woman. Was this what the dead woman had looked like? As he drew, he imagined a past for her. Her name was Mary and she had discovered her husband was having an affair. No, that wasn't it; plenty of people got cheated on and didn't get suicidal about it. He started again. She was Beatrix and she had just been told she had cancer. No, that wasn't right either. People often got better from cancer these days, it wasn't something worth killing yourself over. Her name was Jane and she had just discovered she was adopted at birth but her real parents wanted nothing to do with her. That might be enough to make a person suicidal, he thought. People felt betrayed by things like that. Unloved. He sat back. The sketch wasn't one of his best, but he felt at least he had captured a sense of despair in the eyes. And then he realised they were his mother's eyes and a lump rose in his throat.

His phone rang.

'Thank you for coming round, Tim. You're a good friend. The best.'

Brian's voice was thick with alcohol, the words bumping against each other.

'You okay, Brian?'

'Yeah I'm fine. Nina's here and we're having a drink. I just wanted to say thank you.'

'You're welcome. Anything else I can do, you call, okay?'

'You're a good friend.' Brian hung up and Tim frowned. He was glad Nina was there, but not that they were pissed. Brian was a recovering alcoholic and he hadn't had a drink in months. He'd never driven a train drunk as far as Tim knew. He thought perhaps he should have seen this could happen but what would he have done about it? He couldn't tell Brian what to do. He just hoped it wasn't a long binge and he got himself onto the wagon again quickly. But he couldn't get rid of the feeling he could have said more, something that would have helped Brian understand it wasn't his fault. He wasn't going to find answers at the bottom of a whisky bottle. He sent a text. Brian probably wouldn't read it now but maybe when he was sober it would help.

You're not to blame. Remember that. You're a good man. Stay cool.

It was what his counsellor used to say to him, and he'd eventually accepted maybe his father's violence wasn't his fault, that as the adult his father should have been able to contain his anger instead of taking it out on his son.

He was about to put his phone away when it rang again. He looked at the caller ID. Head office. He didn't want to speak to any of the toffs. They'd be checking to see he was okay, confirming his appointment to see the psychologist, sounding all concerned until they told him to be back at work as soon as possible. He declined the call and stuffed the phone into his pocket.

A man approached carrying a tray and asked if he could share the table. Tim looked around and realised the café had filled with the lunchtime trade. He nodded and moved his cup and plate out of the way. He thought he recognised the man but he often thought that these days, especially around the station. He saw a lot of people in his job. He watched as the man put his lunch on the table and leant the empty tray against the leg of his chair and started eating his sausage roll with a knife and fork. Tim watched, fascinated. Who ate sausage rolls with a knife and fork? The other man looked up, and Tim didn't look away fast enough. He saw recognition dawn on the other man's face.

'You're the ticket collector,' he said, putting his cutlery down.

Tim nodded. 'Guilty as charged, Tim Engleby,' he said.

'Ray Dreyfus.' He put his hand out and Tim shook it firmly because his gran had always said you couldn't trust a man who had a weak handshake.

'I hope the – er – train being late didn't inconvenience you too much,' he said. God, he sounded like the announcements script on all the Virgin rail services.

'No, it was fine. Well, not fine, obviously, that someone died, but I wasn't late for my appointment.'

'That's good.' Tim didn't know what else to say but Ray kept looking at him, so he stumbled on. 'Do you work in London?'

'No.'

Tim watched in horror as Ray's face seemed to collapse and tears welled in his eyes. 'I came to see a specialist. A doctor,' he said.

'Oh. And–'

'I have cancer. Inoperable cancer.' Ray frowned and squirmed in his seat, pulled out a hankie and wiped his face.

'Sorry. You don't want to hear about it. It's just that it's been rather a shock.'

'You talk if you need to,' said Tim. It seemed to be his destiny today, to have people needing to talk to him. Not that Brian had done much talking. Perhaps he could help this chap more than he'd helped his friend.

Ray had pulled himself together. He gave Tim a bleak smile and got up. 'I think I'll go for a walk,' he said, and left.

Tim watched him go. Maybe a cancer diagnosis was enough to make you want to top yourself after all.

By the time he thought that and wondered if he should do something, the other man was nowhere in sight.

Tim didn't know what to do with himself. He still wasn't ready to go home, but he couldn't sit in the busy café any longer. It was as if something was compelling him to stay near the station. He wasn't sure if it was because he felt the need to be near trains and the familiarity of the place or if it was more about being around people. There was an energy about stations he never found anywhere else.

He was concerned about Brian and now also worried about this man with cancer. His gran had always said he was a sensitive sort who absorbed other people's feelings. Today, he'd quite like to put them down again and work out what he felt about the whole suicide thing. He grabbed his jacket and edged off the stool. He knew quite a few of the station staff but he didn't want to see them and have them asking questions about what had happened. Instead, he went and sat in the park outside and pulled out his sketchbook again. Drawing helped him work out what he was feeling and then find a way to deal with it. Another thing to thank his counsellor for. Tapping his pencil against his teeth, he thought about what he wanted to draw and turned to a new page and starting doodling.

The doodles turned into a woman standing in front of a train. There was a tightness in his chest.

Stop thinking about it. It won't do any good. It won't change anything. He scribbled the image out and shut the book.

He watched two pigeons fight over a piece of a polystyrene food container, then looked around, pulling up the collar of his jacket against a rising breeze and made himself smile. *Be grateful for what you've got.*

The wind scuffed litter along the ground, and all around him people were rushing to and fro. Behind him on Marylebone Road, cars, buses, lorries, and motorbikes were streaming along trying to find a small advantage in the traffic. And here he was, alive, healthy, and sitting in the middle of this great city. He took a selfie, planning to make a painting from it later, then closed his eyes for a moment, imagining himself on a stage talking to people about his art and them applauding him for his great and exciting talent.

He opened his eyes when he felt someone sit on the other end of the bench. He glanced over, annoyed he'd been disturbed. He looked again, stared. It was the girl from the train, the one he'd watched from the other end of the carriage. She was wearing make-up now and she'd changed her clothes but it was definitely her. Her eyes were a bit puffy, like she'd been crying but she was still beautiful. She was unaware of him, staring at the ground in front of her and playing with the handle of her bag, folding it over and over, letting it go and folding it again. Her nails were bitten, he noticed, and the skin of her hands dry and raw like she washed them too often. His gran's hands had been the same.

Looking away, he tried to calm down. Should he go? He was always uncomfortable around beautiful girls. Even when he and Tess had been going out for months, he was sometimes tongue-tied around her. It was as if her beauty had made his words sound stupid and unworthy.

He was just about to leave when the girl let out a sob and buried her head in her hands. Tim stayed where he was. He wanted to reach out and touch her shoulder, to offer comfort but she might take it the wrong way, so he pulled out a tissue – his gran had told him always to have one with him – and held it out to her. When she didn't take it, didn't notice it, he gently pushed it into her hand.

She blew her nose noisily and said thank you without looking at him. Tim edged back to the other end of the bench once more.

He found beautiful women terrifying but he found a woman in need almost irresistible. It was like a knee-jerk reaction; she needed something, he provided it. Leaving was no longer on the agenda. So he sat and waited, every so often glancing in her direction.

'Thank you,' she said again after several minutes.

'I haven't done anything.'

'But you haven't run away screaming either,' she said. She'd raised her head but hadn't looked at him.

'No, I'm still here.'

'So you don't think I'm a loony then?'

'Should I?'

She smiled, still staring straight ahead. 'I don't know. Maybe I am.' She turned and did a double-take. 'You!'

'Me.' Tim blushed.

'You're the guy on the train.'

'And you're the girl on the train.'

'Yeah, but you ignored me. You didn't even look at me.'

'Oh yes I did.'

She smiled, but tears started spilling down her cheeks.

'What's the matter? – it can't just be that I didn't look at you when I checked your ticket.' He made a puppy-dog face.

'No, although it did break my heart.' She gave a little laugh that turned into a sob that caught in her throat. 'I just made such a tit of myself and watched all my dreams go galloping out the door.'

Tim moved a little closer. 'What happened?'

'I had an audition for *The X Factor* and I screwed it up big time. I mean, I was so bad they asked me to stop before I'd finished the song.' She started folding the strap of her bag again.

'Oh.' Tim sat quietly, waiting to see if she wanted to say any more. His gran had always said if you give people the space, they'll tell you everything. But the girl didn't go on. She wasn't crying anymore but she was taking deep breaths as if trying to stay calm.

'What did you sing?' asked Tim eventually.

'Doesn't matter. It was shit and I'm never singing again.'

'I wouldn't do that if I was you,' said Tim. 'I mean, you must love singing and be good at it to get an audition. Be a shame to let one setback get in the way of a dream.'

She looked at him but didn't say anything, so he went on.

'I do a bit of painting and who knows, one day I might even sell some, but everyone has setbacks. I'm sure even Beyoncé has bad days. Would've been a tragedy if she'd quit at the first hurdle.' Tim had never told anyone about his dream of selling his work before. Perhaps this girl had a gran who told her about giving people space to talk, thought Tim.

'What's your name?' he asked.

'Alice.'

'Alice what?'

'Alice Cooper. Why?'

'Any relation to Alice Cooper?' he asked.

She smiled. 'No. It wasn't even his real name.'

'I know. He was Vincent Furnier. I prefer Alice Cooper.'

'Why'd you want to know my name anyway?' she asked.

'So I can listen out for you on the radio and say, "I met her once, before she was famous. She'd just been turned down by *The X Factor* and now they're regretting it".' He smiled. 'Don't give up, Alice Cooper.'

Alice laughed. 'You're the loony, not me. But thank you. You're sweet.'

Tim blushed more deeply and held his breath. Suddenly he was aware of her again as the girl he hadn't been able to make eye contact with on the train. And here she was, calling him 'sweet', sitting right next to him on a bench on a summer afternoon in London. He wanted to draw her, or take a photo so he could paint her later. Anything that meant he didn't have to focus on actually being there now.

'So, Mr Ticket Collector, do you always sit here in the afternoons in case someone comes along and needs cheering up?'

Tim swallowed. 'No.' His suddenly sweaty palms seemed to have drawn all the moisture away from his mouth, which was as dry as a pub in a brewery strike. *Come on, Tim,* he thought, *say something funny. Or not funny, just say something, or she'll think you're a jerk.* 'I was drawing,' he said. *Oh, God, I've mentioned it again! What a stupid thing to say. She's either going to think I'm bragging, or she's going to ask to see it. Or both. Shit.* 'Normally I'd be on my way to Manchester now,' he said, hoping she'd ignore the art bit.

'But not today. Is it because of what happened this morning or do you have magical powers and you knew about my potential suicide this afternoon? Sorry – that was a pretty off thing to say.'

Tim didn't know how to answer. Yes, it was because of the morning incident, no he didn't have magical powers, and yes, he agreed it was a pretty bad joke – or at least he hoped it was a joke. He looked at her in confusion and wanted to kick himself. How often did he meet girls he fancied these days? And here he was, fucking it up because he was so shy he couldn't talk. He wanted to scream. 'Want a drink?' was all he managed.

He felt his skin burning under Alice's scrutiny. It seemed to take hours for her to decide. Hours in which Tim had plenty of time to imagine her laughing at him, asking why on earth a girl like her would want a drink with a guy like him, point out that she was worthy of far better, could have, in fact, anyone she wanted, and had no need for a nobody like him.

'Yeah,' she said finally. 'That would be nice.'

Which Tim heard as, 'Yes, I haven't got anything better to do until my train leaves.'

Tim looked back with longing at the pub he had just left. Not the pub, Alice, who was still sitting at the table. She was the first chick he'd met since Tess that he really wanted to get to know. She was hot, but it was more than that. She interested him with her mixture of self-confidence and self-doubt. Sure, he would like to see her naked, he couldn't deny it, but he also wanted to unravel the mystery of this Alice Cooper.

He shrugged himself deeper into his jacket. The temperature had plummeted with the sun going down. He turned his thoughts to Brian. He'd been practically incoherent on the phone. Tim had found it difficult to understand what it was he wanted, and was dismayed to find it was him. A friend to talk to now Nina had gone and the events of the day were hitting him. Tim couldn't let his mate down; his gran had always said, a friend in need is a friend indeed. Or was it in deed? He had no idea what it meant either way, but he did know friends were important and you didn't ditch them for a bit of skirt. Not that Alice was that.

He hurried through the estate past teenagers sharing a joint who jeered at him and got back to their puff.

A woman stepped out of a doorway. She stood under a dim light, her bleached hair glowing either side of the darker strip of her parting. 'Ten quid for a blow job,' she said, in a raspy smoker's voice.

'Not tonight, thanks.' He hugged his jacket tighter and quickened his step.

At Brian's door he paused. Part of him wanted to run back to the pub to see if Alice was still there, if she was real.

He knocked. The door was ajar. Tim pushed gently and went in.

'Brian, it's me, Tim. You there?'

No answer.

The lights were off and Tim couldn't find a light switch. He left the door open so the landing light shone in weakly. He looked into the bedroom but there didn't seem to be anyone in there. From what he could make out, the bed was still made. He felt his way along the hall into the kitchen which was lit in strobes by a blinking street light.

'Shit – what the–?'

Brian was slumped over the kitchen table, vomit pooled around his face. His eyes were closed and he wasn't making a sound. Tim rushed over and felt for a pulse, leant down and listened for a breath.

Shit, he thought again, and pulled out his phone. He dialled 999 and asked for an ambulance. He found the light switch and noticed Brian wince as the light came on, but his eyes didn't open.

'Come on, man, wake up.' Tim patted him on the cheek. He

moved Brian's face out of the puke and cleaned it as best he could, talking all the while, telling him what he was doing.

'I'm here to help. Let's get you looking beautiful again.' He almost gagged at the smell of vomit and alcohol fumes.

Where was the bloody ambulance? It had been at least fifteen minutes since he'd called. At last he saw the blue-and-red flashing lights reflecting on the ceiling. He opened the window and called out, relief replacing his anxiety. Now someone else would take responsibility. Someone who knew what they were doing.

'What's the story here?' asked one of the paramedics as he came in.

'I don't really know. He's a train driver and someone jumped this morning. He called me earlier and said a friend was here and they were having a drink. He called again about forty minutes ago. I came round and found him like this.'

'Just alcohol? Does he take any drugs you know of?'

'Nah. No drugs. He's dead against them.'

Tim looked around and saw an empty bottle of vodka and a nearly empty one of bourbon. There were several beer and cider bottles by the sink. 'I'd guess it's that,' he said, pointing.

'Best get him to hospital for fluids then,' said the paramedic to his colleague. 'You coming?' he turned to ask Tim as they manhandled Brian onto a stretcher.

'Well – okay. Yeah, sure.' How could he say no? He wondered what Alice was doing. He was sure he'd never see her again, not leaving the way he had. Resentment flickered and died. What was the use? He had to help his friend, no two ways about it.

In the ambulance, he gave Brian's details as best he could. He had to guess his birthdate and didn't know his middle name, had no idea who his next of kin was, nor whether he had any existing illnesses. He wondered if he should tell them he was a recovering alcoholic, but in the circumstances, it didn't really seem to matter; there wasn't a lot of recovering going on right now.

At Ealing Hospital the paramedics wheeled Brian into a corridor and left to find a staff member to hand over to. His eyes opened momentarily, unfocused. Saliva stretched down his chin. Tim looked away. Brian wouldn't want to be seen like that.

He waited, leaning against the stretcher in the absence of anywhere to sit. The light immediately above had blown, leaving him in a pool of shadow. In the distance, he could hear voices, the beeps of machinery, a squeaky trolley being pushed along the lino floor.

He jumped when Brian gurgled as if he was going to puke again, but he just mumbled something and settled back into semi-consciousness.

Tim thought again of Alice. Perhaps she was waiting for him to call. He pulled his phone out and found her number in his contacts. There she was. He tapped the screen and heard her phone ring. His heart started beating faster.

A doctor in a flapping white coat parted the plastic doors at the end of the corridor and approached. Tim ended the call before she answered – would she have answered? – and slipped his phone back into his pocket.

'Alcohol poisoning? Were you there? How much did he have to drink? Has he vomited at all?'

Tim was about to answer but the doctor glanced at the paperwork in his hand and said, 'Oh, yes. I see. Terrible shock he's had, although drinking himself into a coma isn't the best way to deal with it.'

Tim agreed and was about to say so when a nurse arrived and strapped a hospital band onto Brian's wrist and started pushing the stretcher back the way they'd come.

'Should I come too?' he asked.

They didn't reply, so he followed. At the plastic doors, the nurse turned to him and pointed to a seating area on the right.

'You can wait there.'

'How long will it be?'

Again, no response and then they were gone, the sound of their voices retreating down the hall. One said something and the other laughed. Tim was annoyed. This was no laughing matter.

In a corner of the waiting area was a TV showing a shopping channel, the sound turned off. A sign next to it said *For the comfort of all, DO NOT TOUCH the television.* Tim wondered what not touching the TV had to do with anyone's comfort, and then lost interest and looked about. An old man was coughing into his hand, the younger man with him eating a family-size packet of crisps. An Indian couple were cradling their children on their laps. Tim couldn't tell which one of them was ill or injured. A mother and son sat talking quietly, his thickly-bound ankle resting on another chair. That was it; early Monday evening in A and E. Tim thought it would probably be busy later with the drunks and the sick who hadn't made it to their doctor during the day. He looked at his watch. Alice was probably halfway home and he'd never see her again. He knew it had been too good to be true. Chicks like her didn't go for guys like him. He swallowed his disappointment and sat, hands in his armpits, staring at the floor.

He was nodding off when his phone rang.

'How's your friend?'

'Alice?'

'Yeah, it's me. I'm still in London. Didn't know how long you'd be.'

'Alice – you're – Alice!'

'Course I am. Who else would I be? Are you okay? What's happening?'

Tim told her about finding Brian and waiting at the hospital.

'Want company?'

Tim smiled. 'You'd come here?'

'Sure. Why not. Got nothing else to do except go home, and I don't really want to yet.'

Tim's smile faded. She was bored, and hanging out with him was marginally better than going home.

'What I meant was, I'd rather come and hang around with you than go home, if you want me to.'

'Yeah, I'd like that.' Tim's smile reappeared. 'I'd like it a lot.'

'See you soon then. Don't go anywhere.'

Tim paced. He couldn't keep still. Alice was coming to see him. He hoped they kept Brian long enough so he was still there when she arrived. What if they discharged him and Brian wanted to go straight home? He couldn't let him go on his own, but he could hardly take Alice with him.

The woman and her son looked at him and the mother's brow creased. Tim realised he was probably annoying them with his ceaseless pacing but he couldn't stop. The Indian family was called and they rose and disappeared into another room. Everyone watched them go and then looked at the clock ticking away on the wall above the rack which held useful leaflets about AA, NA, MS, PND, MND, SLAA. You name it, there were letters to obscure what it actually was.

The crisp-eating guy raised his eyebrows and said something to the older man who shrugged and looked back at the TV. A teenager came in and went to the reception window where a frazzled-looking clerk took his details and told him to wait. He was holding his arm above his head. It was wrapped in a tea towel but blood was seeping through it. Tim remembered his trip to hospital when his dad had stomped on his hand – he'd had the same tea towel, held his hand above his head in the same way – and suddenly he wanted to leave. His hand started throbbing at the memory of it. He wanted to see Alice, but not in this place. He'd forgotten how much he hated hospitals; the pain he saw on people's faces, the smell of fear and antiseptic, the overlit drab rooms.

He told the receptionist he'd be waiting outside for any news of Brian and exited through automatic doors. He took a deep breath and looked across the car park to Uxbridge Road. Alice would be coming from that direction. He imagined her walking towards him while he watched, her coat flying open revealing the clothes hugging the curves of her body. He saw himself taking her in his arms and pulling her towards him, breathing in the sweet floral smell of her perfume, looking into her eyes, leaning down to kiss her.

'Your friend is awake and asking for you,' said a voice behind him. Tim swung round to see the nurse who had taken Brian away hugging herself in the cool evening air.

'Thanks,' he said and took a last look towards the road before following her back into the hospital.

Brian was sitting in bed in a curtained cubicle. A drip stand held two bags of fluid that were flowing into Brian's arm through clear tubes. His eyes were red-rimmed and unfocused and Tim wondered if they'd pumped his stomach yet, or if they even still did that. He remembered his father had once had to have it done, not long after his mother had left and alcohol had been his constant companion. Tim had called 999 when he'd come home from school and when they arrived, heard the ambulance men talk to each other about pumping his stomach. Tim had had an image of a pump handle like the one he'd seen on an old Western, a woman in a long dress, a shawl around her shoulders, pumping water from a standpipe.

'Hey, man, how you doing?' He grabbed a plastic chair and pulled it closer.

'Sorry – sorry I did this to you. You're a good friend,' Brian slurred without looking at him.

'It's okay. You'll be fine.' Tim hoped he was right. 'Want me to get you anything?'

'Nah. They're going to keep me in overnight, they said. Coz of what happened and all.'

'Have you – I mean, do you – are you thinking about it, the jumper?'

Brian looked into the distance. 'Trying not to, but it's hard. I keep seeing her eyes boring into me and then she wasn't there anymore... you know.'

'Yeah. I know, man. Might be a good idea, staying in for the night,' said Tim. 'Have people around in case you feel like talking.'

'Yeah.'

They lapsed into silence. Brian closed his eyes. Tim looked around wondering how far away Alice was, when she'd be there, if she was really coming.

He watched the busyness of the emergency department through a gap in the curtains, pulled out his notebook and started sketching as he listened to the sounds and the rhythm of the hospital. The staff wrote notes, chatted to each other, spoke on the phone, tended to patients. He felt dislocated from reality.

Tim assessed his drawing. A nurse leaning against the desk reading case notes. It wasn't finished but he liked the image he'd created. A moment of calm in a busy emergency department.

And he thought again about Alice and what it might be like to kiss her. She was sinuous, sensuous... ordacious? He wondered how it was spelt so he got his phone out to check it. *Audacious.* Lively, unrestrained, uninhibited. That was her. But she was also intelligent, ambitious, soft and gentle, holding a nugget of fear and shame close to her centre. He hadn't known her long but he was sure he was right. She was all those things and more.

His phone vibrated in his hand – he'd had to turn off the sound when he came in to sit with Brian.

'Tim – I'm here, where are you?'

'Alice! I'm with Brian in A and E.'

Brian opened an eye and looked at him. Tim smiled at him and spoke into the phone.

'Go to the waiting area and I'll come out.'

'Off you go, mate, I'm fine. See you soon. And, Tim – thanks again,' said Brian.

Tim squeezed his arm. 'See ya, mate. Call me, okay?'

As he walked down the corridor he felt the adrenaline rush through his body. She'd come all the way to this place to see him, to spend more time with him. The confidence he'd felt after a few drinks had evaporated with the alcohol in his bloodstream and he didn't know what to say to her. He rehearsed lines on his way back to the waiting room but they all sounded cheesy.

She had her back to him, looking at the TV. He called her name and she spun round, her face lighting up and making his heart skip a beat, just like they said it did in books when you saw the one you loved.

'Shit, you're beautiful,' he heard himself say and she laughed and came and put her arms around him. He hoped the people in the waiting room saw this gorgeous woman was there for him and then he lost himself in her perfume, the touch of her skin, the softness of her lips.

4

RAY

Ray couldn't concentrate on the newspaper. He rarely read them these days, but not being a regular commuter, it had seemed like the thing to do at the station. Buy a paper to read on the train. It was almost a conditioned response. Maybe it was all that kept print media going, all those sheep who did the same thing, day in, day out, not because it was desired, but because they didn't think. He preferred to get his information from the BBC news when he got in from work, opened a bottle of Sauvignon Blanc, poured a glass for himself and Russell and sipped his wine as he prepared a plate of cheese and crackers.

Russell always got in a few minutes after him. They'd kiss hello, Russell would move through the flat like a tornado, throwing his briefcase into a corner in the bedroom, opening windows, peeling off suit and tie, pulling on jeans and T-shirt. It was funny, thought Ray, how he didn't feel like he was home until Russell had cluttered the place up and flopped down in front of the TV in his loose-limbed way, remote in hand. Only then did Ray feel like he could breathe properly, that his world had taken its proper shape. In spite of Russell's untidiness and his inability to talk about his feelings, Ray loved him completely and still couldn't believe Russell, ten years younger than him and a hundred times better-looking, loved him back.

He stared at the headlines. It was all about the EU referendum. Remain or leave. Ray was firmly in the Remain camp. Britain was no longer the centre of an empire with markets hungry for its goods and resources in colonies around the world to plunder. They needed the EU even if it meant more rules and regulations than you could poke a stick at and the sense, sometimes, that the whole thing was like a juggernaut with a slightly defective gearbox.

The train lurched and came to an abrupt stop with a screeching of locked wheels. Ray grasped hold of the window ledge, pressed his feet into the floor and held his breath. They came to a halt amidst newspapers littering the floor and eyebrows being raised but no one said a thing. All eyes turned towards the windows as if the answer to the question no one had voiced would appear on the grimy glass.

Ray, who had somehow held on to it, put his paper down on his lap and wiped his hands on his hanky. He folded it carefully and put it back in his pocket, took out his glasses case and the special little cloth and cleaned his glasses which he had recently had to start wearing. It made him feel old, needing glasses, but Russell had helped him choose the frames – heavy and dark – and said he thought Ray looked distinguished and sexy, had even asked him to wear them when they made love.

He fiddled with his ring, rolling it round and round on his finger. The ring Russell had given him last winter as a token of his commitment. It was a silver Claddagh ring, two hands holding a heart. Ray had given Russell a plain gold band inscribed on the inside with Ray <3 Russell. It was a bit corny but it was all that would fit. Ray had actually wanted to write that Russell was the best thing that had ever happened to him and he hoped they would grow old together.

A click and a scratchy sound preceded a tinny voice. 'We are sorry for the delay which is due to unforeseen circumstances. At this time we cannot say how long it will be. We will keep you posted. Sorry for any inconvenience.'

The woman sitting across the aisle from him looked at the man opposite her. 'Body on the line, I suspect. Wonder how long we'll be stuck here?'

The man to whom the comment was addressed looked at her but made no comment.

'Poor bugger,' she added, too late.

The man still offered no response and the woman shrugged and got back to her book.

Ray's heart was beating fast. A body – really? His first thought was that it was so early. He'd always imagined people desperate enough to kill themselves would wait until later in the day. After dark even, when things can sometimes look worse than they are. The lonely time when you imagine everyone else is at home with a partner or their family, tucking in to a home-cooked meal instead of something picked up from M&S on the way home and heated in the microwave, eaten alone with too many glasses of wine. His next thought was that it might make him late for his doctor's appointment. He was about to look at his watch when he bit his lip and let his hand fall back into his lap. What a callous thing to think, he chided himself. If it was a body (he shuddered at the idea), it was the desperate act of a person grappling with their demons. Someone who could no longer see a way out of their predicament, no path back to the light. He wasn't a religious person but he found himself, in the absence of anything more useful to do, repeating the Lord's Prayer to himself. It was the only thing he could remember from

Sunday school all those years ago apart from the hardness of the pew under his non-existent buttocks and the sting of a ruler across the wrist when he was caught daydreaming.

He noticed he was feeling tight in the chest and closed his eyes. He recognised the signs of stress. He lived with it almost constantly these days. Right now he was unsure if he was more upset for the jumper or himself.

His doctor had said the cancer was discrete and there was no point in doing more than watching and waiting but Ray wasn't happy with that. He had nightmares about being engulfed by alien beings, amorphous, ugly, voracious. It didn't take Freud to work out what they were about. He was scared. Who wouldn't be? So he was on his way to Harley Street for a second opinion.

He had asked around at work, men he thought might know about these things, who were of a certain age, and Michael Montague from Compliance had given him the name of this doctor.

'He's *the* man to go to for these things,' Michael had said. These things being prostate cancer. He couldn't even bring himself to say it.

'How do you know?' Ray had asked. He wanted the source, wanted to make sure it wasn't his wife's hairdresser who had mentioned him, or a friend who had since died from his cancer.

'Remember Anthony Ballard? He had it, went to see this chap, now he's right as rain. Fighting fit. Plays eighteen holes of golf twice a week and can still beat me at tennis.'

Ray noted that Michael still couldn't bring himself to say the C word, or even the name of the urologist he was recommending. He'd written the name and number down as if not saying them aloud offered some magic protection from being affected. Infected.

'Great, thanks,' Ray had said, and entered the name and

number into his phone before throwing the piece of paper in the bin.

'Don't mention it. Let me know how you go. See you on the golf course,' said Michael.

That'd be right. *Let me know if you get better but not if you don't.* Ray didn't play golf and couldn't imagine himself starting in celebration of being successfully treated.

Out the window the green fields and hedges were bursting with summer flowers. The cows in the field were being herded towards a milking barn, heads down, udders swaying, the farmer studiously ignoring what was happening not a hundred yards away.

Suddenly he felt like weeping. He was terrified and all alone. Russell was like Michael; he couldn't talk about Ray's cancer either. He'd got all tight-lipped and pale when Ray first told him he thought something was wrong and refused to go to the doctor with him. Ray had found him crying in the bathroom later and hadn't mentioned it again. He hadn't even told him he was taking the day off to see Dr Moncrieff today. He sighed, took more deep breaths.

The young woman sitting next to him wearing an army surplus coat several sizes too large, got her phone out and made a call.

'Hey, Maddie – you'll never guess what – the train ran into someone. Like a real person. And now we're sitting in the middle of a field and no one's told us what's going on and when we'll get going again or nothing.'

Ray winced and closed his eyes. What was the world coming to? What was so fascinating about a death it had to be broadcast in real time to your friends? And anyway, it was only rumour so far that there had been a suicide. Maybe it wasn't even a suicide – maybe someone had wandered onto the tracks in a state of inebriation or under the influence of drugs.

Maybe it wasn't a person at all but one of the cows from the field.

'Yeah, I know. Shit. Yeah, okay. Oh, yeah – thanks. I'll let you know. I'll call you back. Laters.' The young woman put her phone down in her lap and picked it up again immediately, scrolling through her texts, sent a few back to chosen recipients, typing with her two thumbs as fast as Ray could type with ten fingers. How did they do that, these people who had been raised on a diet of phones and American sitcom 'kulcha'? He shook his head and the woman looked at him, angled her phone so he couldn't see what she was writing and shifted away from him as far as the seat would allow.

'It's all right,' he said, 'I can't read anything without my glasses.' He smiled in what was meant to be a reassuring way but she rolled her eyes and got back to her phone.

Anyway, I wouldn't want to read your mindless tosh, he added to himself. *You probably can't spell your own name, read trashy magazines and your mother's looking after your children so you can have a day in the Big Smoke finding a daddy for the next one.* God – where did that come from? He wasn't usually so judgemental. It must be the stress. The cancer.

He felt like weeping again just thinking about those cells invading his body. It terrified him. What if they'd already spread, were even now eating away at other parts of him? He'd heard you don't recover if it spreads to other organs like the stomach or the liver, but his doctor hadn't even checked that. He'd just said he was sure the tumour was discrete. Discrete! Contained. Unattached. Separate. Different. Exactly how Ray felt these days. He and his tumour had that in common. He almost laughed at the irony. A cluster of cells had marched in and taken up residence in his body where they didn't belong. Multiplying. Growing.

Ray took his handkerchief out again and wiped his forehead.

Was it just him or was it getting hotter in the train? He wished Russell was with him. He wished they could always be together. He thought, as he often did, about their first meeting at the dismal party of a mutual acquaintance. They'd been in the kitchen refreshing their glasses.

'How soon do you think I can leave without hurting Eugene's feelings?' Russell had asked.

Ray had looked at him, this tall, good-looking young man and his heart had all but stopped. 'Oh, I think we should give it another half hour before we make a break for it,' he said, and Russell had laughed.

For Ray it was love at first sight but he hadn't dared hope it might be reciprocated. Especially when he discovered Russell was going out with a woman. Tall, elegant, aloof Lucy. He was happy enough to discover he and Russell had a common interest in architecture and they'd started visiting stately homes together and spending the evenings afterwards discussing them over dinner and a bottle of wine. There had been invitations to Russell's house – he still lived with his parents in their enormous mansion – and social occasions with his family. Ray had been happy to be included, especially since his own family wanted little to do with him. Everything would be perfect if it wasn't for this bloody cancer. If only Russell could man up about it and give him a bit of support instead of Ray looking after him and his feelings all the time.

No, that wasn't fair. Russell looked after him in other ways, and his father had died of cancer, that's why he couldn't bear to see Ray going through it. Although Jeff, Russell's father, had been a sixty-a-day smoker since he was a teenager; lighting a cigarette before he got out of bed. There was always a cigarette in his hand, and he drove his Bentley, cigarette in mouth. There were ashtrays in the toilets. So it shouldn't have been a surprise when he got lung cancer, but it was. As if money and status should have protected him against something as pedestrian, as proletarian as lung cancer.

When Jeff had been diagnosed, Ray had stepped in to help. He made dinners, bought wine, walked the dogs. He needn't have done any of it, they were wealthy and had a housekeeper for that sort of thing but he wanted to be useful, wanted to show his gratitude for their hospitality, for having him there for Christmases when he didn't want to see his own relatives. Jeff's whole family seemed to take a deep breath in when they heard the diagnosis and didn't let it out again until he was dead six months later. They even moved differently, like they were gliding about underwater, and they avoided being in a room together, as if they wanted to give each other more space. God forbid they might actually touch and provide physical solace. And in those six months they were so polite to each other, as if saying anything more than 'please' and 'thank you' and 'would you' and 'could I' might open the floodgates to a torrent of feelings that hadn't just been buried for years, but embalmed and set in concrete. Ray had never realised such a repressed group of people existed outside his own family. But when Jeff had died, Russell had let out a long-held breath and relaxed, talked to Ray about his fears. They weren't yet lovers although Lucy had disappeared during Jeff's illness. Ray was the shoulder waiting to be cried on, the supportive friend.

Ray let his head rest against the back of the seat and felt his lips lift into a smile as he remembered the moment when their relationship moved from friends to something more. The way Russell looked at him as if really seeing him for the first time. It was such a cliché, but exactly described how it had felt – that he, Ray – was suddenly being seen. And not just seen. Appreciated.

And not long after, That Night. Russell had looked at him over the table, the muscles at the corners of his eyes tightening slightly. Ray held his breath, felt the heat rise in his chest and hoped he wasn't blushing like a thirteen-year-old virgin. He'd swallowed and forced himself to return Russell's gaze. Thank God they were having dinner at Ray's flat because suddenly Russell almost flew across the table and grabbed him, finding his mouth and kissing him deeply. Ray smiled at Russell's hardness and his own and felt, for a moment, a profound gratitude. Then he was taken over by pure lust.

He opened his eyes, looked around guiltily and placed his newspaper over his lap to hide the bulge in his trousers, hoping no gasps of pleasure had escaped his lips as he remembered undressing Russell and seeing his beautiful body for the first time. And the sex that came after. Oh, the sex.

He was relieved to observe that everyone was behaving as usual – reading papers, checking phones, dozing, heads back, mouths open. He dabbed his forehead again and looked out the window.

If they didn't get going soon he'd definitely be late for his appointment with the urologist. And after that he had to see his accountant. Barry had been doing his tax forever, since way before he'd moved out of London but Ray hadn't seen him for quite a time and was rather behind in his accounts. He sighed and wished he'd kept his eyes shut and allowed himself to drift around in his memories longer, but now they were gone and he was once again taken over by anxiety, a sense of doom and dread.

He needed to move. He'd love to get off the train and walk through the dew-soaked grass, smell the sweet cow dung and feel the weak sun on his skin. Instead, he rose and stretched his arms over his head, tucked his shirt in again and started down the train, careful not to knock into the various arms, legs and bags spilling into the aisle.

A couple of seats along a hand touched his sleeve as he

walked past. 'Excuse me – are you going to find out when we might get going?'

Ray spun round to see who had spoken. A Chinese woman was looking at him.

'Er, I hadn't thought about it. Just stretching my legs.' He looked at his watch. They'd been there for over forty-five minutes. Surely it couldn't be much longer. Not that he really knew; he'd never been in this situation before. Once, when he was still living in London, he'd been waiting for a train at the Tube and there'd been an accident at the next station. He remembered the platform getting more and more crowded and wondering why the staff didn't stop people coming down the escalator – he was worried people would be pushed onto the tracks. He'd shuffled and pushed his way to the back of the platform and stood there, overheating in his winter coat until eventually a train came, and another and another. He'd finally managed to squeeze onto the fourth train only to feel so claustrophobic he had to get out at the next stop and take a bus the rest of the way to work.

'I don't suppose there's a buffet car on this train, is there?' asked the old lady next to the Chinese woman. 'I'd love a cup of tea.'

Ray nodded towards the front of the train. 'Yes, I think there is – a food shop they call it these days.'

'I expect you're right. They don't call things the same as they used to, do they?'

'Do you want me to get you a tea, Iris?' asked the Chinese woman.

'Would you mind, Mei-Ling? Only I'm a bit shaky on my legs.'

Mei-Ling smiled. 'Of course. And I'd love a British Rail pork pie right about now! I bet they don't make them anymore. Heart attack in every bite!'

Ray laughed. 'Surely you're joking. Those things could have been used as cannonballs in the Napoleonic Wars. In fact, they probably were.'

The ladies laughed. Ray excused himself and moved on. He wasn't a regular commuter these days but he was struck by the fact that people were talking to each other. It wasn't the norm. In his experience people were very good at maintaining their privacy in the tightest of crowds. They were champions at looking past the shoulder of the person they were crammed against, or of sitting next to someone on a train without ever being seen to take any interest in them. People who sat in the same seat every day for years and didn't know even the tiniest detail of their neighbour's life but who noticed them missing the minute they weren't there. The mood on the train this morning wasn't festive by any means, but people were talking to each other, pulling together in adversity. Perhaps this day, this suicide, would change things. Maybe the people here today would feel a greater sense of connection to each other from now on. Connectedness had become very important to him in his own life recently.

He entered the next carriage and looked around. A woman was snorting into a hanky, watched by a man who looked like he'd been knocked back into his seat by the force of the woman's breath. A blonde woman and her daughter were chatting, as were a few others in the carriage. He shrugged. No, they'd probably all ignore each other again tomorrow. Not that he'd know, he wouldn't be there. Tomorrow he'd go to work on his bike as normal. But would it be normal, or would today change everything for him? His heart thudded against his ribcage.

The doctor peeled off his rubber gloves and threw them into the special bin. Ray went behind the screen to dress and heard Dr Moncrieff flicking through the reports and images he'd given him. As he perched on the patient's chair again in front of the imposing desk, the specialist sat back in his chair.

'Well, there's no doubt it's cancer but I agree with Dr Adams' approach to treatment. I can't in good faith recommend anything different.'

Ray sat on the other side of the broad desk, concentrating on his breath. This was good news, the doctor told him. Congratulated him, in fact, as if Ray had achieved this surprising result through some specific action he'd taken. So why did he still feel panic rising? When he'd made the appointment he had thought of questions to ask but they'd all fled, leaving him with nothing to do but nod.

The doctor stood and offered his hand. The consultation was over. Ray walked out mechanically, told the sympathetic receptionist he didn't need to make another appointment, and walked out into Harley Street and the blaring of a car horn as the driver shook her fist at the person who had pipped her to the post for a parking spot. He looked at his watch but barely registered the time. A thought nudged him. He had to get to his accountant. He'd planned his day in London to kill two birds with one stone – cancer and tax. It had seemed a good idea when he made the appointments but now all he wanted to do was lie down and pretend none of this was happening. Or go somewhere and get very drunk.

His feet seemed to decide on a course, however, while his mind was elsewhere. He started walking towards Marylebone Road. The tightness in his chest made breathing difficult. He needed to sit down, but he was afraid that if he did, he'd start thinking. So he kept walking along streets he didn't know, passing strangers whose faces offered no consolation. He fantasised about Russell coming to get him, taking him in his arms and comforting him.

'Get a grip,' he urged himself, clenching his fists.

It was no use. Tears wet his cheeks and on he walked.

Somehow he found himself outside his accountant's office. He almost smiled at the realisation he'd got himself there. Somewhere in the back of his mind the rational Ray still functioned.

He stood for a few moments trying to gather his thoughts. There were still none to be had. His mind was a blank, a wall standing between his conscious self and the panic he suspected was behind it.

Then, wiping his face and taking a deep breath, he entered the offices of Worthington and Jones, Tax Accountants.

The reception couldn't have been any more different to Dr Moncrieff's. Where the doctor's office had soft tones and comfy sofas, this one had hard orange chairs and a nylon carpet which caused little electric shocks when you touched any metal.

The receptionist nodded to him, told him to grab a seat and got back to her phone. From the jarring bleeps and dings being emitted, he suspected she was playing a game.

He stood with his hands behind his back, looking at a poster on the wall. It was an Escher, the perspective all wrong so the staircase looked like it was going both ways at the same time, as did the people on it. It was confusing and annoying, but also fascinating, and he couldn't take his eyes off it. It was somewhere for his thoughts to sit.

'Ray, long time no see,' said a voice, and he turned to see Barry Worthington, his accountant, striding towards him.

'Barry.' He shook the offered hand.

'I hope you don't mind but I've asked my new man to oversee your accounts. Normally, as you know, I'd give them my attention but with – what is it – three years' worth? Four? I need a bit of help!'

At that moment Ray couldn't have cared less who did his tax. If Barry had said his pet duck was going to have a look at his accounts he wouldn't have batted an eyelid.

'I'll check it all when he's finished, of course,' Barry continued, obviously taking Ray's silence for displeasure.

'Fine. No Problem.'

Ten minutes later, he was sitting opposite a youngish man with black-rimmed glasses and a severe parting. He had smooth, clear skin and amber eyes, and Ray wished he could touch his face, trace a finger along the contours of his cheekbones. He looked vaguely familiar too, but realised he could have sat opposite him all the way from Milton Keynes and still wouldn't recognise him.

'Did you bring all the papers?'

Ray snapped out of his fantasy and opened his briefcase, pulling out a manila folder. 'It's all there.' He slid it across the desk.

The accountant turned to his computer and tapped away, accessing Ray's past returns. He checked he still lived at the same address, asked a few questions, typing the answers in quickly, without looking at the keyboard. Ray had always wondered how people managed that. What if you started off with your fingers on the wrong keys? – you'd create a page of jibberish, with every letter replaced by the one on its left. He shook his head, trying to clear it of the random thoughts that had replaced reason.

When the accountant had run out of things to ask he looked at the manila folder as if desperate to delve into its secrets. It was another thing Ray had never understood – how someone could get excited about numbers and finances.

'Well, if you don't need anything else–' He stood, held out a hand. 'I look forward to hearing from you when you've gone through it all. Thanks.'

In the foyer the receptionist mumbled a bored farewell and Ray sidled out the door with a 'Cheerio.'

He looked up and down the road. A bus came into view with Euston written on the front and he decided he might as well catch it.

London rushed by, people walking the streets, entering and leaving shops and offices, holding hands to their eyes against the unexpected glare. *How many of them have cancer and don't know it yet*, he wondered, thinking back to the days not so long ago, before his diagnosis. Days that now felt carefree and happy merely because they were unclouded by the knowledge of tumours and procedures and doctor's offices. Even when he had gone to his GP he hadn't expected to be referred to a specialist. He'd thought he had a urinary tract infection or kidney stones perhaps. Not prostate cancer.

He shifted in his seat and gripped the handle of his briefcase in both hands to stop from falling into the well of fear the words opened before him. Taking deep breaths, he forced his attention once more to the buildings he was passing, to the people in the streets, living their lives.

At Euston, he entered the station concourse. His stomach rumbled and he decided to have something to eat before getting on the train, preferring the idea of café food rather than the overpriced offerings on-board.

Half of London must have had the same idea. The cafés were crowded with lunchtime trade and once he had his sausage roll and drink, he had to ask permission to share a cramped table with a young man who was sitting with a coffee.

As the other man turned, Ray realised it was the ticket collector from the train that morning.

~

Afterwards, when he was well away from the station and the young man, Ray wondered what had possessed him. He'd broken down and told him – Tim, he'd said his name was – he had cancer. And not only that, but that it was inoperable. He felt ashamed, could feel the warmth of his blush at the memory of it. Poor young man, as if he hadn't had enough to cope with already today with the suicide and everything. Ray's heart was racing and he was breathing as if he'd been sprinting. The embarrassment. And the reality was, he had lied. Dr Moncrieff hadn't told him the cancer was inoperable. He'd told him he wasn't going to operate. At this stage, he agreed with the other urologist Ray had seen, that they should wait and see. There was no good reason to cut anything out.

Ray had been disappointed. He wanted rid of this thing, this tumour didn't belong in his body. He didn't want it there a moment longer. But as he was telling Tim about it his fear spoke for him, saying what he believed the doctors really meant; they weren't willing to operate because it was too far gone and they didn't want to tell him that it was useless. That he only had months to live. He was angry with himself; he should have insisted on surgery.

He walked, trying to outpace his fear and an hour later he found himself on Hampstead Heath, puffing from the exertion of the uphill climb but feeling calmer. He turned and looked at London below him, cranes marking the sites of new skyscrapers, sunlight glinting off the glass buildings in the city. The Gherkin standing like a black missile, a bold, aggressive building. And the Shard, soaring towards the heavens, so full of hope and light and space. He inhaled deeply and felt, for a moment, hope and light and space fill him too. And then he remembered the little nugget growing in his body and the fear returned.

He turned his back on the view and started walking again. Although it was a weekday, there were quite a few people about. Two teenage boys were trying to fly a kite with little success – even up here there was little wind. A couple was enjoying a romantic picnic, paté and cheeses set out on plates, the crackers in an open packet. Champagne sparkled in plastic flutes. The couple kissed as if no one was watching, their hands in each other's hair. Ray had to look away as a lump rose in his throat – he wanted what they had. He wanted to embrace his lover without a care in the world. He was angry and disappointed that Russell couldn't face what was happening, couldn't support him in his hour of need. He turned and walked quickly away.

At the ponds, he stopped. As a teenager, perhaps eighteen or nineteen, he used to come here with Steven to swim, to hang out with friends and get away from the censorious gazes of all the straight people in London. To have a break from his parents who didn't understand – didn't want to understand – his sexuality. They'd thrown him out not long after that summer, when he wouldn't be bent back into the shape they wanted him to be, wouldn't lead the life they'd mapped out for him. Wife, children, steady job.

He watched. Men lay on the grass enjoying the sun, jumped, whooping, into the water, swam and bobbed around. He wondered how Steven was. They'd parted about the same time Ray's parents had chucked him out, occasionally bumping into each other in the intervening years at gallery openings or friends' parties. All that had stopped when Ray moved out of London. He'd heard Steven was HIV positive – he always had been more of a risk-taker than Ray, and more promiscuous as it turned out. Ray didn't know if he was even still alive although he presumed he was, the drugs being what they were these days. He knew plenty of men who were quite healthily with HIV.

'Hello there. Are you coming in?'

Ray spun round to see a man, shorter than him with blond hair and startlingly blue eyes, looking at him. Daniel Craig eyes.

'Don't hang around out here, the action's all in there,' the man said. 'I'm Aidan by the way.'

'Ray. I was just out walking.'

'Well, you walked and you got here. Come on, you look like you could do with a sit-down.'

Ray did want to sit down. He wanted to sit with Aidan and relax and forget about everything else, just for a few minutes.

'I don't have my trunks. I wasn't expecting to be here.'

'Trunks aren't necessary,' said Aidan. His eyes twinkled when he smiled. He held out a hand to Ray, who took it and allowed himself to be led to the grassy area beside the water. Aidan spread a towel out and they sat.

'You look like you've got the weight of the world on your poor tight shoulders,' said Aidan, beginning to massage them. Ray stiffened at his touch and then gave in to it, feeling the other man's thumbs find the knots of stress and fear in his muscles and begin to knead them out. He sighed.

'Bad day at the office?' Aidan's voice was soft, concerned.

Ray looked at his briefcase. It was all but empty now he'd given the papers to the accountant. He could see why someone would think he'd been at work. Maybe he should go along with the lie, pretend all was well, that he had, indeed, had a tough day at work. But Aidan seemed to care. He was still massaging his shoulders and bit by bit, Ray felt himself soften, release. He wanted to lie down on the towel and let Aidan do his magic.

'Take off your shoes,' said Aidan. 'Let's get you more comfortable.'

Yes, thought Ray. *He knows what I need.* A tear gathered in the corner of his eye and a great sob caught in his chest. He keeled over, lying in a foetal position.

'Oh, poor girl, it's worse than I thought.' Aidan lay down too, spooning Ray and stroking his hair, his back, whispering to him that it would be okay, he was there to comfort him.

Slowly, Ray calmed down. The sob was expelled in deep puffs of breath. He surrendered to Aidan's hands and his soft breath on the back of his neck as he kept up the platitudes.

Ray felt Aidan's erection against his back as he gently rubbed himself against him. A leg wrapped itself over Ray's and Aidan's grip became tighter. Ray was surprised but he couldn't honestly say he was shocked. This was the Men's Pond, after all. What he was shocked by was the need he suddenly felt, by the heat in his own body and his erection straining against his trousers.

'Atta boy.' Aidan smiled. 'Shall we go somewhere a little more private?'

Ray could hardly talk. His heart hammered against his ribs.

They stumbled to a quiet patch behind the dressing rooms, into the privacy afforded by some bushes. Aidan knelt down and unzipped Ray's trousers, taking his penis in one hand, cupping his balls in the other. 'Well, hello, big boy,' he said, and moistened his lips.

Ray looked down, saw his hand on Aidan's blond hair.

He gasped. This was all wrong. He wriggled, trying to move away but Aidan took it for pleasure and kept gently squeezing his balls and now looked up at Ray with those Daniel Craig eyes before taking him in his mouth.

Ray let out a whimper of pleasure and then pulled away.

'I can't.' He started zipping his trousers. 'I'm sorry.'

He didn't look at Aidan as he turned and ran.

He ran until his lungs were bursting. He slowed to a walk, chest heaving. He realised he'd left his briefcase behind but nothing would have made him go back for it. He felt ashamed and guilty. How could he have let it happen? Was he so needy he'd fuck the first person who showed him kindness? That wasn't who he was. It was what the cancer had made him. Weak, pathetic. He kicked a stone on the path and looked to the sky and fought back tears.

An old man walking his dog gave him a wide berth and Ray gave him the finger, which made him feel even worse.

He pulled out his phone and booked an Uber. He had to get to Euston and onto a train home as soon as possible before he did anything else he'd regret.

Ray had had a pet rabbit called Lionel when he was young. He couldn't remember why he named it Lionel – maybe it was after Lionel Blair. He and his mother had watched *Give Us a Clue* devotedly during his childhood. Lionel, the rabbit, had lived to a ripe old age and had always seemed content to live in his hutch, being moved about the lawn so he always had fresh, sweet grass to eat. When he was old and frail he'd escaped. Ray had found his body days later in a nest of dry leaves and grass he'd made for himself under the laurel bush at the back of the garden. Twelve-year-old Ray had decided he must have known he was dying and wanted to go off and do it on his own. He thought about that as he stood on the doorstep of his parents' house in 'up and coming' Wandsworth. When he was a child, no one wanted to live there. Now hardly anyone could afford it. He wondered what his parents' semi was worth these days.

Lionel. Housing affordability. He didn't seem to be able to hold on to one coherent thought. His mind was throwing useless memories and facts at him and he was unable to filter them. And what on earth made him turn his steps towards Wandsworth now? He turned back towards the street, viewing the garden path, all four feet of it, as the drawbridge between hell and purgatory. His mother opened the door.

'Ray – is that you?' she asked his retreating back.

Damn. Not fast enough.

'Yes, it's me.' He swung round and pulled his face into a thin smile while his insides headed towards his feet.

'I didn't know you were coming.'

'No, neither did I.'

His mother stood in the doorway wringing her hands in the particular way that always made Ray feel sorry for her and want to reassure her everything would be all right. He wondered if she'd done it all her life, or just since she'd met his father.

'Shall I come in?' he asked. It was convention, wasn't it, to go into the house when one visited even if it had been a mistake to come.

'Your father's in the loft sorting things.'

Ray nodded. His father was always in the attic. It was his equivalent of a garden shed. For as long as Ray could remember his father had disappeared there rather than spend time with his family. Quite what he was sorting, Ray wasn't sure. It had been boxes of stuff from his parents' house after they died, but that was years ago. Surely he couldn't still be going through that?

His mother still occupied the doorway. Ray took a step towards her and she recoiled, flattening herself into the narrow hall. He stepped past her carefully, took off his jacket and shoes and turned to give her a peck on the cheek. She hadn't moved but as his lips approached, she tilted her face slightly to receive the kiss.

'Who is it?' came his father's voice down the stairs.

'Ray,' said his mother.

'Me,' Ray said at the same time.

'Oh.'

'Just came to say hello,' Ray called to his father.

There was a noise in response that could have been an

acknowledgement or it might have been his father exclaiming over a new and rather disappointing find in one of his boxes.

Ray shrugged and followed his mother into the kitchen where she fluttered around between the sink and the table as if she couldn't decide what to do.

'What's he sorting now?'

'He goes to auctions and buys job lots. He says one day he's going to find something really valuable someone's tossed out by accident.'

Ray rolled his eyes. 'These days everyone watches *Antiques Roadshow*. Trust me, no one is going to throw out anything that might turn out to be a priceless artefact.'

The creases round his mother's eyes and mouth deepened in what Ray recognised as her pained look. 'It keeps him busy.' She turned to the sink, squeezed out the dishcloth and started rubbing at the already spotless draining board.

Ray sucked in a deep breath that felt like it came from the soles of his feet and drew up all the strain and disappointment, the repressed anger and unspoken shame that was the fabric of the household. He'd thought, when he came out to his parents, that he'd been the cause of it, but when he reflected on it later, it had always been the same. His father's remoteness, his mother's anxiety; the distance between them set the tone for family life. He wondered now if he actually liked any of them. His sister was as emotionally cut off as their father. She and Ray hadn't spoken much over the years, in spite of their childhood closeness. A closeness Ray suspected had more to do with offering each other a bit of warmth and comfort than because they actually had anything in common. After she'd come back from India having 'found herself' she'd decided to ditch the family. He hadn't needed to go to India to know what he needed – he'd made it a goal to be as little like his parents as he could but he had maintained contact, however limited. He was perhaps more forgiving than his sister. He'd courted outgoing friends who dragged him out when he wanted to retreat into himself, who had demanded not only his presence but his conversation, his involvement, connection. It had at times been almost too much for him, but he was proud of himself, the life he had built, the community of friends he had surrounded himself with. And his relationship with Russell.

With his next breath he tried to inhale kind thoughts about his mother. She was doing her best. She had always done her best.

'Are you staying for tea?' she asked. 'Only I haven't been shopping. You should have told me you were coming. I'd've got something in.'

Would it look odd if he left now, having just arrived – if he went into the hall and put on his shoes, his jacket and slipped out the front door? Would it matter? He couldn't imagine himself doing it. His mother's disappointment would follow him down the road, sit with him on the train, add a heaviness to his steps as he walked home from the station and accompany him to bed ensuring he didn't sleep.

'Perhaps we could order a takeaway,' he said.

'Oh, no. We never get takeaways. You don't know what they put in those meals. Your father says they spit in them.'

Ray sighed. 'All right, how about we rustle something up from whatever you've got in the fridge?'

His mother looked in the fridge, went to the larder, back to the fridge. 'I haven't been shopping, I told you.'

'Well, what were you and Father going to have tonight?'

His mother looked in the larder again, as if hoping some food had miraculously appeared since last she looked. She shrugged. 'Your father was going to take me shopping, but he must've lost track of time.'

Ray wondered how often that happened. 'Why don't you

order your shopping online? It's very easy. I can show you if you like.'

'Oh, no. I couldn't do that. I like to smell the fruit and veg. They give you the bad stuff if you don't handle it yourself. And what if they don't have what you want and you're expecting it to arrive and it doesn't?'

He sighed again. He'd forgotten how much sighing he did at his parents' house. It was better than shouting. 'I was just thinking it would be easier for you, seeing as you don't like going out on your own. You wouldn't have to wait around for Father.' Ray could feel the old anger rising. Anger at his mother's passivity, his father's insensitivity. He took a deep breath.

'You look tired.' His mother always changed the subject when she didn't like the course the conversation was taking.

Ray sank into a chair. He felt a strange sensation starting in his nose. A pinched feeling almost like the beginning of a sneeze, that spread to his sinuses. A pressure, not unpleasant, that reached behind his eyes and out to his temples. He felt the wetness on his cheeks and the weight of his mother's arms around his shoulders.

'What's the matter, love?'

He couldn't speak, was lost in the warmth of his mother's embrace. This was what he had come for. This was why his feet had led him to Wandsworth. His mother. The comfort she could give. He could be needy and scared and she would provide succour. He leant into her and allowed himself to cry. He hung on to her, hands around her waist as she stood beside him holding him tight.

'What the hell's going on?' His father came into the room and sat heavily in the chair at the head of the table.

His mother pulled away abruptly. Ray almost fell sideways off his seat.

'Ray's a bit upset, that's all,' she said, wringing her hands.

'Hmm. What's for tea?'

Ray didn't hear his mother's response. He made his way to the downstairs toilet and locked himself in. Sitting on the loo, head in hands, he bit his lip to stop himself from screaming. It had always been the same; his father came first. Demanded it. Made life so unpleasant if anyone dared put their needs before his that, over time, they'd all given in. Maybe his sister had been right after all to cut off all contact. At least she'd spared herself the hope it would ever change and the disappointment when it didn't.

He felt stupid for thinking it would ever be any different, for allowing himself to be vulnerable in this house.

He washed his face, looked at himself in the mirror, drew his shoulders back and lifted his chin.

Back in the kitchen his mother was standing by the cooker, stirring something. An empty baked bean tin sat on the countertop. Two slices of white bread were ready to go into the toaster. His father was reading the newspaper.

'I've got cancer,' said Ray.

His mother dropped the wooden spoon and turned to him, her face drawn into a mask of shock. She looked across at his father who shook his newspaper and turned the page.

'I just thought you should know,' he added into the lengthening silence.

His mother put her hand out to him across the kitchen but didn't move from her spot by the stove. Eventually his father put his newspaper down.

'AIDS, is it?' he asked.

Ray clenched his teeth. 'No, actually. Not all–'

'That's enough. I don't need to hear any more about you and your – your men friends.'

'–gay men get AIDS,' Ray finished. His father flared his nostrils and looked away. Ray noticed the redness of his anger rising above his shirt collar and wondered what was going to happen.

'Have you seen a doctor?' asked his mother, a deep crease appearing between her eyebrows.

'Two, actually. I came to London for a second opinion today. It's prostate cancer.'

'And?' There were tears in his mother's eyes waiting to fall the minute she heard the bad news.

'And nothing,' said his father. 'I've had prostate for years.'

'Cancer?' asked Ray.

'What other sort of prostate is there?'

Ray and his mother gasped in unison.

'I didn't know that. Why didn't you tell me?' She was hovering between the stove and her husband, clearly unsure what she should do.

'And what, precisely, would you have done if I had told you? Worried, asked me every minute how I was feeling, made me feel like a bloody invalid, that's what.'

Ray felt his mother's frustration. She had been deprived of worrying over something that mattered for a change. She looked like she'd been slapped and he found himself, as he so often did, wanting to protect her. But he knew if he did anything she would be accused of weakness by his father, of not being able to stand up for herself. So he watched as she went and put a comforting hand on her husband's arm which he moved away from her touch. She looked hurt and tried words instead.

'Oh, Stan, if only I'd known. Surely there must be something I can do?'

'There's nothing.'

'But I could look after you.' She turned to Ray. 'Tell him, Ray – tell him how I could look after him.'

His father shook his head and snorted. 'See what I mean? Now you'll never shut up, will you, woman?'

'That's a bit harsh,' said Ray, and his mother looked at him in surprise. He realised he had never actively supported her before and felt ashamed.

'Oh for pity's sake, shut it the two of you. I don't need anyone to look after me.'

'It's just–' his mother started. She stopped when Stan glared at her.

Ray begrudgingly admitted to himself his father had probably been right to keep his cancer to himself and realised, too late, he should have done the same. He had opened himself up to daily phone calls and offers of unspecified help for months to come. He felt a weariness seeping into his bones. But he also felt angry. This had been his hour, his opportunity to receive his mother's care. However she might act later, she had been holding him when he needed it, had been providing what comfort she could. Until his father had spoiled it.

'So it's prostate adenocarcinoma is it?' he asked.

His father nodded. 'That's what the doctor said.'

'And the Gleason score?'

'Seven. Always been seven. Not getting any better, not getting any worse.'

'And when, exactly, were you diagnosed?'

'About twenty years ago.'

Ray took a long, slow breath. His hands curled into fists. 'You bastard. You selfish bastard.' He had the pinched feeling in his nose again, the pressure in his sinuses. He didn't want to cry. He drew his lips in and clamped his jaw.

'How dare you say that to me.' His father rose abruptly from his chair, fists clenched.

'Now, now, you two. Be nice to each other,' said Ray's mother. They both ignored her.

'So you think it's all right to keep these things to yourself. You probably think you're being brave or strong, toughing it out on your own. But if I'd known – do you have any idea what it's been like for me these last few weeks? I thought I might be dying. If you'd bothered to tell anyone what was going on for you, I wouldn't have been so terrified. But, no. You have to go on in your selfish, self-absorbed way keeping everyone at arm's length, hiding away in your fucking attic. You're pathetic.'

Ray's father straightened himself to his full height and jabbed Ray in the chest. 'Get out of my house you disgusting poofter. That's why you've got cancer – all that bumming.'

Ray started laughing hysterically. 'So how did you get it? One rule for me and another for you, is it? Or are you a secret "poofter"?'

'How dare you? You make me sick. Get out. Now.'

'It's okay. I'm going.' He looked at his mother who was holding her hands over her face, the tears escaping between her fingers. 'Sorry, Mother. I'll call you.' He gave her a quick hug. She didn't respond.

Closing the door quietly behind him, he took a deep breath. He had never stood up to his father before and he felt elated.

By the time he reached the end of the street the lightness Ray felt on leaving his parents' house had been replaced by guilt. Not for what he'd said but for the fact that his father, never an easy man, may take it out on his mother. He wasn't aware of any physical violence in their marriage but there were other kinds of domination and he knew his father to be capable of nastiness. He wondered what his mother had ever seen in him and why she hadn't left. He felt sorry for her – she was the victim in all this. Had she learned it as a defence or had she always been like that, so they were a perfect fit, right from the start? Not that it made what his father did acceptable. He was a bully. An abuser.

Ray felt the shock of the word and for the first time acknowledged that it described his father.

He dug his hands deeper into his pockets and walked faster. He would never understand his parents' relationship and he certainly couldn't fix it. Or his own relationship with them.

He thought again about his father's admission that he had cancer and the implied criticism of Ray for being worried about his own diagnosis. Why couldn't he have shown the tiniest bit of empathy? If he'd said, 'Sorry to hear that, son, but I've been living with it for several years now and I'm still going strong,' Ray would have been shocked, of course, but also soothed.

He imagined the conversation that could have happened:

'That's encouraging,' he'd have said. 'Do you feel well, despite the cancer?'

'Fit as a fiddle. Doesn't stop me doing a thing.'

'That's great. Well, I'll certainly worry less now.'

'That's the way, boy, that's the way,' Stan would have said, giving him a smile or a squeeze on the arm. His fantasy father.

Now, though, the wedge between them had been driven deeper than ever. Ray shook his head and wiped his eyes. His father was a damaged man who locked himself away from his family physically and emotionally, so when would he stop wanting his love and acceptance?

Ray looked at his watch and cursed under his breath. What on earth had possessed him to go and see his parents? Now he'd be late home and his phone battery had died. He looked around for a phone box but the only one around had been vandalised, graffiti covering the windows and the receiver dangling by its metal cord. He wouldn't be able to let Russell know and he'd have all sorts of questions to answer when he got home. Russell would be curious to know where he'd been, what he'd been doing, who with. Not in a jealous way – far from it. In fact, Ray had wondered early on if he even cared enough to want to know what he did when they weren't together. But now there was an expectation that they told each other their plans, shared their day's highs and lows. What would Ray say to him about this day? It had started badly and got worse? He was terrified still, even though the doctor had said there was nothing to do and little to worry about? That his father was in fine fettle living with his cancer?

He looked at the departures board at the station and checked his ticket was still in his pocket. Twenty minutes to wait. Time for a glass of wine or a cup of tea.

He opted for the tea, not wanting to go home smelling of alcohol.

He realised with a jolt he didn't want to go home at all. He was tired of Russell's inability to support him emotionally and exhausted by his own anxiety and the effort it took to keep it from the man he loved. He felt the heat of righteous indignation rise in his chest. Russell's fear of illness suddenly seemed like nothing more than selfishness. Surely if he truly loved Ray he should put that aside in order at least to talk about what was happening.

As Ray walked towards the train there was determination in his stride, a stiffness to his spine and a resolve in his heart. He was going to demand what he needed and Russell was not going to be allowed to slide off the hook.

By halfway to Milton Keynes, Ray was slumped in his seat, his resolve in tatters. He understood Russell's fear, he empathised with his avoidance. He would like to do the same; there was something seductive about ignoring bad news, hoping it would go away or assuming someone else would deal with it. The trouble was he couldn't do it. He'd never been able to walk away from a problem or distract himself so totally that he forgot it. Maybe Russell's ability to do so was one of the things that had attracted Ray in the first place; his father lay dying and Russell could go out and enjoy himself as if he hadn't a care in the world, and go back to his father's bedside refreshed, to hold the old man's hand while he slept or listen to him as he wheezed out a memory too precious to die with him. Russell had announced after the funeral that he didn't have it in him to go through it with anyone else, that the energy it had taken to overcome his fear and revulsion of the whole dying process with its indignities and leaking bodily fluids, had depleted him forever. But surely, thought Ray as he sat on the train, surely he could muster a little more from his reserves for the man he loved?

Was that it – did Russell not love him enough? It was what Ray was afraid of. Russell, ten years his junior, looked like a model with his blond hair that flopped over his baby-blue eyes unless he put product in it and swept it back from his temples. Ray couldn't be said to be a great catch, being stocky and prone to weight gain. He took pains to stay in shape, but his hairline was receding, leaving him with a forehead growing ever taller. He sighed and leant his head against the window.

'I'd offer you a hanky except I gave mine to a woman on the train this morning. Terrible thing it was – a suicide on the line and the lady had a panic attack.'

Ray looked at the man opposite him. 'Sorry?' he said.

The man pointed to Ray's face. 'Bad day?'

It was only then Ray realised he was crying again. He reddened and tugged a tissue out of his pocket. 'Bad day – yes,' he said quietly, embarrassed. He blew his nose. 'I was on the same train – awful thing to happen. Poor bloke.'

'I heard it was a woman. A youngish woman. Younger than me, anyway.'

Somehow that made it even worse and Ray shook his head

sadly. 'It makes one's own problems seem insignificant, doesn't it – someone taking their own life?'

'Puts things into perspective, that's for sure,' said the other man. 'I'm Trevor, by the way,' he said, extending his hand.

Ray shook it. 'Ray,' he said.

'Well, Ray, all I can tell you is the events that happened earlier have made me rethink my life and what I want out of it. A death can do that, can't it?'

He thought for a moment. What did he want out of his life? He had a job he loved and was comfortable financially but his relationships seemed to have started unravelling. He and his father had had a stand-off and more or less said they never wanted to see each other again, he'd had little to do with his sister in years, and he'd almost had sex with a man who wasn't Russell.

'I suppose so.' He looked away, wanting to halt the conversation. It was another half hour until they got to Milton Keynes and he didn't want to bare his soul to this stranger, nor hear the other man's story. He needed to try and understand his reluctance to go home, and decide what he was going to say to Russell. And to work out if the two were related. Fortunately, Trevor got the hint and sat back to read his paper.

By the time they pulled into the station, Ray was ready.

'Bye,' he said to Trevor, who was also leaving the train. He felt he should say more, but nothing came.

'Take care,' said Trevor. 'Hope tomorrow's a better day for you.'

Ray smiled tightly. 'You too.' He stepped onto the platform and walked away quickly.

The lights were on in the flat and even before he opened the front door, Ray heard Russell's voice. Dismayed there might be someone else there, he stopped to listen. There was a pause and Russell's voice again, more urgent now. Ray couldn't make out the words but he knew the tone well; Russell was worried. And given that his was the only voice Ray could hear, he must be on the phone. Ray put his key in the lock.

Before he could turn it the door opened and there was Russell, eyes wide.

'Where have you been?'

Ray felt the wave of accusation sweep towards him. He was the cause of Russell's anxiety and Russell didn't like feeling worried. He took a step backwards and knocked into the plant pot outside their door; the peace lily shook.

Russell always became angry the minute his anxiety was laid to rest. He was like a child whose mother had left the room and wouldn't talk to her when she came back because of the fear she'd caused him. *I don't want to be his mother*, thought Ray. *I want us to be equals.* He looked Russell in the eye.

'I've been in London. I didn't think you'd be interested. So I didn't tell you.' Who was being the child now? Ray felt like stamping his feet with the unfairness of it. And suddenly it didn't matter. Nothing mattered. He was too tired to have the argument he felt was coming, too tired even to tell Russell what had happened. He wanted to lie down.

'Oh, Ray – that's not fair. I do want to know, I just...' Russell stood with his arms by his sides.

'Why don't you let me come in,' said Ray, and Russell stood aside for him, then followed him through to the living room. Ray dropped his bag, shucked off his jacket and sagged onto the sofa.

'Why didn't you call?' asked Russell, hands on his boyish hips. Even now, Ray noticed those hips.

'My phone ran out of steam.' This was how they spoke, assigning old-world language to new technology. Suddenly it seemed juvenile. Once it had been fresh, amusing. Now it felt hackneyed.

'I was worried. I called Mike to see if he'd heard from you. He said he hadn't spoken to you for weeks. What's going on – he's your best friend?'

Ray closed his eyes and leant back into the soft cushions. He wanted to answer Russell but no words came. How to tell him that Mike and he had had a fight when Ray had accused Mike of coming on to Russell and he hadn't denied it. His best friend had been trying to seduce his partner?

'Ray – what the fuck is going on? You're so bloody secretive, and when you do say anything it's always negative these days.'

Ray took a deep breath, thinking about Russell's words. He couldn't deny them but why had he chosen those things to accuse him of when there were so many things he could have said. Positive things, like 'thank you for protecting me from your cancer', or 'I appreciate all the little things you do for me', or even, 'I'm grateful you ask so little of me'. He bit his lip for a moment and opened his eyes again.

'Why do you say these things?'

'Because they're the truth.'

Ray gazed into Russell's eyes. 'But you know lots of things that are true and don't say them. Why these things?'

There was a pause. Ray and Russell stood on opposite edges of it, staring in.

'Because–'

'They hurt me. You hurt me. Is that what you want?'

'No... Maybe.' Russell threw his hands in the air and shook his head. 'I don't know.' He moved to the window, looking out over the rooftops, his back to Ray. 'I want us to be okay. I want us to love each other like we did before–'

Ray heard the words but they sounded so rehearsed he couldn't believe them. Or maybe he didn't want to believe them. Did he want to go back to how it had been before? Or did he want more? He'd always felt he was the lucky one having Russell in his life, so he'd been the housewife, doing the chores and the looking after.

'Before what – the cancer? There, I said it. Now go and have your panic attack.'

Russell turned to him looking like he'd been slapped.

'That was low. I know what you did today.'

Ray blanched. He knew Russell must be talking about his appointment, that he'd put two and two together when Ray told him he'd been in London but his guilt made him wonder what else he knew. Surely he couldn't possibly know about Aidan? Ray took a deep breath.

'I need a drink,' he said, and went into the kitchen.

There were two glasses of wine poured, condensation forming droplets on the glass, and a platter of sweaty cheese and biscuits on the table. Looking at it he thought of Russell getting home before him, wondering where he was, making the decision to greet Ray the same way Ray usually greeted him. He felt the love that went into getting it all ready. The same love he felt when he prepared it each day. He sank into a chair, rested his head in his hands, and started sobbing. Russell put his hand on his back, the reassuring weight guiding him away from the grey swamp of his despair back towards dry ground. The sobbing stopped, he hiccupped a couple of times, the breath catching in his throat.

'I thought I was dying,' Ray said, looking up into the steady eyes of his lover.

'Don't, please,' said Russell.

'Don't talk about it, or don't die?'

'Don't die. I've been so scared that I'm going to lose you.' A tear gathered on Russell's lower eyelid, hovered, fell.

Ray felt something release in his belly. Russell loved him. Whatever their future held, they would face it together.

'Fuck cancer!' he said.

'FUCK CANCER!' Russell yelled.

5

ALICE

Alice hated trains. There was something about them that made her angry and sad at the same time. Too many people trying to ignore each other, perhaps. Or the tragic carpet design; the mottled blue as if trying to make travellers think of water, like they were going on a cruise rather than chugging along on dry land, and the red streaks through it as if someone had painted the bottom of their shoes and dragged them through the carpet. It looked a bit like someone had puked on them. And the thought of all the other bums that had sat on the too-bright seats and the dirt encrusted in the fabric. She rose slightly and pulled her skirt down her thighs. It was too short to offer much protection from the grime, so she pulled her army surplus coat on in spite of the fact that she always got too hot in it.

She sat back in her seat and adjusted her headphones. Adele sang of love and betrayal, her sultry voice adding to Alice's sense of the futility of life. If someone as talented and sensuous as Adele couldn't make a relationship work, what hope was there for her, a twenty-three-year-old nobody whose life was spent cleaning old people's backsides when they'd shat themselves.

She put on some rap and nodded her head to the beat.

The train had been sitting in the middle of a field for ages now. The blue-and-red lights of police cars and ambulances flashed in her peripheral vision. She put a hand up to screen them out and scrolled through her messages and decided to call Maddie. She told her about the suicide, and Maddie sounded suitably impressed, wanting details Alice couldn't provide. As she ended the call, she shifted away from the man next to her who had obviously been listening in. She texted Lou and Cherie, but again, the old pervert was making her uncomfortable, peering over her shoulder. She angled her phone away from him. Sad old creep who probably tried to pick up young girls to make himself feel attractive and alive. Stupid sod. She edged farther away, gave him a death stare and got back to her texting.

Looking around, she saw an Indian guy over the aisle who looked like he was praying, eyes closed and lips moving. The trill of her phone distracted her and she smiled as she read Lauren's text, and started replying. When she looked up, the Indian dude was staring at her. He looked away quickly, but not before she noticed that he had beautiful amber eyes behind his glasses. Alice was so surprised she forgot to look away.

'Wonder how long we'll be here,' she said to cover her embarrassment.

He looked shocked that she was speaking to him, and shrugged. 'It is difficult to say with these things.'

'Has it happened to you before then?'

'Oh, no, I just meant I don't know how long it takes for the police and–'

'Were you praying before?' asked Alice, raising her eyebrows.

'Yes, I was praying for the soul of the poor man who saw no alternative but to kill himself.'

'It might have been an accident. He might've fallen.'

'From where?' asked the man, looking out the window. 'There is no bridge near here and he cannot have fallen from the sky, I think.'

'Stranger things have happened.' Unable to think of anything else to add, she turned back to her phone. What a stupid thing to say. He'd think she was really dumb. Not that it mattered – she couldn't fancy anyone who was so religious. Even a man with such lovely eyes.

Yawning, she leant her head against the window and closed her eyes. It had seemed doable when she first agreed to the extra shift; finish night duty and get on a train to London. She needed the money. A few caffeine tablets and she'd be fine. But she hadn't banked on the night she'd just had, with two of the old biddies deciding to do shit-art in the middle of the night, and her having to clean it off the walls. Still, she couldn't blame them. She would probably do the same if she was confined to a home and spent all her waking hours sitting in a chair staring at daytime TV. She liked to think it was their little rebellion. She preferred them to rebel on other people's shifts, but they didn't care who had to clean up. They didn't even know what they were doing. Still, at least Mrs Beauchamp hadn't hidden her shit in her sock and put it back in her drawer like last week. Alice had laughed at that. Mrs Beauchamp's daughter, Deidra Kelly, was such a refined lady and her mother hid shit in socks. Which just showed that in the end the posh buggers with their hoity-toity airs and graces were no different to anyone else.

With a shudder and a few clanks the train started moving, slowly at first, as if it needed to stretch and warm up again. Bit like her mum who did yoga to a video every morning. Alice wished she earned enough to move out. She closed her eyes and made a wish – *let me be successful today. Let this be the first day of the rest of my life.*

She checked the time on her phone. She could have gone

home and slept for a couple of hours in the time they'd wasted. But she had taken the extra shift partly because she knew she wouldn't have slept anyway and might as well have something to take her mind off the day. And here it was. The day that was going to be the first step to her new life. She crossed her fingers. Suddenly a shiver went along her spine. What if the suicide was a bad omen? She stifled a groan.

'Don't be so bloody superstitious, you idiot.' She clenched her fists. But having thought of the jumper, she couldn't get him out of her mind. She wondered what had driven him to suicide. A failed relationship? The lack of a relationship? She was experiencing that right now, for the first time since she was fourteen. She always had a guy in her life, although most of them turned out to be toerags. Sometimes, although never for long, she even regretted breaking up with Karl, two months before. He had been far too self-absorbed and didn't have a romantic bone in his body. He hadn't even sent a card on Valentine's Day; she'd had to dash out and buy one at lunchtime so she had something to show her friends that night. And a bunch of roses. She hadn't realised how expensive they were. It was then she knew he had to go. She sighed, her head lolling in time with the clattering of the wheels.

The door at the end of the carriage opened and the ticket collector started slowly along the aisle, checking tickets, smiling, having short conversations with the other passengers. He was tall and quite good-looking. His shirt was coming untucked on one side in a cute sort of way; she wanted to pull it out all the way and look at his body. She sat straighter, tucked her hair behind her ears, shrugged herself out of her coat and pulled her shoulders back, just enough to make her breasts seem a little fuller.

'Morning,' she said as he took her ticket.

He nodded in her direction but didn't actually look at her,

and he was gone. Not even a word. No smile. Rude bugger. She turned and watched him take the old lady's ticket, have a bit of a chat, and then he moved out of her sight along the carriage.

Maybe he fancied her, and that was why he didn't look at her – perhaps he was shy. Or gay. Or in a committed relationship with someone who got jealous if he looked at an attractive girl. She slumped in her seat again. She was a catch, so why was it that Mr Right hadn't found her yet and swept her off her feet? Fuck the ticket collector. Who wanted to go out with someone who couldn't get a better job than that?

She pulled a book out of her bag. *Illicit Love* by Pauline de Winter. It was the third book she'd read by her, and she loved them all. So romantic, but spicy too. This Pauline de Winter certainly knew her stuff. She must have lived such an exciting life. The things the lovers did together, too, made her blush, but in a good way. The women were strong, not the sorts that needed saving, but not so independent they didn't know a good thing when it came along. And the men were always bold, but not too bold, handsome, but unaware of it, courteous without being pussies. And, of course, they always adored the heroine. Oh, how Alice wanted a man like that. She opened the book and started reading.

He lifted her onto the chaise carefully. She felt his powerful arms around her and turned towards him, her face inches away from his. He smelled musky. She could feel his breath on her cheek, his heart beating, strong and steady.

'Are you sure this is what you want, Katherine?' he asked.

'Yes,' she breathed, unlacing her bodice, revealing her pert breasts, the nipples already erect, waiting for his kisses.

He looked at her and she heard his breath quicken.

'Come to me,' she said.

He lay next to her, his hands on her breasts, squeezing gently, his member hard against her thigh. She felt the heat spreading in her groin and moaned in anticipation as he lifted her skirts and started slowly easing her underwear off.

'Oh, Clifford,' she said, and then, as he found her pink pearl, waves of pleasure engulfed her and she couldn't talk any more.

Alice stopped reading and closed her eyes to imagine the rest of the scene. Lady Katherine Quincy and lowly Clifford Brown, the gardener, making love in her boudoir.

The man next to her coughed quietly and she opened her eyes, wondering if she'd been groaning or sighing or somehow alerting him to the fact that she was feeling quite aroused. But he was deep in his newspaper, reading about Brexit. Couldn't happen fast enough for her. She thought all the foreign health workers who could hardly speak English were a disgrace to the National Health Service. And made getting jobs harder for people like her, born and bred in England. She knew how she'd be voting come June 23rd. Closing her eyes again, she let her thoughts drift back to her book.

She wanted a Clifford Brown, although she'd prefer it if he wasn't a gardener. Maybe a personal trainer so he was fit and tanned with a six-pack. Or a doctor so he was rich. But he'd have to not be a wanker like the doctors who came to the nursing home. They all thought they were God's gift and treated the patients and the staff like they were shit on their shoes. Well, except for Dr Malone, but he was at least sixty and wore a corduroy suit straight out of the seventies. And he wasn't being retro and cool. And Dr Bell was nice too, but she was a woman.

Alice noticed the countryside giving way to the urban sprawl. Somewhere out there was the man for her. He'd find her, claim her as his soulmate. Shame the scenery was so ugly; miles and miles of houses and gardens, factories, parks, high streets with their tired-looking shopfronts, graffiti, abandoned shopping trolleys in a muddy canal, worn-out people dragging themselves to the stations or onto buses for another day at work. She almost understood why the man had jumped in front of the train. But her Clifford Brown would make everything seem okay. With him, life would take on new meaning, colours would be more vibrant, each day would be a new adventure.

She made her way to the toilet to freshen up. She was beginning to get nervous. It was going to be a big day. The biggest day of her life.

∾

As soon as the train came to a stop Alice was out the door, jogging along the platform. She'd had an idea when she was trying to do her make-up in the train – instead of battling with the swaying and getting eyeliner all over her face she'd get her make-up done at a department store, pretending she was going to buy their products. It would take longer than doing her own, but she reckoned it would be worth the time.

She needed to get to Oxford Street so she jumped on the Victoria line and emerged a few minutes later at Oxford Circus. She didn't get to London much. She'd have liked to, but it was expensive, and she was always short of money. She scanned the busy road, but couldn't remember which direction Debenhams was in. She stopped a woman with a shopping bag and asked. She mumbled something at her in an incomprehensible language but a turbaned Indian man who had overheard her question pointed down the road.

'Debenhams,' he said. Alice thanked him and turned towards the department store.

Five minutes later she was browsing the beauty section, awed by the choice, the lighting, the sheer opulence of the place. All the surfaces sparkled, light bounced off mirrors polished to diamond brightness. Women in the uniforms of Clarins, Clinique, Lancôme, and all the other posh brands were beautifully made up, hair perfect. They stood at their counters, idly waving dusters over their displays or turning their products so they all faced the same way. Alice took her time, now she was here, to make her choice. She'd applied her own foundation and blush, she just needed dramatic eyes, for which she needed a youngish sales girl who looked bored and so would welcome the distraction of making someone up. She also had to have a certain look herself, so that Alice knew she'd understand what she wanted.

At the Urban Decay counter, she found her girl.

'Hi,' she said, trying to keep the tremor out of her voice. She felt intimidated in this place with these people who acted like they'd been born there.

'Can I help you?' The girl smiled.

Alice relaxed a bit.

'I've got an important event happening today, and I've come out without my make-up. I was wondering if you'd, you know, do it for me?'

The sales girl's smile fell. 'Like for free?'

Alice bit her lip and said nothing. She'd humiliated herself in this Mecca of beauty. She was shocked to feel tears welling, and turned to go before she embarrassed herself even more.

'What's the event?'

Alice told her.

'OMG – that's fantastic! Of course I'll do it. Got nothing else to do anyway. Monday's are always so quiet. What are you wearing – not what you've got on, I hope.'

Alice pulled her outfit from her bag.

'Great. Love the top. Good colours. I'll make sure your make-up matches.'

Alice wanted to hug her. 'Really?'

'Yep. But if my boss comes, I'm just doing a demonstration and you're going to buy something. Now, what sort of look are you after?'

Alice explained what she wanted: dramatic, but not too out there, sexy but not tarty.

'I'm Alice, by the way,' she said.

'Debbie, pleased to meet you.'

As Debbie did her eyes, they chatted. Debbie, it turned out, had always wanted to be a make-up artist in movies.

'It's just so competitive, I don't have a chance. I don't know anyone in the industry.'

When she'd finished, she held a mirror up. Alice gasped. She'd been transformed. Debbie was a magician.

'Wow, thanks so much.'

'Don't thank me – take my number and let me know how you go! Good luck. I'm so excited for you. And jealous.'

Alice pulled her phone out, punched in Debbie's number and looked at the time. She went cold all over. Having her make-up done had taken longer than she'd thought, and now she'd have to rush to get there on time. And she still had to change. Taking a few deep breaths, she decided to change when she got to the venue rather than traipsing across London in her gear.

'Here, take this. It's a sample, but you might need to do your lipstick again. Hey, and if you could put a word in for me at all...'

'Course I will. You're an angel, Debbie. Laters.'

Alice walked quickly back to the station. She wanted to run, but thought it might make her sweat and her make-up might slip. Her heart pounded. Consulting the Tube map and her instructions for how to get to the venue, she made her way to the Central line platform deep in the hot bowels of the station. She arrived on the platform as a train was pulling out and had to wait ages for the next one, shifting from one foot to the other, trying to calm herself enough to think through the next couple of hours.

Once she was on the Docklands Light Railway, she wished she'd told Maddie what she was doing. She'd have offered to take the day off to come with her. She felt out of her depth and needed a friend. London was so big and so unfamiliar, and she too young and vulnerable and unready. It was an unusual feeling, and made her all the more uncomfortable for being so. The man opposite stared at her without embarrassment and she wanted to run away and hide, even though he was her type – good-looking and youngish and well dressed. She looked out the window, trying to ignore him, but she remained conscious of his eyes on her, and blushed.

'Get a grip, girl,' she said to herself under her breath. If all went well today, there'd be a lot more than just one good-looking bloke gazing at her. She was going to enjoy that.

As they approached her stop she picked up her bag, winked at the bloke, and waited for the door to open.

'Where are you off to then?' asked a voice right behind her.

Shit. How embarrassing. She'd never have winked at him if she thought he was getting off there too.

'ExCel.' She hoped he was going somewhere – anywhere – else.

'Me too. Ever done it before?'

Alice drew herself up to her full five foot three, pulled her shoulders back, and looked him in the eye. 'No. First time.' The train had stopped, the doors opened. 'Good luck.' She marched off.

'It's this way,' said the bloke.

When Alice looked back he was smiling.

'Right.' She felt herself redden again.

'Look, you're nervous, understandably. Let me show you where you need to go. I promise I'm not trying to pick you up.'

Alice didn't know whether to be relieved or offended. What was wrong with him? He'd spent all that time on the train staring at her like he wanted to get into her pants, and now he was telling her he wasn't interested.

'It's okay, I'll find my own way.' She started walking down the platform, then turned back to him. 'Good luck for today.'

'Thanks, but I'm pretty sure I'll be fine.'

Alice thought what a prat he was. An arrogant prat. Why were all the good-looking blokes such plonkers? Seriously, where did he think he was getting off with an attitude like that? Stupid sod. She hoped he got put in his place today. In a big way. She hoped he was completely humiliated.

A crowd hovered around one of the doors, and Alice approached a girl on its rim. She turned away as Alice was about to ask her question.

'This where I need to be for the auditions?' she asked the next closest person, a fat boy in dungarees and a backward cap who looked like he'd just finished the milking. He smiled and said yes. He had crooked teeth and bad breath so she edged away and started her preparation. Slow, deep breaths and several wide yawns to soften her lips and the lower half of her face. She started humming very quietly.

The crowd moved and within minutes she was inside the door. In the foyer were long tables, the people behind them looking bright and welcoming. One of them beckoned to her.

'Name?'

Alice told her and she looked it up on her tablet.

'Okay – here, this is for you.' She handed Alice a lanyard with a number written underneath the famous logo. 'Don't lose this – no lanyard, no audition. It'll be a while until you're called. Lots of people here today. Good luck.'

Alice thanked her and moved on with the stream of people heading towards a vast hall. There were seats in clusters, most already taken. She looked around for a toilet to change in and saw the man from the train nearby. He gave her a thumbs up and disappeared into the crowd.

In the Ladies a couple of girls chatted as they repaired their make-up. They turned as Alice entered, and said hello.

'Nervous?' one of them asked.

'Terrified,' said Alice. 'I was okay until I got here, but now, well–'

'Yeah, it's pretty full-on, isn't it?' said the other girl. She was black and had green contact lenses in that looked amazing. Why hadn't she thought of doing something like that? She knew she was attractive, but she should have done something more to make herself stand out. Suddenly, Alice needed to be alone. Comparing herself to others wasn't making her feel any better. She wished them luck, ducked into a cubicle and changed into her black skinny jeans and turquoise spandex boob tube. When she came out they'd gone. Alice assessed herself in the mirror. Her make-up was still fine. She needed to do something with her hair. Some of the girls out there must have been at it all night doing theirs. She'd spent a fortune having hers straightened and now she scraped it back and tied it high, pulling a few strands out to frame her face and hide her ears, which stuck out slightly. She teased the ponytail into a fuller, messier bunch. Casual but sexy. Once she was satisfied, she put on a bit more lippy and pouted at herself, turning her head this way and that, imagining a photographer taking dozens of snaps. Finally, she blew herself a kiss for luck, poked her tongue out at herself for being such a wanker, slung on her bag and left as another group of girls entered, giggling.

Out in the melee again her legs felt like they wouldn't hold her up. So many people. So much noise. People were talking and laughing with each other, a few were crying, others singing or humming to themselves. What chance did she have? *Breathe.*

Just breathe. You're good, you're well prepared, you can do this. She took a sip of water, found a corner, and began her voice exercises. She'd learned them from YouTube because she couldn't afford a singing teacher, but they were good. All her friends said her voice had really improved.

'Number 984 go to room three, please.'

That was her! It was now or never. Smoothing her jeans and tugging at her top, she took a deep breath and made her way to room three. A girl with a clipboard marked her name off, wished her luck in a bored voice and opened the door.

Across the room sat two people behind a table. Neither of them was Simon Cowell. These were just producers' auditions. She had to get through this round to meet the proper judges, but still she was disappointed. In her fairy-tale fantasy, she'd imagined him marvelling at her voice, wondering why he hadn't heard talent like hers before, and whisking her away to his recording studio immediately. Instead, there was a woman who could have been her mother, in a frumpy jumper and no make-up and – fuck – the man from the train.

Alice's step faltered, but he smiled and invited her forward, told her to stand on the X marked on the carpet.

'Name?' asked the woman.

Alice moistened her suddenly dry lips and said, 'Alice Cooper, no relation to Vince.' It was her icebreaker, but neither of them cracked a smile. 'Vincent Furnier, you know, Alice Cooper?' Why was she doing this? Clearly neither of them had got it, or if they had, not thought it funny. An icy hand clutched Alice's belly.

'What are you going to sing for us?' asked the woman.

'"Back to Black".' Alice wasn't sure if she imagined the groan from the man on the train.

'Right then, when you're ready.'

Alice fumbled with the backing track she'd downloaded.

She'd practised getting it ready so often but now she was so nervous she could hardly hold her phone, let alone get it to do what she wanted. Eventually she was ready. She stood tall, took a deep breath, tried not to look at her audience, opened her mouth and sang with as much emotion as she could muster, channelling her hero, Amy Winehouse.

'He left...'

Alice sat in the pub looking at Tim, the ticket collector, and thinking about what he'd just said. He'd watched her from the end of the carriage but couldn't look at her up close because he was shy around girls he liked. He was good-looking, slim, could do with a haircut, and one of his hands was misshapen, as if he'd been in a fight and broken it, but ages ago. He took a sip of his lager and looked like he was struggling for something to say. She felt sorry for him. She'd never understood why people were shy. She was an extrovert, loved being the centre of attention and never had trouble talking to anyone. If she felt awkward she tended to talk more, not less.

'Why do you work on the trains?' she asked.

'It's a good job, pays quite well. Get to move about a bit.' There was a hint of red creeping up his neck. Alice wanted to take his hand and tell him she wouldn't bite, but it might make him feel more self-conscious.

'But you want to be an artist, right?'

He shrugged and made a sound that could have been the beginning of a laugh. 'Yeah, I suppose so.'

'What sort of stuff do you do?'

'People mainly.'

'Are you any good?' Alice hoped he didn't want her to look at any of his stuff. If it wasn't in a magazine, she wasn't interested.

Shame he didn't want to be a writer. She'd loved the *Twilight* books and read all of them several times. That writer had made a fortune. And Pauline de Winter, of course – she'd be rolling in money. Alice wanted to be rich.

'I dunno. I don't let anyone see it. I'm still learning, I guess.' The blush crept a little higher and he swallowed hard.

Alice thought he looked like he was outside the headmaster's office waiting for a caning. Poor thing. Still, she quite liked it. Most good-looking guys were so aware of it they didn't make any effort, they just expected to be admired. She wanted to hug this one and tell him she'd make everything all right for him.

'Sorry, we don't have to talk about it if you don't want to.' She noted his relief and went on. 'We can talk about me instead!' She laughed so he knew it was a joke, and was pleased when he did too. He had lovely eyes. 'What you said about me singing, did you mean it?'

'What bit?'

'About not giving up.'

'Of course I did. I mean, I've never heard you, but I reckon if you want to be a singer, you gotta sing.'

She smiled. 'Yeah. I don't think I could stop even if I wanted. I sing all the time, even on the loo.'

The blush reached Tim's cheeks, and Alice giggled. 'Sorry – too much information!'

He took a crisp and looked over her right shoulder.

'My mum sang. She was a child star in films and TV. Everything handed to her on a plate. She tells me I've got the talent and all I need is to find an agent to promote me. Aim high, she says. Reach for the stars. It's easy for her to say when she doesn't reach for anything except the TV remote and the wine bottle these days.' Alice realised she was getting heated and stopped.

'My dad's a drinker too,' said Tim.

'Maybe we should introduce them!' Alice laughed. She looked at Tim again and caught him staring at her. He blushed crimson, and she couldn't help herself; she took his hand. 'It's okay, you know, I don't mind you looking at me. Actually, I quite like it.' In fact, she liked it a lot. He wasn't just a ticket collector; he was trying to be an artist, and he was kind and a good listener, and even though they'd only just met, he'd been really nice and encouraged her. He'd made her realise she had to keep singing.

She was glad he wasn't just a ticket collector. She couldn't imagine introducing him to her friends if he wasn't also an artist. They all had boyfriends who were in IT or insurance.

She noticed Tim looking at his watch. Was he bored? She didn't want him to go. 'Fancy another drink?' she asked. 'Not that I'm an alcoholic or anything.'

Tim laughed. 'Sure.'

Several beers later, Tim was talkative and Alice was falling in love. She knew it was really lust, but she wanted to be in love. She wanted to feel cherished, like the heroines in Pauline de Winter's books. She deserved it.

'How come you're so wise, Mr Tim Engleby?' she asked as he set another drink in front of her.

He raised an eyebrow.

'All the stuff you said in the park this afternoon. I do want to be a singer. I can't spend my whole life wiping people's bums and looking for their false teeth.' It was true. She didn't think she could stand another day of it. But then, she often thought that, but when she went in, it was okay. The oldies were pleased to see her, the ones who remembered from one day to the next, anyway. And they didn't mean to shit themselves. She just hoped she didn't get like that when she was old.

'Do you sing to the old folks?'

'Yep. I learnt a few of their favourites off the music therapist who comes in once a week. It's nice to see them smile and some of them sing along. There was this one time when an old lady who hadn't spoken, or even looked at anyone, for months, started singing along and the nurses couldn't believe it.'

'I bet you're good with them. You should be a nurse, when you're not singing. Or be the first singing nurse.'

Alice glanced at him to make sure he wasn't making fun of her, but she should have known he wasn't. He wasn't like that. He meant it. And why shouldn't she do nursing? As a backup to her singing. She didn't have any A levels but there must be other ways to get into nursing. Her, a nurse! What a great idea. She did like working with people, and she did have a knack with the oldies. She got her phone out to write herself a note to look into it.

'Going to give me your number?' asked Tim, but he didn't look at her. They'd been getting on so well, and he'd certainly loosened up with the alcohol, which was what she'd been hoping, but as soon as it got personal again, he was as awkward as a hermit at a rave.

'Yeah, if you like.'

Tim fumbled with his phone. 'I'll give you my number and you can call me and I'll have yours,' she said.

She watched as he keyed the numbers in, and turned away as her phone began to ring.

'Hello?'

There was a pause, and she glanced over her shoulder. Tim looked confused, so she smiled, and talked into the phone again. 'How are you?'

'Good,' he said.

'Me too. I'm out with a fella at the moment, having a really nice time. He's very kind, and good-looking, and I like him a lot.'

There was another pause, but this time Alice didn't let herself look at him.

Eventually, a voice in her ear said, 'I'm out with a pretty amazing chick. She's a singer, or will be, but she probably has a boyfriend.'

'No – no she doesn't,' said Alice. 'She's single and ready to meet someone.'

'Oh.' She didn't let him say any more. She turned round and kissed him on the mouth and was very happy to discover he was a good kisser.

'You know what,' she said when they'd pulled apart. Tim had his arm round her, and she had tucked herself into him. 'I'm glad the audition went badly. I wouldn't have met you otherwise.' She looked at him.

Tim smiled. 'I'm glad I was given the afternoon off, otherwise I wouldn't have met you.'

Minutes later, his phone rang again. Alice watched his forehead crease into worry lines as he listened. *I like him*, she thought. *I really like him. He's so different from Karl. Tim would never forget Valentine's Day – he'd probably paint me a picture or something romantic like that. And he likes me, he said he was glad he met me.*

She felt a warm glow.

'I'm really sorry, but I have to go.' Tim waved his phone at her. 'It was Brian, the train driver. He's in a bad way.'

Alice was annoyed. They'd been getting on so well, and now this. But his friend needed him.

After he'd gone she pulled her phone out and read his number in her contacts list. He'd really given it to her. He wanted to see her again. She smiled and texted Maddie.

Just met v sexy guy

Maddie responded immediately.

OMG! Send pics

No u'll have 2 wait 2 meet him

Pleeeeez!!!

Can't – don't have one

Take 1 now!

He's gone

?????

Had to see a friend in need

All good. Seeing him 2moro 😦

She put her phone away. Maddie would let everyone else know when she got to the pub. Monday they all went to the pub straight after work at six for one of their regular catch-ups. They'd be getting there about now.

She waited, and then, sure enough, the texts started.

Lucky u!

What's his name?

Looks like???

Tell all!!!

Wanna meet him – when???

She didn't answer any of them. Let them wait, sweat it out. Instead, she thought about Tim. Was he her Clifford Brown?

She sat in the pub finishing her drink. She ignored the stares of the men who had come in for a pint after work, the women who cast their gaze in her direction only to look away again and make a comment to their friend. Alice could almost hear them; little tart sitting on her own, hang on to your men. She was used to it, having been told often enough how attractive she was. Usually by a sleazeball trying his luck, but also by nice men, her girlfriends, her mum. She was used to being looked at and liked being appreciated. But it came with its downside; the other women who found her a threat, the unwanted attentions of arseholes.

She went to the toilet and changed out of her audition clothes. As an afterthought she scrubbed off some of the make-up. It was a bit much for early evening drinks, especially on her own. She appraised herself in the mirror. Flawless skin – she had her mum to thank for that – generous lips, cute nose, dark, almond-shaped eyes like her dad, or so her mum told her. She wondered if Tim would prefer her with or without make-up, and decided he wouldn't mind, and anyway, he'd get what he was given. She didn't dress for other people, she did it for herself. Except for auditions. Then you had to play the game.

Thinking back to the audition, a cold rock sat in her stomach – the memory of humiliation, shame. Then she heard Tim's voice in her head: 'They'll eat humble pie when you're famous.' She closed her eyes for a moment, imagined herself on stage in front of hundreds of people, Tim in the wings beaming as the audience clapped and cheered and demanded more.

The door opened and a suited woman came in and smiled at her.

'Hi – busy in here tonight, isn't it?'

'Yeah,' said Alice, although she didn't think it was particularly.

The other woman went into a cubicle. Alice inhaled deeply, took one last look at herself in the mirror, and shouldered her bag. She had decided two things; firstly, she wasn't going to let one audition, however bad, put her off her dream of singing. She'd show those bastards they'd made a mistake letting her slip through their fingers. And secondly, she wasn't going to let Tim get away. He'd suggested they see each other the next day, and she'd make sure they did.

As she entered Euston for the train home, she was struck by the smell of the place – fried food and unwashed bodies; there were homeless people already staking their claim to a few feet of ground, spreading their cardboard and blankets out for another night in the station. She avoided their gaze, angry they were there, that she was forced to see them, that they didn't do anything to help themselves. She joined the commuters looking at the departures board and decided to message Tim before she went home. She pulled her phone out, but before she could text him, Maddie rang.

'We're all dying to know all about him. You can't keep us in suspenders!'

Alice laughed. Trust Maddie. She could never wait for anything, and don't ask her to keep a secret, it was beyond her powers of self-control. Not that Tim was a secret. She'd wanted Maddie to tell everyone.

'Well?' asked her friend.

'Well what? What do you want to know?'

'Everything, of course. How did you meet him, and where? What does he do? What does he look like? Everything.'

Alice could hear the others in the background adding their questions. 'Tall?' 'Rich?' 'Got a brother?'

Alice opened her mouth to answer, and stopped. What to tell them?

'You know I said I was coming to London today?'

'Yes.'

'Well, he's the ticket collector from the train.'

There was a pause. Alice could hear her friend's judgement reaching into it. When she spoke, Maddie's voice had a forced cheerfulness to it. 'Great. That's... great.'

Alice bit her lip. 'Kidding! He's an artist.'

Maddie laughed. 'Geez! You had me going there for a while. What's he like?'

Alice thought about that. He was kind, and good-looking and into her.

'Nice. Sexy,' said Alice. 'Gotta go, Mads, going to see him now.'

'I thought you said you were seeing him tomorrow.'

'Change of plan. See ya.'

Fuck 'em, she thought. Her friends were all so quick to judge. It was Maddie's fault she'd had to lie. Her and her bigwig accounts-manager boyfriend. Alice was glad she hadn't told anyone about her audition – they'd probably all be toasting her failure. She took a deep breath and shook her head. She loved her friends really, they'd been through a lot together – boozy nights, partying the weekends away, new love, broken hearts, illness. But they could be so bloody judgemental.

She looked at the time on her phone. He'd left almost an hour ago. She wondered where he was, what was happening. Would she look desperate if she called him? Interfering? Supportive? She decided to wait a little, and wandered towards

Oxford Street again. It was only seven, perhaps the shops would still be open.

At Debenhams she remembered she'd promised Debbie, the girl who'd done her make-up, she'd let her know how she got on. She made her way to the Urban Decay counter, and there she was, serving a customer. Alice waited, pretending to be interested in the mascaras, until she was free.

'Hi,' she said.

'Can I help you with anything?'

'Debbie, it's me, Alice. I was here this morning – you did my make-up.'

'Oh, yes! Sorry – it's been a long day. I was meant to knock off at four, but the girl who was meant to replace me called in sick. *The X Factor* – how did it go? Need your own personal make-up artist to go on tour with you?'

'Nah. It was awful. I don't mean your make-up. The whole audition was a real shit-fight. They don't listen to anyone properly. Just choose people at random, I reckon.'

'Sorry to hear that.'

Alice shrugged. 'Yeah, well, at least it's over.'

'You can always try again. Or go on *Britain's Got Talent* or something.'

Two girls were trying the eyeshadow testers and Debbie turned to them. Alice was relieved. Talking about it still made her want to curl into a ball and cry. Or shout at someone. 'Yeah. I 'spose. Anyway, looks like you've got another customer. I'll leave you to it. Thanks again.'

Outside on the street, her phone tinkled in her pocket but before she had a chance to get to it, it had stopped. She pulled it out and looked. Missed call from Tim. She called straight back but it went to message bank. Damn. She hated it when people ignored her calls.

'One more time,' she said to herself. 'I'll try one more time and that's it.' She called his number and held her breath. He picked up.

'Are you done?' she asked without preamble.

'Alice?'

'Yeah, it's me. I'm still in London. Didn't know how long you'd be.'

'Alice – you're – Alice!'

She laughed. He sounded happy to hear from her. This amazing bloke was just a few miles away and excited that she'd rung. She offered to go and sit with him at the hospital where he was still waiting for his friend.

She almost skipped to the station, and sang to herself on the train to Ealing Broadway. She asked for directions to the hospital and was told she'd have to get a 207 bus along Uxbridge Road. It seemed to take forever, when all she wanted to do was feel Tim's arms around her.

And then she was there; he was walking towards her, told her she was beautiful, and they kissed and everything was all right.

'How's your friend?' she asked when they broke apart.

'They're keeping him in tonight but he'll be okay. Hope he will be, anyway.'

'Must feel terrible.'

'Yeah. Can't imagine what it would be like to be the last person to look into someone's eyes like that, and then, wham! they're dead.' Tim shook his head and pinched the bridge of his nose.

Alice hadn't meant the suicide; she'd been talking about the stomach pumping or whatever it was they did to people who'd drunk too much, but she didn't let on. 'Me neither,' she said. She didn't want to talk about it, didn't want to put a downer on the evening. And yet, it was because of this person wanting to end their life that she'd met Tim. A death, a new chapter in her life –

did they balance each other out in some way? And if so, where did the train driver fit in – it was, as Tim had said, an awful thing to see right in front of your eyes. How do you live with something like that?

'He'll be okay, though, right? He's got good friends. You for one.'

Tim drew in a deep breath and looked at her. Alice saw the blush creeping up his neck again. He obviously wasn't used to compliments. And he was really shy, even though she thought she'd made it quite obvious he didn't need to be, not with her.

'Yeah, he's got me. And now you're here.'

'Want to go somewhere else then? Your mate's got nurses to look after him now, hasn't he?' she asked.

'Yeah, Brian's okay for now. Let's go somewhere else. Unless you fancy the hospital canteen?'

She put her arm through his and turned him towards the door. 'I think we can find somewhere better than that, don't you?'

'I was only joking,' said Tim.

'I know.' Alice wished she'd laughed. It would have made him relax a bit.

They got an Uber back to Ealing rather than waiting for a bus, and the driver dropped them off at The North Star, the pub he'd recommended. Alice relished the warmth of Tim's hand in the small of her back as he guided her towards a table in the corner.

'What'll you have?'

'My round,' she said, and wouldn't take no for an answer.

At the bar she ordered a vodka and lime for herself and a pint of Dutch courage for Tim.

'A what?' asked the barmaid, laughing.

'Oh, sorry, did I say that out loud?' said Alice. 'It's just that the guy I'm with is a bit, you know, backward in coming forward.'

'Well don't get him too drunk or he won't be able to do anything. There's a fine line between brave enough and stonkered, if you àsk me.'

Alice was still smiling as she put Tim's pint of lager down in front of him and he looked at her but didn't ask what she was smiling at.

She questioned Tim about his life, his job, his likes and dislikes. After another pint, he relaxed and didn't seem to mind being in the spotlight so much. She watched the way his mouth moved as he talked, his slightly overlapping front teeth, the dimple that appeared on his left cheek when he smiled. He reddened when he talked about his painting, and changed the subject quickly, asking her about her singing.

'I'm gonna keep at it,' she said. He reached for her hand and squeezed it. Alice took it as her opportunity to move in closer. She snuggled into his side and sighed.

'What do you want to do now?' asked Tim.

Alice knew exactly what she wanted but she didn't want to scare him away.

'Your turn to choose – I chose to meet you at the hospital, the Uber driver chose the pub.'

Tim pulled away and looked her in the eye, unsmiling. Alice wondered if she'd blown it. Perhaps she'd been too forward, or maybe he liked girls who took the lead. Everything was so hard to gauge at the beginning of a relationship. Was this even the beginning of anything? She saw something flicker across Tim's face, but couldn't read what it was. He bit his lip and looked over her shoulder as if searching for his lines on the wall behind her.

'I don't live too far from here,' he said just before Alice thought she couldn't hold her breath any longer.

'Sounds like a plan. I'd like to see where you live.'

'We could get a takeaway, if you're hungry.'

Alice laughed. 'Yeah, if that's what you want.' Anything to make him relax, she thought.

~

With an Indian takeaway and a couple of cans of beer, they turned away from Ladbroke Grove Station and Westway along a busy road. After a few minutes, they turned right and Tim stopped in front of an old house.

'It's not much. Just a bedsit,' he said.

'That's okay. I wasn't expecting Buckingham Palace.' Alice's heart did sink though. The area was shabby, the three-storey terraces in need of repair, and the front gardens were full of weeds and broken bits of furniture.

She followed Tim up the cracked stone steps to the front door and into the hallway where she was surprised to smell new paint. The walls were pale yellow, the woodwork startling white.

'The landlady let me do a bit of painting. Only finished the day before yesterday.'

'It's fresh,' said Alice. 'Classy.' She tried not to imagine what it had been like before.

Tim looked pleased. 'Must have known you'd be coming.' He led her up the stairs. On the top landing he opened a door and ushered her into a large room with two more doors off it, both closed.

'Bathroom's there if you need it.' He pointed to one of them. 'I'll get plates for this.' He held up the bag of food and headed through the other door.

Food was the last thing on Alice's mind, but she realised Tim wouldn't be rushed. She thought he was as keen as her, or else why would he have suggested coming back to his place? But maybe playing host like this was his way of putting her at her ease, of telling her he wasn't just into her for sex, and she liked that.

She looked about. Inside was definitely better than outside. There was a bay window with a seat built into it, an old sofa and matching armchair in front of a fireplace with a gas heater instead of an open fire. A table with two wooden chairs stood in one corner. There was a poster of Florence and the Machine on the wall, a couple of charcoal sketches, a small bookcase full of paperbacks by people Alice hadn't heard of. The carpet was threadbare, but clear of all the clothes and other junk she let spread about her own room. She liked that he was a tidy type, that he looked after things. She let her bag slip off her shoulder onto the floor.

Hearing the ping of a microwave she turned to see Tim coming back into the room. The smell of curry wafted towards her.

'Here we are then,' he said, putting plates and food containers on the table and pulling cutlery out of his back pocket.

'No bed. Are you a vampire?' she asked.

'What?' His eyebrows shot upwards.

'Like in *Twilight* – Bella goes to Edward's house and he doesn't have a bed because he's a vampire.'

Tim still wasn't getting it.

'Vampires don't need to sleep, see?'

'Oh!' Light dawned, and Tim blushed scarlet and looked anywhere but at Alice, who clapped a hand over her mouth.

'Sorry – I didn't mean – oh God. I just noticed that – where *do* you sleep?' She felt her own blush heating her cheeks. What a stupid thing to say.

But Tim was laughing, gripping the edge of the table, tears in his eyes. 'Sorry,' he gasped, 'but you should have seen your face just then.'

Alice smiled. It wasn't often she was lost for words, but none came now. She sat down and enjoyed watching Tim's laughter. If he hadn't been relaxed with her before, he was now.

'Sorry,' he said again, when he'd managed to stop. 'It's there – a pull-down job. It saves space.' He pointed to what looked like a tall cupboard.

'So how does it work?' asked Alice, going over and inspecting it. She ran her hands down one side trying to find a button or a lever. She felt Tim behind her, reaching over, their bodies so close she could feel the warmth of him, smell the faint, end-of-the-day aftershave on his skin. He took hold of the top of the cupboard and pulled the bed down. The duvet was held in place by two straps. Alice undid them and sat down.

'It's comfy,' she said, smoothing the cover.

She looked at Tim who was staring at her. She smiled and lay back, holding a hand out to him. He took her hand and she pulled him to her, pleased he didn't resist, that he lay along the length of her, fitting himself to her curves. Alice sighed and stretched, and felt Tim's eyes on her. She started undoing his shirt, slipped a hand inside and felt the smoothness of his skin. He removed his trousers as Alice wriggled out of hers.

Tim took her top off and started stroking her breasts. She quivered as he kissed her all the way along her neck, setting something off in her belly.

His phone rang. He looked over at it.

'Not now.' She pulled him close, kissing him greedily. Tim's hands stroked the length of her torso and she shuddered, her nipples hardening.

The phone rang again. 'Sorry,' he said. 'I'd better get it. It's Brian.'

Alice rolled away from him, crossed her arms over her chest.

'Yeah, course I will, mate. Okay. See you soon.'

Tim sat up. Alice knew what was coming and was suddenly

furious. How dare that man expect Tim to leave her and go to him. And how dare Tim even contemplate it. She was giving herself to him and he obviously thought of her as a worthless chick to be played with and dropped on a whim? No one treated her like that and got away with it. And to think she'd thought he really liked her. What a fucking joke.

She got out of bed, started gathering her scattered clothes.

'I'm so sorry, but I can't leave him. He's discharged himself. I gotta go.' Tim reached out to her.

Alice was too angry to respond. Tim started getting dressed, hopping around on one foot as he pulled a pair of jeans on.

'I'll call you,' he said. 'Can I?'

'Do what you like.' She took her clothes into the bathroom and got dressed. When she came out, he was standing by the door. He reached for her but she swept past him and down the stairs.

'Alice... please...'

What was she going to tell her friends?

6

SANDEEP

Sandeep rubbed his eyes and replaced his glasses, then bowed his head in silent prayer. What a terrible thing, to take one's own life. It was a sin. God would not let that man into Heaven. He would be damned for all eternity, his soul burning in the fires of Hell, destined never to be reborn. Sandeep stopped, realising that yet again, he had strayed into his Hindu roots. His new religion did not believe in rebirth. He thought it a shame – the only problem with Christianity, in fact. The idea that his soul, imperfect and prone to minor sins as it was, would be cast into purgatory until the end of the world, whereafter it would be reunited with his body until the end of days, was little comfort. He prayed for salvation for the man who had killed himself. He hoped that when he died he would go straight to Heaven and walk in the presence of the Lord.

He raised his head and opened his eyes. They had stopped in the middle of a field. He didn't spend any time in the countryside these days and the greenery reminded him of his parents' village in Maharashtra after the rains, when the parched land guzzled down the deluge and became almost obscenely fecund overnight. As a child, before he and his parents had left India, Sandeep had seen it for himself and understood that God was in this place. In those days God was Shiva, the one to whom his mother prayed, to whom the shrine in their home was dedicated. After the rains they thanked Indra, too, for his continued bounty.

He felt a mixture of sadness and anger when he thought of his parents. They would not even try to understand his new religion, much less accompany him to church. His mother had cried for weeks when he told her he was going to be baptised. His father had threatened to beat him but he wouldn't be shaken from the right path. And anyway, he was thirty years old, a full head taller than his father and twice as broad. These days they didn't talk about religion at all but he felt his mother's yearning when he was home, waiting for him to come back to her and her false gods.

He sighed and turned his thoughts away from all that. He had a long day ahead – one of his boss's clients was way behind in his tax returns and the inland revenue – revenue and customs, he corrected himself – was after him. Barry had passed the problem on to him, so he was going to be knee-deep in receipts and paperwork all day. And he was having dinner with his parents which also meant staying the night at their house and enduring more of his mother's disappointment over breakfast. He slumped further into his seat.

A phone trilled and a young woman sitting over the aisle in an army surplus coat many sizes too big for her looked at it and typed furiously on the screen. When she looked over their eyes met and Sandeep looked away, embarrassed.

'Wonder how long we'll be here,' she said, and Sandeep realised she was talking to him.

He shrugged. 'It is difficult to say with these things.'

'Has it happened to you before then?'

'Oh, no, I just meant I don't know how long it takes for the police and–' He realised he had no idea who else was involved in situations such as this.

'Were you praying before?' asked the woman, eyebrows raised.

'Yes, I was praying for the soul of the poor man who saw no alternative but to kill himself.'

'It might have been an accident. He might've fallen.'

'From where?' asked Sandeep, looking out the window. 'There is no bridge near here and he cannot have fallen from the sky, I think.'

'Stranger things have happened,' said the woman, and turned back to her phone, leaving Sandeep wondering what things she was referring to. Perhaps the miracle of the loaves and fishes, still one of his favourite stories from the Bible – and little David taking on Goliath was another good one. He had thought they were metaphors written to teach people something, but Dave, the leader of their study group, explained that the Bible was the Word of God, and literal. There was evidence these people had lived in just the way it was written and that miracles were what set Jesus apart. Whether they were real or not, there was a mystery and magic in them that Sandeep was drawn to. When he was little he'd always loved his grandmother telling him stories from the Mahabharata, the great battle between the Pandavas and the Kauravas. He particularly liked sitting on Aji's lap, imagining the elephants lined up in their battle dress, the chariots, the soldiers with their spears and the archers with bows and arrows at the ready. And he loved the bit where Krishna revealed himself in his true, divine form to Arjuna, who had thought he was just a charioteer. What a surprise it must have been to Arjuna, and yet, he, Sandeep, had known it all along! It always made him feel clever to have outwitted Arjuna, just as Krishna had. He smiled, and thought perhaps it was time to make a trip back to India to see his Aji. She was too old to come to see him and had always been unwilling to leave her village. Maybe he would read to her now, since her eyesight was failing, and together they could remember the victory of the Pandavas. He decided to look into flights.

The whoosh of the connecting doors made him look up. The guard came through the carriage, clearly trying to avoid speaking to anyone and this time Sandeep left him alone. The last time he'd asked what had happened and learned of the death and although he wanted to know when they might be on their way again, it seemed callous to ask. Death kept to its own time frame and had to be honoured. He wondered if the body would be buried in a proper graveyard or whether it would be condemned to dwell forever away from God's grace, in unconsecrated ground. And was it a body anyway – what did the remains of someone look like when hundreds of tons of train had run into them? He shifted in his seat and bowed his head again. This time he was praying for the driver, the last man to look into the eyes of the deceased. Sandeep prayed he would find comfort in God's loving care and forgiveness.

Raising his head, he gazed out into the field and thought how much Abby would like wherever it was they were. She'd talked about maybe moving out of Milton Keynes to the countryside when they were married. She'd been raised on a farm and was used to helping with the animals and baling the hay or whatever they did with it. The idea made his blood curdle. He may have been born in a village in India but his parents had transplanted him to another country, to the greatest city in the world and he could not countenance the idea of a backward step, for that's what it would be. It had been bad enough having to move to Milton Keynes for his previous job and now not being able to afford to buy a house back in London.

The girl in the oversized coat was reading, her cheeks red.

He hoped she was all right – one casualty was enough for one day. The man next to her cleared his throat and she glared at him and tried to shift further away from him although she was already crammed against the window. He wondered how the two of them would cope if ever they went to India, where the concept of personal space was so different – almost non-existent. Whole families lived in one or two rooms, or extended families built extra rooms onto existing houses so they could all be together. In his parents' family home in the village, cousins and brothers and sisters had all shared one room, sleeping top to toe on the mattresses, arms and legs thrown over each other in sleep's intimacy.

He sighed and got back to the problem of what to do about Abby. Or rather, how to tell her they would not be living the country idyll if he had a say. He loved her, of that there could be no doubt. He had met her when he started attending the church where she was also a parishioner. She'd been going there since she had moved to Milton Keynes four years previously and had taken him under her wing, him being a novice in the ways of Christianity. He'd only stumbled into the place because there wasn't a temple nearby and he was lonely and wanted to meet people. And it was such a friendly congregation. At first, the singing and dancing had been rather confronting. He wasn't used to people behaving in such a way in a place of worship. He wasn't sure what he'd been expecting, but given the usual British stiff upper lip he hadn't been prepared for the informality, the fun they were having. It took him a while to get used to it but in the end it was intoxicating. As was Abby with her wide hazel eyes and open smile. He would go home after the service and spend the rest of the day thinking about it. About her. They were one and the same to him, he realised. You couldn't have one without the other. Abby and the church. His respite from the busyness of business. His sanctuary. As long as he put his foot down about moving to the country.

With a jerk and a bit of clanking the train started moving again. Sandeep checked his watch. He'd be two hours late to work. He'd rung his boss to let him know he was on his way, and the reason for his lateness, the words faltering on his lips. Normally if he was late, which he rarely was, he'd stay to make up the time but his mother had been adamant that he was to be there at six on the dot tonight for a special dinner she'd been preparing for one minor festival or another. He had stopped listening when she was telling him about it. He felt a pang of guilt. He should be a better son, a better Christian. He decided he'd get her a bunch of flowers and maybe a box of her favourite Indian sweets.

There was the question of introducing them to Abby as well. He hadn't admitted to his parents he was even seeing her, let alone planning to marry her. The last time he and Abby had spoken about it she'd burst into tears, accusing him of being ashamed of her. That wasn't it, as he'd been quick to reassure her. The truth was, he knew his parents would take it badly. Even now, with his baptism only weeks away, his mother still talked about arranging him a marriage. She said it was her right as a parent, his duty as a son.

'Why did you leave the village if you just want to hold on to all the old customs, eh?' Sandeep had asked on his last visit.

'Because it is right. Look at your father and me. We are happy. Our parents chose for us. You are too young to know what you want and you work too hard to meet anyone. Are there even any Indians in MK?'

That was the other thing that counted against Abby – she was most decidedly not Indian. She had the palest skin he had ever seen and such beautiful, thick chestnut hair.

'Of course there are, Mataji,' he'd said, but she'd just

harrumphed in the annoying way she had and somehow changed the subject.

Neither of them had dared mention the religion trump card. They had both backed off just before one of them hurt the other too deeply, although Sandeep certainly felt the barbs in his mother's words. Once again, at the end of the evening, Sandeep had gone to his childhood bedroom angry, misunderstood and staring into the chasm between his mother's desires and his own. His father left them to it these days, preferring to watch cooking shows on TV.

Biting the inside of his lip, he told himself he was lucky to have both his parents still and that he should try and look forward to seeing them. And tonight he would tell them about Abby and deal with the consequences.

On the journey from Euston to the office, Sandeep was still feeling emotional. It seemed unfair that he was able to walk, enjoy the warmth of the sun on his skin, look forward to a day at work when a woman (he had overheard this awful fact from the man next to him in the train, which in an indefinable way made the suicide even worse) had died in such a terrible way and would never again enjoy God's bounty. He hadn't known this person, of course, but surely there must have been glimpses of a better life, or memories of one at least? He was deeply saddened by the bleakness that must have led to such a decision. Even the thought of seeing his parents later suddenly seemed like a gift.

He pulled his phone from his pocket. He needed to talk to Abby. She always had the right words to educate him in the ways of the Lord and make him feel better.

'What is it – you never call me during the day. Is something wrong?' she asked.

It was true. Theirs was not a relationship that required constant nurturing. They saw each other at church, prayer group, Bible study and once a week for dinner. They hadn't slept together and Sandeep's few attempts in that direction had ended as awkward fumbles. Abby was saving herself for marriage. At first it had been an issue for Sandeep, although not one he could discuss with Abby. Although no Casanova, he had enjoyed sexual relations with two previous girlfriends, and missed the intimacy. There was something glorious about two people trusting each other with their most private desires, engaging together to produce such exquisite pleasure. He could understand how some people thought it was a path to the Divine. But Abby knew the ways of the church and she smiled in a coquettish sort of way when she mentioned their wedding night, which gave him hope that once they were married their love life would be active. Not that it was the only reason he wanted to marry her.

'I need to talk to someone – to you. A terrible thing happened this morning.'

He told her about the incident and his response to it in detail, cupping his hand around the microphone to cut out the din of traffic and make himself heard. Abby remained silent at the other end. When he'd finished she made an odd noise, as if she was clearing her throat and exhaling sharply at the same time. Sandeep wondered if she'd caught a cold since he'd seen her at church the day before.

'You have to realise, Sandy' – he hated her calling him that, but she said it was an endearment, and anyway, she preferred it to his real name – 'that this person committed the unpardonable sin for which there is no salvation.' She said it in a soft voice, as if she was talking about the weather or something inconsequential, but the words struck Sandeep like a blow.

'But the despair she must have been experiencing to do such

a thing – maybe she could see no other way. Perhaps I can pray for her soul.'

'The un-pard-on-able sin.' Abby spoke slowly, annunciating every syllable as if he hadn't understood. 'Self-murder. Call it what you will, Sandy, but her soul will not get into Heaven whatever you do. It would be a waste of time. Forget about it, put it behind you. There's nothing you can do for her now.'

Another blow, this one harder, almost knocked the wind out of him so he had to lean against a shop window and catch his breath. Her words were so harsh, cruel even. Surely a loving God would understand that some people, however hard they tried, couldn't attain perfect faith in Jesus. He himself was still trying very hard, with Abby's guidance.

'Sandy, are you still there?'

'Yes. Thank you. I'd better go, I'm at work now.'

He slipped his phone into his pocket and walked on, his heart heavier than it had been before. Not only had Abby, his guide, his teacher, been unsympathetic, he had lied to her. He wasn't at work. He was still in the street, as she would have known by the sounds of traffic in the background. She would, no doubt, reprimand him for it next time they saw each other, and suggest they pray together for the Lord's forgiveness.

Sandeep ran his hands through his hair and stopped, closed his eyes for a moment to calm himself, then hurried on until he came to a church whose doors were open and in he went. It was an old building, with wooden pews and stained-glass windows. The smell of incense in the still air enveloped and comforted him. Candles burned in front of paintings and images of saints; a priest in robes prayed at the altar. It was as unlike his modern unadorned place of worship as it was possible to be, but there was something calming about the way the light shone through the coloured windows, and the flickering of the candles. He sat, bowed his head and prayed. Maybe Abby had been wrong about

all people going to purgatory if they took their own life –
perhaps there were sometimes extenuating circumstances, and
anyway, Sandeep didn't believe it was wrong to pray for
someone's soul, whatever had happened.

When he got to his desk a while later, feeling guilty he had
taken the extra time, calming though it had been, he stared at
the to-do list he'd made the day before as was his habit. He
ended every day with a review of what had been achieved and
a plan for the next day. One of his university professors had
suggested it in his first year and he'd been doing it ever since.
It gave shape to his days and a sense of accomplishment. He
had learned, over the years, to have one particular item on
every list – half an hour to deal with the unexpected.
Something always cropped up and before he had planned for
this spontaneity, he often didn't manage to get through his list
without staying late. Today, however, he was two hours late and
had to leave early. It was going to be difficult to finish
everything. He felt a surge of anxiety and had to wipe his
sweaty hands on the towel he kept in a drawer for such
occasions.

His boss popped his head round the door. 'Ah, Sandeep,
there you are. Are you okay?'

'Yes, thank you, I'm fine. Sorry to be so late.'

Sandeep had always been acutely aware of the pecking
order. Barry Worthington was the boss, and he, Sandeep, was a
minion. A hard-working, intelligent one, but a minion
nonetheless. And bosses deserved respect.

'Not at all, not at all. Terrible thing to happen. Poor man.
Well, poor you, too, going through it.' He cleared his throat. 'By
the way, I just got a call from Ray – he's also running late for his
appointment, as luck would have it. Probably a good thing – give
you a bit of time to gather yourself. You don't look too good.'

'It was a lady, actually.' Sandeep didn't know why he had to tell Barry, but it seemed important. A degree of respect for the woman.

Barry scratched his head. 'How awful.' He shook his head sadly. 'Anyway, I'll leave you to it.'

'Thank you, sir,' said Sandeep.

His boss raised an eyebrow at him.

'Sorry – thank you, Barry.' He'd been reminded on numerous occasions not to call him *sir*, but it was a habit Sandeep found difficult to break. He watched his boss go, thinking that he'd been more sympathetic than his fiancée.

A few minutes later, Sandeep was back to looking at his to-do list when the phone on his desk buzzed. 'Ray Dreyfus to see you,' announced Monica, sounding as bored as always.

Sandeep stood and straightened his tie.

When Ray entered, they shook hands but Sandeep didn't invite any small talk. His client handed over a folder full of receipts and invoices and closed his briefcase with a click.

'I hope that's everything,' he said, and looked expectantly at Sandeep.

'I'll call you if I need anything else,' he said, and opened the file. He had a job to do and it was important to get going on it as soon as possible. Fortunately, his client seemed keen to go as quickly as he could, so Sandeep put his head down and started going through the figures.

As Ray opened the door to leave, Sandeep put his headphones on, found the Gregorian chants on his phone and got stuck into Ray's accounts.

In spite of the chants and the soothing screen full of numbers in front of him, Sandeep couldn't concentrate. Abby's words kept intruding: *unpardonable sin, no salvation, there's nothing you can do for her now*. That must mean existing for all time in a no-man's land of – of what? Nothingness? Away from the comfort of others and the Lord. He sat in a lather of confusion. He was well aware that in his mother's religion suicide was also a sin that brought great shame to the family but he also knew people had a chance, many chances, in fact – to redeem themselves over lifetimes. This woman may have set herself back on her road to enlightenment, but she could eventually get there. Maybe it had been her karma to die in such a way in this lifetime, to pay for past sins. Sandeep thought it was a kinder view than Abby's eternal damnation.

Sandeep clenched his jaw and squeezed his eyes shut for a few moments, forcing thoughts of the dead woman from his mind so he could focus on the task at hand. Then he chose a playlist of Hindu chants, including his favourite, the 'Gayatri Mantra', and for the next five hours, only stopped intermittently to stand and stretch his arms over his head and bend from side to side – another tip he'd been given and stuck to over the years.

At four in the afternoon, Barry stuck his head around the door again. 'How are you going with Ray's accounts – I hope he's given you everything you need?'

'Yes, everything's here. I've almost finished the first two years.'

'Thanks for agreeing to take it on – I know personal tax isn't what you're used to, but he was one of my first clients when I started the practice years ago, and I've never had the heart to send him on his way. He's a bit like my lucky mascot, if you see what I mean.'

Sandeep didn't, but he wasn't about to admit it. He had wondered why a corporate accounting firm such as Worthington and Jones was doing an individual's tax return, especially when the amounts, so far at least, were rather paltry. He'd far rather get his teeth into the audit of the big engineering firm they'd just tendered for. Big numbers, complex tax strategies, offshore accounts, international threads to follow. It was why he'd got into accounting. He thought of himself as a financial detective, and a quite a good one too.

'It's fine, sir – I mean, Barry. Really, I don't mind at all.'

'Excellent. Well, I'm going to squeeze in a few holes of golf with Sir Peter before I go home. See you tomorrow.'

At his first job several years ago, Sandeep had been on the team that did Sir Peter's company tax and knew all about his particular penchant for tax avoidance and hiding profits in offshore accounts. Nothing outright illegal, but shady, and it had troubled Sandeep so he'd requested to be moved to another project. And when Peter Welch became Sir Peter, knighted in the Queen's Birthday Honours list for services to British business and global relations, he thought the Queen or her people should check more thoroughly before bestowing such honours.

'Have a good time,' he said as Barry retreated out the door.

By the time he left at five, Sandeep was frustrated by the slow progress on Ray's tax backlog. He put it on his to-do list to address the following day, added a couple of other small but pressing items and the half hour for unexpected occurrences. After today's events he considered extending it to an hour but decided against it – half an hour had always been ample until now and although it hadn't served him well enough today, he reminded himself of one of Abby's sayings. *One swallow does not a summer make.* Everything would be back to normal tomorrow, with the added bonus that he would have told his parents about Abby, and their plan to marry.

Leaving his list under the paperweight on his desk – he always wrote them out by hand for the satisfaction of placing a tick by the finished items – he nodded his farewell to Monica who had her back to him doing something at the photocopier and left the office to spend the evening with his parents.

~

Sandeep smoothed his hair down as he stood at the front door of his parents' semi in Hounslow. He felt like a naughty schoolboy waiting to see the principal whenever he visited them these days, these moments on the doorstep full of tense anticipation.

'Sandeep! What for are you not using your key? You are not a guest, are you? Why always behaving like one?'

'Hello, Mataji,' he said, smiling and thrusting the flowers he'd bought for her into her hands. She couldn't pull him into one of her crushing, incense-smelling embraces if she had her hands full. He'd thought, as a boy, his mother must keep several Indian incense factories in business – a sweet-smelling, smoky haze hung over every room and the furniture and their clothes were impregnated with its cloying odour. Now he lived on his own he didn't have to suffer the jokes of his fellow pupils, students, colleagues. But Abby always commented on it when he'd been to see his mother. She reminded him each time that she had a sensitive nose.

'What am I needing flowers for, Sandeep?' said his mother as she put them on the hall table. 'Come, come – Abby is here already, waiting, waiting.'

Sandeep gulped. His legs started tingling. First the left, then the right, then his whole body felt as if someone had poured a fizzy drink into it. 'Abby is here?' he managed to get out through lips tightening in fear. How could it be? Had she finally snapped and rung his parents, told them everything? She'd been pressuring him for a long time to tell them about her but would she really have taken the matter into her own hands?

'Whatever is the matter, Sandeep – are you ill?'

'No.' He gulped and swung round to look at his mother. 'No, I'm fine. What do you think of her?'

'She is a lovely girl. Just right for you. So clever, so pretty-pretty and good family.'

Sandeep felt his heart settle into its proper rhythm again. 'So you like her?'

'Yes, yes. Of course.'

He could hardly believe it. Why had he been so reluctant to introduce them all these months? All his mother wanted was for him to be happy, and to her marriage was the key to his happiness. Whether the girl was black, white or blue, Hindu, Christian or Jew was of secondary importance. He should have known. He should never have doubted her love for him.

'Come, come – she is waiting.' His mother beckoned him towards the living room.

At the door, she stopped. 'Now, Sandeep, let me look.' She put her hands on his upper arms and peered into his face, brushed a stray lock of hair off his forehead. 'Make me proud, Sandeep, please.'

He lifted his chin, smiled at his mother and said, 'Of course, Mataji.'

He calmed himself with a quick prayer and followed his mother into the living room.

He saw his father sitting in his Parker Knoll by the electric coal-effect heater and made his way over to him, stepping over the occasional table by the lamp and leant down to kiss him on both cheeks.

'Yes, yes,' his father said, nodding.

Sandeep turned and scanned the rest of the room for Abby. There were two women sitting next to each other on the sofa. The older one wearing a midnight-blue sari and the younger wearing a pale-pink blouse and a dark skirt. Both had long black hair. Neither of them was Abby. Sandeep's forehead creased in confusion. He glanced around the room.

'Sandeep, let me introduce you to Mr Devdas Iyer.' His

mother was standing by a tall, thin man with a narrow moustache clinging to his top lip.

It was as if his body remembered his manners and propelled him forward to bow and take the older man's hand when he offered it. Certainly his head wasn't working. What was going on? Abby was meant to be there but she was nowhere to be seen, and these people were occupying his parents' living room instead.

'Allow me to introduce my wife, Mrs Madhuri Iyer,' said Mr Iyer, gesturing to the older woman who looked at him without a smile, 'and my daughter, Miss Abhi Iyer.'

Sandeep's heart stopped. He could almost feel the colour drain from his face. He swallowed a couple of times and ran his hand down his already straight tie. How could he have been so stupid? Of course his mother would never have accepted Abby – and Abby would never have gone behind his back and invited herself to their house. In fact, she seemed quite disinterested in having anything to do with his parents, he now realised. She said they didn't even need their approval for the marriage, them being adults and all, and she showed little inclination to meet them. And his mother was determined to arrange a match for him with a nice Indian girl, this evening being just another in a long line of introductions. He threw her a glance and didn't respond to her self-satisfied smile before assuming the dutiful son demeanour as he turned to the women on the sofa. He greeted the mother and the daughter, who kept her eyes down but acknowledged his greeting with a small nod.

'Now, sit, sit, everyone,' said his mother as she swept out of the room only to return seconds later with a tray laden with food, plates, serviettes.

'Sandeep, see to the drinks.' She nodded towards their guest. 'Mr Iyer's glass is empty again.'

Sandeep, raised to respect his elders and make polite

conversation with guests, played his role even as he fantasised about forcing all the samosas into his mother's mouth at once.

As the minutes dragged by and Mr Iyer steadily lowered the contents of the Johnny Walker bottle, Sandeep found himself glancing more and more often at the quiet girl sitting with her mother. Even over dinner she hardly looked up, and never met Sandeep's eye. He found her intriguing. She looked after her mother's every need without being asked, answered when spoken to but otherwise remained silent. He wondered what she thought of it all, this awkward introduction, and wanted to ask her, wanted to take her away from these parents and their hopes and expectations and talk to her about what she actually wanted, what she dreamed of, what she thought of this charade.

'I'll clear the table, Mataji,' he said when they'd eaten all they could of his mother's excellent dinner. She'd pulled out all the stops and filled the table with several curries, a biryani, chutneys, raita, saffron rice, chapatis. For dessert there was kulfi and gulab jamun in sweet rose syrup. Sandeep needed to move after all the food.

'I'll help,' said Abhi in her first spontaneous utterance.

Sandeep saw his mother and Mrs Iyer exchange a look of smug complicity that made his stomach clench. It made him want to tell Abhi to sit, that he didn't need her help, but he stopped himself. This might be the only chance they got to speak alone so he ignored the excitement in his mother's face, the expectant look in her eyes and took a breath to calm himself.

'Thank you.' Jaw clenched, he started stacking the plates.

'We'll have tea in the living room when you've finished.' His mother gave him a knowing wink and then raised her eyebrows and glanced quickly at Abhi. Sandeep nodded but didn't acknowledge her childish semaphore.

He rinsed the plates and stacked them in the dishwasher and started on the pans and glasses which his mother decreed had to be washed by hand. Abhi took a tea towel from where it hung over the handle of the oven and waited by the sink.

'So, Abhi–' He was suddenly nervous. He hadn't noticed how beautiful she was until that moment. Now he was fascinated by the way the light lay across her cheek, shadowing it and making her lips seem fuller. Her hair, he now saw, was loose and thick, several strands lying over her shoulder, not plaited as he had assumed when it was pushed behind her back. Her hands holding the cloth were delicate with long fingers, the nails cut short.

She looked at him for the first time and her face broke into a wide smile. Laughter lines fanned out from her eyes.

'Isn't this the pits?'

Sandeep was caught off guard and said nothing.

'I get hauled along to these things at least once a month. I'm surprised there are any single Indian men left to introduce me to but somehow Mataji finds them.' She shook her head, a small smile on her lips.

Sandeep sucked in a deep breath. She looked at him. 'Sorry – I didn't mean to be rude – I assumed–'

'No, it's okay,' he said. 'I feel the same. My mother has to hoodwink me into coming home these days.'

They stood in silence for a while, Sandeep washing the dishes, Abhi drying them and putting them on the kitchen table. It wasn't an awkward silence, one of those that stretches on with neither party able to think of anything to say. It was companionable. The parameters had been set – they would never meet again so there was no rush to know everything about each other, yet anything they did want to talk about would be dealt with on this one occasion only.

'So, what do you do?' asked Sandeep eventually.

'I'm a pharmacist,' said Abhi. 'At University College Hospital. How about you?'

'Accountant. Small but growing firm just round the corner from there.' He sounded like a recruitment officer and gave a little laugh to show that he also had a sense of humour.

Abhi laughed. 'So we're both good Indian children who have gone into safe professions.'

Sandeep thought about that. He'd always been good at maths, but he'd preferred the pure sciences. He couldn't remember his parents actively putting pressure on him to go into accountancy but there had been comments ever since he could remember about going into a profession offering stability and allowing him to earn enough money to look after his parents in their old age. He'd toyed with the idea of studying physics at university, but a quiet, insistent voice in his head had stayed his hand. What would he do with a physics degree? Join the ranks of the overqualified unemployed, it said.

He shrugged. 'I suppose so, but I'm not unhappy, are you?'

'Not at all.'

Sandeep noticed the way the light danced in her eyes when she smiled.

'What else do you do – I mean when you're not at work?' he asked, more to stop himself gazing at her than because he wanted to know.

'The usual – see friends, go to movies, get away for weekends in the country or to Paris – I love Paris.'

'Oh.' Abby had been to Paris before they met. She hadn't liked it. It was expensive and full of French people who didn't speak English, she'd said.

'How about you?'

He was surprised to find he was embarrassed to tell her that all he did was go to Bible study and take his secret girlfriend out for dinner once a week. He'd never been to Paris and the last film he went to was *Tinker Tailor Soldier Spy* four or five years ago.

'What's so special about Paris?' He realised he sounded petulant rather than interested.

She didn't seem to notice, or ignored his tone if she did. 'It's beautiful – the river, the buildings, the food, the art galleries. The people seem so much more sophisticated than Londoners – I can't quite put a finger on why.'

'Maybe because they speak French,' said Sandeep and Abhi laughed. He hadn't meant it to be funny but he liked the way she laughed, the little creases that appeared beside her eyes. He wondered how old she was, and how desperate her parents were to find her a husband.

'Where's your favourite place?' she asked.

He wanted to tell her it was Berlin, or Dubrovnik. Somewhere that boasted a proud culture, strong people, unusual cuisine. The truth was he hadn't travelled. The only times he'd been overseas since they came to live in England were the two trips with his parents, back to their village to visit envious relatives. He hadn't enjoyed them; having lived in the cleanliness and sanitation of London, he thought India dirty and was horrified at the way people lived on the streets and in the train stations. The beggars had given him nightmares, and the relatives always seemed to have their hands out – either pawing at his nice clothes or asking for gifts.

'I like my house,' he said, at last.

'Where is that?'

'Milton Keynes.'

The laughter bubbled out of Abhi. Sandeep stood watching her. She had such even, white teeth. When she leant forward and put her hands on the table to catch her breath, he saw the pale-pink lace of her bra, the gentle swell of her breasts. He felt a stirring in his trousers and looked away quickly. He shouldn't be feeling what he was feeling. He had a fiancée in Milton Keynes. She loved him, so she said. And he loved her, didn't he? He realised that this Abhi in front of him was the Devil trying to tempt him. He cleared his throat.

'I'm glad you find it amusing,' he said.

She looked at him from under her fringe. Those big brown eyes with the hidden depths. 'I'm sorry,' she said. 'Truly.'

'And you laugh when you meet people from Bristol, or Manchester?'

'No, of course not. I've just never met anyone from Milton Keynes before. It's the place with the concrete cows, isn't it?'

'It is. But they do not define the place any more than the statue of Nelson defines London.'

She looked away and busied herself with drying a saucepan. 'Sorry. I really am.'

Sandeep felt uncomfortable. It wasn't like him to be rude but he had to keep this temptress at a distance. He started putting the dried dishes away, making sure, when he had to pass her, they didn't touch. And yet he longed to touch her, to feel the weight of her hair, the smoothness of her skin. Skin that was the same colour as his, not Abby's pale freckled flesh. He felt himself flush at the thought of flesh. He'd never seen Abby's body. She wore conservative clothing, covering herself from neck to knees. He'd seen more of Abhi's flesh when he'd glimpsed her breasts than he had of his own girlfriend's. His breath quickened at the memory of those breasts and he was angered by the faithlessness of his body.

'Have I offended you?'

'No,' he said too quickly.

'I have, haven't I?'

Sandeep sighed. He couldn't tell her the truth. 'It is I who should apologise. I had a bad day and all I really wanted to do tonight was go home and crawl into bed. I am not good company.'

He saw an immediate change in Abhi. It was as if everything about her softened.

'Anything you want to talk about?'

What would he tell her – that he was having impure thoughts about her? He wanted to make her laugh again just to see the corners of her eyes crinkle?

'No. It'll all be fine.'

He busied himself preparing the tea tray and took it in to the sitting room where his parents and Abhi's were talking about *MasterChef*.

'I think they should cook more Indian food,' said his mother, and Mrs Iyer nodded in response.

'Perhaps there should be a *MasterChef* India,' Mr Iyer slurred. He had a large glass of brandy in his hands.

'Abhi and I were thinking of going for a walk,' said Sandeep, handing his mother her turmeric and ginger tea.

She smiled up at him. 'Good idea, my son. You two young ones must have a lot to talk about.' She stopped short of winking at him, instead glancing at Mrs Iyer who raised her eyebrows and smiled, complicit in this matchmaking charade. 'But don't go far – it's dark.'

'It's only half past eight, Mataji,' said Sandeep. 'We won't be too long.'

He helped Abhi on with her coat, feeling a frisson of excitement as his hand brushed against her arm. His earlier theory about her being the Devil come to tempt him was fast crumbling. How could she be when she was so caring, so easy to talk to, when her hair fell in that particular way over the swell of her breast?

But he heard Abby's voice in his head. 'The Devil hides in plain sight. He is a charmer until he has you and then he rips everything good out of your life, strips you of God's grace and condemns you to purgatory.' He opened the front door and was careful not to touch Abhi again as she passed him on her way out.

The night was mild, the clouds low. To the right was Hounslow, to the left, Heston, Norwood Green and the fields either side of the M4 he had played in as a boy. Osterley House and its grounds, where he used to take his first girlfriend for romantic picnics and frantic fumbles under a cedar tree, was straight ahead along Jersey Road past the posh houses.

Abhi turned in that direction and he followed. As they walked she asked more about the suicide he had told her about as he made the tea – or rather, his reaction to it. He considered her questions carefully, was as honest as he could be in his answers. The truth was, no one had ever questioned him so closely about anything nor seemed so attentive when he answered.

'I am not surprised you can't stop thinking about it,' she said. 'How awful to feel so desperate you'd want to end your life in that violent way. It's quite horrible.'

It was exactly what Sandeep had thought, and yet he hadn't said as much to her. He tucked it away, though, treating with caution the words she used to fool him into believing she was as good as she appeared to be. If he was quiet she'd trip up, make a mistake and reveal herself to be, as Abby would tell him, a She-Devil.

'I'm sorry,' she said when he didn't respond. 'I have asked too many questions. You must deal with it in whatever way is best for you. But if I can help, please say the word.'

The ground seemed to shake beneath Sandeep's feet and he got the fizzy feeling in his legs again and in his stomach. But this was not adrenaline. He recognised it as the Fall. He'd felt it before. Twice. Once with Tracey and again with Karen. It was a giddy, flying sensation really, not a fall at all and he certainly, at this stage anyway, wasn't scared of falling. He was soaring on the wings of love, of desire, of hope, and nothing could hold him down.

He didn't dare look at Abhi in case she guessed what he was feeling and hated him for it. Or laughed at his adolescent crush. He knew his desire was written in the way his body leaned towards her, the expression on his face, the longing in his eyes.

Taking a deep breath, he forced himself to think of Abby, his fiancée. This was madness. He couldn't love her as he did and be falling for another, surely? It must be a trial, a final test before they were joined forever in marriage. Strange, though, how he had never felt this way about Abby, had never had the sensation of being swept off his feet and into the limitless blue sky. Surely that meant theirs was a mature love, not the stuff of movies and teenage romance novels. He smiled, safe in this new insight. He made a promise to himself that when he got through this ordeal he would agree to anything, even living in the country if it was really what Abby wanted. He prayed silently for strength.

'It's getting late. We should turn back,' he said after a few minutes during which neither of them had spoken.

Abhi looked up at the sky. A plane flew overhead, landing lights twinkling. 'It's a beautiful night, though, and I was hoping we might get as far as Osterley Park. I used to go there as a kid sometimes and dream about living in that beautiful house, wearing big dresses with bustles, all English-like, and having servants to bring me whatever I desired. Which was usually ice cream – real ice cream, not kulfi.'

Sandeep took a sharp breath. Had he not imagined the same things? Not the dresses, but carriages with horses and people calling him 'sir' and falling over themselves to fulfil his every desire? Bringing him English treats, accepting him as one of their own – even admiring and respecting him?

'Are you okay?' Abhi looked into his eyes.

'Fine. Yes, fine.' Sandeep planted his feet carefully to stop himself from taking her hand and running to the house and gardens that had been the setting for their childhood fantasies. Perhaps they had been there at the same time, had seen each other and smiled.

'Once,' he said, 'when I was about ten, we went on a visit to India and my cousin had a jar full of fireflies. He used to shake it to make them fly and light up. It was cruel I suppose, but to a boy like me it was magical. He took me hunting for them so I could have my own firefly light and I cried when, after a few hours, they died. After we came home, I found a jar and begged my parents to take me to the gardens of Osterley House to hunt for fireflies again. My father told me they didn't live in England, but I wouldn't believe him.' He looked at Abhi and laughed. He wasn't sure why he'd told her that story. 'Silly things boys do, eh?'

'Not silly, no. I don't think it's ever silly to hope. It was a little piece of India, and a connection to your cousin.'

Sandeep felt her words gather round his heart. How did she know these things? It felt like she could see right into his soul and explain to him these feelings that had no name. Perhaps she would be able to help him make sense of his feelings for Abby too. He smiled at her, about to tell her about his finacée, even as he felt a pain in his heart at the thought of saying the words. Her beauty made them catch in his throat and they would not venture forth. He stood, lips slightly apart, silent.

'So what do you think – can we make it to Osterley House?' Abhi looked in the direction of the stately home.

'I think we must...' Sandeep wanted to say I think we must go back, but his mouth wouldn't form the end of the sentence.

Abhi grabbed his hand and squeezed it. 'Come on. Last one there buys dinner!'

She let go of his hand and started running. Sandeep stood for a moment feeling the imprint of her hand on his, wanting to feel the softness of her skin again. And then her words sank in, *last one there buys dinner*. But they had already had dinner so did she mean she wanted to see him again, that they were to have dinner together, just the two of them? He started running after her. He needed to clarify his position. He was engaged to be married, he already had an Abby and didn't need another one. But as he ran he realised he might not need another Abby, but he wanted one. This one. Desperately. A She-Devil she may be but he didn't care anymore. If it meant he went to hell, at least he could be with her.

He slowed to a walk and watched her run. He had never seen anything so remarkable, so perfect. She'd hitched up her skirt and her legs were long. Her hair swung from side to side with each step. She turned, and stopped under a street light.

'Too fast for you, am I? I knew it. Too much sitting in an office and not enough exercise.'

'Oh, that's what you think, is it?' He started running and overtook her, arms and legs pumping. But after a minute his lungs were screaming and his legs felt like lead. He stopped, leaning over with his hands on his knees, panting. She caught up with him, barely out of breath, and laughed.

'I told you so,' she said as she jogged past. 'I win.'

'Wait. We are going the wrong way for Osterley House – we should have taken a right turn back there.'

Abhi grinned. 'Okay. We'll go Dutch. But I would have won if I'd known the way.'

Now, thought Sandeep. *Now is the time I must tell her that I am not a free man, I cannot have dinner with her.* But his voice had deserted him again and all he could do, when Abhi took his hand, was hold it and revel in her touch.

'So, how many introductions has your mother actually organised?' Abhi looked at him as they passed under another street lamp, and Sandeep had to take a long breath and remind himself to keep moving even though he suddenly felt like he had lost all his bones and was turning to putty.

'A dozen, maybe,' he said in a voice that sounded strange to his own ears; strangled.

'Only a dozen? You're getting off lightly. You must be my thirtieth.' She laughed, showing straight white teeth and the tip of her pink tongue. Before he could stop himself, Sandeep imagined it licking his skin. He groaned. No, no, no, he must not think these things. He must not want these things. But he couldn't stop himself. He didn't want to.

The gates to Osterley House were locked and Sandeep was disappointed they weren't going to be able to see the house after all. Abhi, however, had other ideas.

'We can climb over them, they're not high.'

Sandeep looked around. They may not be high but there must be CCTV cameras around, or security men with dogs.

'What are you waiting for?' Abhi climbed over, jumped down on the other side and started walking along the drive.

'It's illegal – we could get into a great deal of trouble–'

'Oh, come on. Live dangerously.'

Sandeep's heart quickened as he climbed the gate and caught up with her. He wanted her to take his hand again but she was walking fast and hardly seemed aware of him at her side. Now there were no street lights and the clouds were obscuring the moon and stars, the trees either side of the path dark silhouettes against the charcoal night. Their footsteps were loud on the gravel, competing with the sound of Sandeep's pulse in his ears. What if they were discovered? He might lose his job. Or worse, Abby might hear of it and wonder what he was doing late in the evening walking through Osterley Park with another woman.

Not just any other woman. Abhi. Beautiful, kind, intelligent, daring Abhi. He wanted to laugh out loud, to raise his eyes to the heavens and thank the goddess Parvati that he was with such a woman. Even if it was only for this night and nothing happened between them he would have the memory of it, of her, always.

He paused – he'd wanted to thank Parvati. Not God, not Jesus, but Parvati. And in that moment he realised that whatever happened in the future, his recent foray into Christianity was no match for the religion of his past, his family, his culture.

The drive looped to the left round the end of the lake and across the grass they could make out the dark bulk of the house. Without a word they left the path and stopped in the shadow of some trees.

'I suppose we'd be pushing it a bit if we went all the way to the house,' said Abhi.

Sandeep agreed, glad he didn't have to be the one to point it out. 'We could sit here for a while, though, if you'd like?'

He took his jacket off and lay it on the ground. They sat, Abhi with her back against the tree trunk.

'I had my first kiss here,' she said.

'Who was it with?' Sandeep felt a pang of jealousy he knew was irrational but left a sour taste nonetheless.

'A boy called Arun. It was awful. He was so good-looking and such a dreadful kisser. It put me off for ages.'

Sandeep laughed, relieved.

'I didn't know you lived near here,' he said.

'We don't know much about each other, do we? I was brought up in Hanwell. Mum and Dad still live there. I moved out a couple of years ago in spite of their protests.'

'So where do you live now?'

'Battersea. I share a house with two friends.'

Sandeep wanted to ask about her life, every detail, but what was the point? Tomorrow, after work he would go back to Milton Keynes and see Abby who would hold her breath when he put forward an opinion in case he got it wrong and she had to correct him. He often felt her tense beside him, as if readying herself for an apology or an excuse. He had never sat with her in a park talking about first kisses and childhood dreams of ballgowns and servants and ice cream.

'What do you want out of life, Sandeep?' Abhi interrupted his thoughts.

This was the time. He must tell her he had what he wanted – a good job, a good fiancée, a community that welcomed him. But when he thought about those things and about Abby, his heart sank. His job was mundane, his church community hadn't been terribly welcoming until Abby showed an interest in him and Abby herself was more interested in pointing out his shortcomings than in finding out what made him tick. She had never asked him what he wanted in life, although she had told him what she wanted. What they wanted. And he had gone along with it because he was grateful to her for saving him from loneliness. He saw it all now. They didn't love each other. Now he even doubted his interest in her religion. He had sought out a religious community because he had been raised to believe in something outside of himself, but he'd never really had a faith, had never really come up to the mark. He spent a lot of time trying, praying he would one day feel the hand of God, or hear His words, but it had never happened. He finally realised that he was Abby's project and had gone along with it because he needed to be accepted, to feel a part of something. It was a harsh assessment, he knew, but suddenly he saw it for what it was. And now he had to tell her. He would have to sit her down and try to explain it all. He cringed inwardly. The thought of hurting her caused him physical pain but his eyes had been opened here tonight and they wouldn't be closed again.

'You have a strange habit of going quiet on me,' said Abhi. 'Have you got a secret?'

Sandeep sighed and clamped his mouth shut against the

words that leapt to his lips. He wanted to tell her all that he had been thinking but he couldn't even look at her. He didn't want to be disloyal to Abby who had been a good friend to him, who wanted to marry him, and whom, if he hadn't met Abhi, he would have spent his life with.

'Hey, you there.' Abhi put her hand on his arm, softly.

He turned to her and her mouth was on his, her tongue parting his willing lips and he responded, his whole being aching for her. He wrapped her in his arms and felt their bodies soar through the night sky, dipping and weaving amongst the stars.

'Better than Arun?' he asked when they landed on earth again.

'Just let me double-check.' She smiled and leant in to kiss him again.

7

IRIS

The sudden stop made Iris's heart beat fast so she forced herself to focus on her gnarled hands in her lap to distract herself. When had they got like that? She minded more about them looking old than she ever had about going grey or getting wrinkles. Hands were meant to be busy, useful. Not these ugly old things. She used to have such beautiful hands – long tapered fingers, nails always painted, even when the children were small. Reg had loved her hands, said they were one of her best features. Them and her big blue eyes, her cooking, her flair for putting people at their ease, her ability to stretch his meagre income as a clerk for the water board and provide for the family. She sighed. Reg had been a good husband, she couldn't have asked for better. They'd scrimped and saved and bought their own house and paid it off as quickly as they could, neither of them comfortable with owing money to the bank. Yes, they'd had a good life together. She felt tears gather in the corners of her eyes and wiped them away with her finger. She missed him, that was for sure, but she had Charlie now and most of the time she was happy.

She looked out at the field they had stopped in. The grass

was long and tussocky, ready to trip anyone walking through. She thought about how her slender ankle had snapped when she lost her footing on the street outside her house. One minute she was fine and steady, limbs intact, and the next, she was lying on the pavement clutching at her leg, clamping down on her lips so she didn't scream out loud. While she was in hospital she'd wondered why the council had men going about with noisy leaf blowers, swooshing the autumn leaves into piles where they waited until a lorry came along to vacuum them up – or until someone tripped and fell on them. When had brooms and wheelbarrows gone out of fashion? She still had bits of metal in her leg from where they screwed it back together, and it ached something awful in the cold weather. No good dwelling on it though.

She turned her attention to the field again. There wasn't much to see. The farmer had taken the cows in for milking and now there were just a few birds picking at the ground hoping to catch a worm or an earwig or whatever insects lived in fields. She closed her eyes for a moment, and suddenly there were silent tears pouring down her cheeks.

'Are you all right?' asked a gentle voice.

Iris's eyes flew open and she saw a young Chinese woman looking at her. Disorientated momentarily, she blew her nose to give herself time to think.

'Yes, thank you, dear. I think so.'

The woman didn't look convinced. There was a frown line between her eyes. And now Iris saw she wasn't so young after all – she had light crow's feet developing, and creases either side of her mouth. She'd have jowls in a few years. Shame. She was a pretty little thing now. She put her hand to her own face without thinking, felt the soft skin draping over her cheekbones and jaw. Ageing was a cruel trick.

'Can I get you anything?'

'No, dear. Don't mind me. I'm just a silly old lady feeling a bit sentimental, that's all. I'll be right as rain in no time.'

She wondered if that was true. Would she be all right? She had no idea anymore. She'd thought her life was sorted, but the last few days with her daughter had thrown everything into the air, and she didn't feel she had any control over where it would all land again. It was a new feeling for her, and terrifying. She'd always known what she wanted and worked out how to get it. It was another thing Reg had admired in her – perseverance. Now she worried she was getting senile. It was her worst fear, going doolally and everyone laughing at her behind her back and resenting her for having to do things for her because she couldn't remember how to do them for herself. Like getting dressed and wiping her own bottom after she'd been to the toilet. She wouldn't let that happen.

'Take deep breaths,' the woman said.

Iris realised she'd been shredding her tissue. She looked at the mess in her lap and swallowed a wave of fear. Surely one of the first signs of senility was not knowing what you were doing, and she hadn't even remembered getting a tissue out. She looked and saw her panic reflected in the Chinese woman's deep-brown eyes.

An announcement came over the tannoy: 'We are sorry for the delay which is due to unforeseen circumstances. At this time we cannot say how long it will be. We will keep you posted. Sorry for any inconvenience.'

Iris shook her head. 'How awful. What a terrible way to go.'

'Yes, very sad.' The Chinese woman looked at the floor and back at Iris. 'My name's Mei-Ling, by the way.'

'Oh, that's a pretty name.' It was also a strange name, thought Iris. She liked the fact that England was multicultural, it made things interesting and colourful, but sometimes found it difficult to get her tongue round the different names. 'I'm Iris.' In saying her name, she felt she'd anchored herself back into her life again. She smiled. 'Thank you, dear. You're very kind.'

Mei-Ling inclined her head. 'I haven't done anything.'

'You have – you've made an old lady smile.' Iris took her hand but didn't know what to do with it. It felt too intimate a gesture for what had passed between them and yet to shake it would seem awkward. She let it go again and looked away, embarrassed.

'I'm glad,' said Mei-Ling quietly and sighed.

Iris waited.

After a few moments, Mei-Ling said, 'I'm going to see my parents tonight to tell them I'm expecting a baby, their first grandchild. And at my age and in my circumstances, probably their only.'

Iris peered at her more closely. How old was she? She only looked to be in her mid-thirties. People had babies well into their forties these days. She'd even read about an Italian woman who'd had sextuplets at sixty-two, which was immoral, as she would have told anyone had they asked for her opinion. Which, of course, no one had, because what would an old woman know?

'I'm sure they'll be pleased.' Iris would have liked grandchildren.

'They wanted me to have a large family so that in their old age they'd be looked after, and surrounded by noise and laughter.'

Iris didn't know much about China, except it was communist. And big. And until recently people were only allowed to have one child, which seemed like a shame to Iris. Children needed brothers and sisters to round the sharp edges of selfishness off them. There'd been a girl at her school all those years ago who'd been an only child and she never shared her lunch with anyone, or helped with homework.

The other thing she'd learned about China was when her daughter flirted with Buddhism in her late teens – she'd said something about the Chinese making the Dalai Lama leave Tibet when they decided it was part of China rather than its own country. She'd gone on to give her a long lecture about Buddhism. Laura would have called it a discussion, but Iris knew a lecture when she heard one. Discussions meant two people were talking.

'Well, one grandchild's better than none,' she said.

Mei-Ling gazed into the distance, and Iris turned and looked too, almost expecting to see two elderly Chinese people in the cow field. Instead, there were now police vehicles, a fire engine and an ambulance, lights flashing, and people in boiler suits wandering around looking at the ground.

'I've let them down.' Mei-Ling shrugged.

'I'm sure they're proud of you.' Iris wasn't sure of anything of the sort, and kicked herself for saying something so trite. She had a rule – if all you can offer is a platitude, better not to say anything.

It seemed Mei-Ling hadn't heard, however, because she was still staring into the middle distance, a sad expression on her face. 'I really don't know why I'm telling you all this.' She smiled.

Iris nodded. 'Maybe it's because a life has ended here today. It focuses the mind, doesn't it? We spend our lives avoiding death but it comes to find us and we can no longer pretend our lives will go on forever.' She was talking as much to herself as to Mei-Ling.

'You're right – death is so final. We should make every moment count. Make those we love happy.'

Iris was unsure how the conversation had got to this point, but it certainly wasn't the first time it had happened. The ability she had to put people at ease often led to strangers telling her their life stories. She was a good talker, but a better listener, and enjoyed hearing about lives and ideas that were often – usually – so different from her own. Reg used to say MI6 should employ her because everyone told her their secrets, and she would never have to resort to torture. She just waited and listened. Fully. Completely.

'What do you do, dear?' she asked.

'I'm a social worker in a mental health unit part time, and a counsellor in a private practice,' said Mei-Ling turning back to her. 'Although you wouldn't know it, would you, when you hear me go on.' She smiled, showing slightly crooked teeth. 'I'm meant to be the one who does the helping, not the one who needs help.'

'Everyone needs to talk sometimes, dear. It's human nature. And sometimes talking to a stranger is easier than talking to your best friend. And certainly better than talking to your family.' She shuddered involuntarily.

'Not so good for you, either?' asked Mei-Ling.

'Not so good, no.' Iris still wasn't sure exactly when things had gone wrong with her daughter, but they had certainly gone from bad to worse on this visit.

'You don't have a Chinese accent,' she said, not wanting to talk about her family troubles.

Mei-Ling smiled. 'When I started school I didn't speak a word of English. There were other immigrant kids there too, but we all wanted to be normal, to be seen as white, I suppose. So within the first term, most of us were speaking English with English accents. Those who didn't were the ones who got picked on. I sometimes felt guilty when I saw them being bullied, but I also thought they were stupid and pig-headed for not trying to fit in. Later, I felt guilty I did nothing to defend them.'

'What could you have done? You were a child yourself.' Iris thought how sad it was that children could be so cruel. She was also glad Mei-Ling didn't have an accent; she had a hard time understanding the Chinese woman who ran the shop at the end of her street. Or was she Vietnamese?

They fell silent for a while. Iris started thinking about what Mei-Ling had said about her circumstances. She studied her new friend as the younger woman searched for something in her bag.

'My son's gay,' said Iris. 'He hasn't admitted it, but he lives with his partner. He must think I'm blind or stupid. Or maybe naïve. When I go over there there's two toothbrushes in the bathroom, one big double bed in the main bedroom, narrow little singles in the other two rooms, no personal belongings in either. Why can't he just be honest? I like his friend, Luke. He's an interesting man, and very caring. Always cooks my favourite dinner when I go. Barry – that's my son – he pretends Luke just happened to be over, and Luke goes along with it.'

Mei-Ling nodded. 'Perhaps he thinks you would be shocked, or reject him.'

'Is that what your parents would do if you told them? Is that why you're concerned about their reaction to the baby?' Iris looked at her closely.

Mei-Ling took a deep breath but didn't look away. 'I'm not–' but she didn't go on. Then her face relaxed. 'How did you know?'

'I have a Gaydar – isn't that what they call it these days?' Iris laughed. 'Gaydar, what a silly word. Anyway, you didn't do anything to give it away, so don't worry, I'm sure your mother and father won't have guessed. As a rule, parents are very good at not seeing what they don't want to in their children.' Iris patted Mei-Ling's hand. In fact, when her own children were younger she'd prided herself on intuiting what was going on in their lives. Now she wondered when she had stopped being able to read her daughter. Or had Laura just got better at keeping things from her?

Mei-Ling shook her head. 'I hope you're right. I don't think my parents will ever accept that Jenny and I are together.'

'There's another thing people are too good at, if you ask me – concentrating on the things they don't like rather than all the other things. Too much hate in the world these days.' Iris sighed.

Once again they lapsed into silence.

Iris watched all the police who had arrived in the field. Most of them were standing around doing nothing. There were no people to direct, no crowd to contain. Just a train full of commuters, all behaving calmly and quietly, following a set of rules not written anywhere but which everyone abided by. She wondered if the same number of police would attend if she killed herself. She'd thought about it often enough after Reg died and day after day she felt like a vice was squeezing her lungs so each breath was a gasp, and every memory was a punishment. No, there would have been no police. She would have died in her bed having taken the pills she stockpiled. Only the thought of a neighbour finding her had stopped her. And then, after months of feeling like she was living underwater, she'd noticed the lady in the corner shop smiling at her as she gave Iris her change, and Iris had smiled back. The next day she'd noticed that her breath was a little easier. And a while after that, Charlie had come into her life.

Charlie! She rummaged in her handbag. 'I can't seem to find my address book,' she said.

'Do you need it right now?' asked Mei-Ling.

'I should let the neighbours know what's happening. And check on Charlie.'

Mei-Ling nodded. 'Are you sure it's in your handbag? Maybe you put it in your overnight case.' She pointed to the bag at her feet.

'Oh, yes. Silly me.' Iris fished it out of the case. It was old and much used, the leather covers barely holding the pages between them anymore. As she flicked through it she noticed how many of the names she'd crossed out over the years and felt sad. All those friends dying and leaving her to carry on alone.

She got her mobile out. She still didn't like these newfangled things, but she had to admit they had their uses.

'You know you can store phone numbers, don't you?' said Mei-Ling.

'Yes, dear, but I prefer doing it this way. Otherwise, if I lose my phone, I've lost my friends.' She carefully punched in each number, holding the phone as if it was an alien object. She cupped her hand round the mouthpiece as she spoke.

'Doreen? Is that you? It's Iris here.'

Her eyes roamed around the carriage as she listened to what Doreen had to say.

'No, I know. Awful. I just–'

Doreen was speaking so loudly Iris was sure everyone around her could hear what the other woman was saying, the urgent, forceful tone of her voice. She caught Mei-Ling's eye and shrugged, as if to say, *she always goes on like this*.

'I'm sorry to hear that, Doreen. I was just telephoning to tell you I'm on my way home.'

She listened for a moment. 'Yes, I know I said I wouldn't be back until Thursday but my plans changed. How's Charlie?'

After another pause, 'Yes, I know, but he frets, I know he does. Thank you, dear.'

She pressed the red circle and sighed as she let the phone fall into her lap.

Mei-Ling smiled. 'Your friend likes to talk, doesn't she?'

Iris laughed. 'Oh, yes. She's old and lives on her own. Any opportunity and she's off, telling whoever's listening about how she was evacuated to Somerset in the war and the latest bargain at Aldi, all mixed together, but she's been a good friend over the years.'

She turned towards the window again but instead of watching what was going on in the field, she found herself thinking again about her son. Did he really think she'd turn her back on him if he told her he was gay? If he did, he really didn't know her at all and that saddened her. She'd tried to teach her children to be open-minded and tolerant. Obviously she'd failed. She'd often wondered if she should be the one to raise the issue, but it was his life, his choice to tell her or not. She had dropped hints, made positive comments about gay men. She'd even been on a Gay Pride march some years ago with her friend Betty and sent him a photo of them under a rainbow banner, but he hadn't taken the bait. It had driven a wedge between them, this lack of honesty. Not that she wanted to live in his pocket, nor have him in hers, but it felt like he'd shut the door to a large part of his life in her face and it hurt. And if the death this morning had proved anything, it was that life was too short to wait around for other people to do things. She sat straighter, pulled her shoulders back and made a decision. She would tell him she knew. She wouldn't wait any longer for him to come out of the wardrobe or wherever he thought he was hiding.

That settled, she felt like talking again.

'Do you live in Milton Keynes, Mailing?' She wondered if she'd got the name right. It was so unfamiliar. Why didn't she just call herself May? That was a sturdy English name. She hoped she hadn't got it all confused.

'Not completely – since the IVF and everything, Jenny and I are trialling living together. I'm still trying to get used to the commuting and not having all the excitement of Camden Town on my doorstep. It's a big step, moving out of London.'

'That's nice, though, isn't it, moving in with your friend. How long have you known her?' asked Iris.

'We went to school together. We've known each other forever, and now we're going to be parents!' Mei-Ling smiled.

'I hope it all works out for you both.'

'Thanks. I don't think I've ever told a stranger so much about myself,' said Mei-Ling, frowning.

'I'm not a stranger. Some people you meet you just get on with, and others, doesn't matter how long you know them, you can't get along.' *And some*, Iris thought to herself, *you think you know and get along with and one day they turn on you.* Like her friend, June, years ago. She still wondered about her sometimes.

She rummaged in her pocket and brought out a tube of mints. 'Want one?' She offered the packet to Mei-Ling. They sucked on their sweets for a while in companionable silence. Iris gazed around at the other people in the carriage, the man with a newspaper on his lap, a worried look on his face, the woman next to him who was tapping messages into her phone as if her life depended on it. Maybe it did. You never knew, did you? But soon her mind was back with her daughter. What had happened, or more to the point, when had it all gone so wrong?

Laura had been such a loving little girl, and loved too. Her blonde curls and big blue eyes had seen to that. She always had a smile on her face and a kind word on her lips. She never even gave Iris anything to worry about through her teens, the way some girls did. Betty's daughter got pregnant at fifteen and refused to give the baby up for adoption. Betty and her husband took him on when Justine got tired of being a mother and wanted to go out with her friends again. No, Laura was a fine teenager and got a good job at Boots when she left school. It was when she turned thirty she started getting all moody. Iris couldn't understand it. One minute she'd be all happy and helpful and the next she'd fly off the handle or storm out in tears. It wasn't as if she wanted for anything; she had a good husband, a nice house, she was managing a chemist shop in Milton Keynes where she'd moved when she got married. They had a holiday abroad every year, and were planning to have children. And then these silly moods.

What hurt the most was that they used to be close but Laura stopped talking to her about anything that mattered, wouldn't tell her what was going on. Iris wondered if she was depressed and suggested seeing her doctor. That was a bad argument. Laura fair flew at her, saying that if she was depressed it was because of her and her prying. Iris clutched her stomach remembering the pain she'd felt at those words. She popped another mint in her mouth and sucked hard.

Over the years they'd found their way back to each other again. Laura had been a pillar of strength when Reg died. She'd loved her dad and felt his loss deeply, but she was there for Iris. *That's the term they used these days*, thought Iris. *She was there for me. I wasn't there for her or Barry. I tried to be but I couldn't do it.* She shifted in her seat. Was that the moment when the balance in the family altered – when they had to help her because she couldn't help them?

'My children see me as a useless old woman,' she said, and Mei-Ling looked appropriately shocked.

'I'm sorry to hear that,' she said.

Iris felt on the edge of tears. Nobody respected her now that Reg was gone; and her recent visit to her daughter had confirmed that Laura didn't think she was wise. In fact, she seemed to think she was on the verge of dementia. Or perhaps only hoped she was. For a moment Iris almost wished her memory was going so she could forget the last few days.

'Oh, for a forgettery,' she murmured too softly for anyone else to hear.

At Euston, Mei-Ling helped Iris gather her belongings and step down from the train.

'I'm so pleased to have met you, Iris.'

'Me too,' said Iris. 'And now you run along to your meeting. I hope you're not too late.'

She wanted to say more, to assure her that her parents would love her no matter what, but she didn't know that, and her idea of parents loving their children unconditionally had been shaken over the last few days. She wasn't sure she even liked Laura anymore, let alone loved her. She put a hand to her cheek, wincing at the tenderness of the bruise, and sighed. Watching Mei-Ling trot off, she lifted her bag, fished for her ticket in her coat pocket, and headed for the barrier. A crush of people tried to get through, rushing now the train had finally arrived, all going in their different directions – to work, or shopping, to visit a loved one, or to go home, like her.

No, she decided not to go home immediately; she wasn't in town very often these days, and Charlie would be all right for a little longer. She'd go to one of her favourite places, one she and Reg had found quite by accident years ago when they'd started cycling, the children having grown up and left, leaving a gap in their time as well as their home. So at weekends they cycled into the city, or took a train into the countryside and pedalled along the lanes until they found a pub. That was all before they discovered Reg's heart probably wasn't up to riding bikes, or, indeed, keeping him alive. She bit her lip, remembering her husband's first heart attack. The fear. Their lives had changed after that. Iris threw the salt out, and cooked low-fat meals, and encouraged Reg to do a little careful exercise each day. Yet still he died. Five years, it had been. Five long years.

From Euston it required a train and a bus to get there, but she'd do it; she could take it slowly, and have a cup of tea in the lovely café once she arrived.

She lifted her chin and smiled. She was going on an adventure. She was an independent woman taking herself off for a day out. When had she last done that? Too often her hip hurt when she walked long distances, and her doctor had told her that when older people like her were stressed they were more prone to accidents. She'd taken his advice to heart; these days if she felt in the least emotional, she stayed indoors. She couldn't risk falling in the street again at her age. Her friend Betty had fallen coming out of Lidl and broken her hip and never left the hospital. An infection set in and she was gone. Iris sighed. She missed Betty. But today, even though she was feeling a bit wobbly – not physically, but emotionally – after what Laura had done, she would throw caution to the wind and treat herself to an outing. It would make her feel better to be out and about.

The Chelsea Physic Garden always delighted her. Small enough and flat enough to walk round easily, it hid away behind houses and a high wall so it felt like visiting a secret place. The medicinal trees and shrubs from all over the world had been collected over the centuries.

After Reg died, she'd had a brass plaque inscribed and paid a donation to have it screwed to their favourite bench on the patio outside the café.

Reg Worthington, My Medicine. 1934-2011

It was better to remember him here than in the awful cemetery overlooking the motorway. He'd have wanted her to keep coming to the garden, to sit on their bench and enjoy a cup of tea and a bit of sun. And there were always other people who were willing to stop and chat about the plants and what they might be used for. It was so much more interesting than the cemetery or her local park with its patchy grass and uneven paths that might cause an old lady to fall.

Iris took her tea over to the bench and gazed around contentedly. This place soothed her. She and Reg had returned time and time again to wander along the paths, share a pot of Earl Grey, dream of visiting the places the plants had come from: Australia, the West Indies, China. So many places they'd never been. One day Reg had found a label on a small bush stating its origin as Devon, England. 'We'll go there, shall we, and see where this little specimen came from?'

Iris had laughed so hard she almost fell sideways off the seat. 'Exotic Devon,' she managed to gasp out eventually, and Reg took her hand and said, very seriously, 'It may not be exotic, but if it's capable of producing a little beauty like this, it's good enough for the likes of you and me.'

Iris stopped laughing. She had to agree with him. They were ordinary people with ordinary needs; there was no point in going to the other end of the world when they had all they needed much closer at hand.

She sighed and got to her feet with the intention of going to find the little bush from Devon and pay her respects, but she felt dizzy and had to sit down again and wait till it passed.

'Are you okay?'

Iris turned to a woman standing to her left with a floppy straw hat and soil-streaked gardening gloves in one hand. Mei-Ling had asked if she was all right too. Did she suddenly look older or less capable because of what had happened at Laura's?

She pulled her shoulders back and lifted her chin, looked at the gardener and smiled. 'I'm fine, thank you, dear. Just got up too quickly.'

The woman nodded and went back to her work.

Iris sat a while longer, gathering her thoughts. She didn't want people thinking she was a feeble old woman who needed their help. She didn't want to *be* a feeble old woman who needed their help. She could think of nothing worse than being dependent on others, which was perhaps why she'd been so dismayed when Laura had made her suggestion and so shocked at the reason why.

She shook her head to rid herself of thoughts of her daughter; she didn't want to spoil her time in the gardens. Two men had taken a table close to her bench and were talking quietly, heads almost touching. Iris couldn't hear what they were saying, but they started laughing, and one lay his hand over his friend's in a moment so intimate Iris had to look away again. They reminded her of Barry and his friend, Luke.

Her phone rang, and she fished in her bag to look at the screen. A picture of Laura's face stared at her from behind blue-framed glasses. Iris gasped and dropped the phone back into her bag. She wasn't ready to talk to her daughter. She stood again, more slowly this time, steadied herself for a moment against the back of the bench, her hand resting on the brass plaque, then made her way to the exit. The Devon shrub would have to wait for another day.

Out on the street again, she walked slowly to the bus stop. She considered going to see her son at work since she was in town, but decided against it. He didn't like her visiting unannounced, especially at the office. She sighed. Once upon a time Barry had loved being with her. They'd gone to the cinema together, and for walks. He'd lived at home until he was twenty-seven, saving to buy his own house, the one he was still in. He didn't like change. Her friends had all told her she and Reg should make him leave, but she liked having him there. The house felt empty when he left. And that was when Reg was still alive. Now it felt like a morgue. Friends had suggested she sell the house and move to Margate, or

Whitstable maybe. She and Reg had talked about it before he died. But she knew she'd never leave now. She knew all the neighbours, even the young ones who were moving in as the old ones died off or went into homes. It wasn't the same anymore, but it was home.

She was suddenly exhausted and decided to take a taxi home and not have to wait for the bus. Her ankles were swollen and her shoes rubbed. She hated her body letting her down.

'Don't you start feeling sorry for yourself, Iris, old girl,' she said to herself. 'Give in to self-pity and you're on the slippery slide.'

'Sorry?' The woman next to her at the bus stop looked concerned.

Iris didn't realise she'd been talking out loud. She apologised, and shut her mouth firmly. She didn't want anyone thinking she was a lunatic, talking away to herself. Mary had been taken to some sort of institution and never come home again. That was two or maybe three years ago. Iris had seen her son a few months after Mary had disappeared, and he'd told her his mum had Alzheimer's. Terrible thing to happen to someone. Mary was younger than her. Iris had been terrified for weeks that she was forgetting things and would be put away too.

Half an hour later she let herself in her front door. Relief at being home overcame her, and her eyes felt watery.

'Charlie!' she called as soon as she was inside. 'Charlie, I'm home.'

She found him asleep on the sofa, snoring. Sitting next to him, she put a hand on his back gently so as not to cause alarm, and shook him awake.

'Charlie, I'm home. How have you been?'

He looked at her with mournful eyes, then looked away.

'Don't be like that, Charlie. I've had an awful time. I know you don't like it when I leave you, but please don't punish me for it. I'm sure Doreen's been taking you out and feeding you well. Anyway, I'm back now, and I won't leave you again.'

He turned towards her again and yawned.

She didn't want to get up, but she was dying for a cup of tea and a wee, so she pushed herself out of the sofa and limped into the hall. Charlie followed. She passed the phone, blinking with messages. She suspected they were all from Laura, wondering where she was. She carried on into the kitchen, filled the kettle and plugged it in, went to the loo, came back and got the tea and a packet of biscuits out. She realised now she'd had nothing to eat since the night before at Laura's, and only a weak cup of tea on the train when Mei-Ling had insisted on getting one for her. She hadn't even finished the one at the gardens. She sat in a kitchen chair waiting for the kettle to boil. Charlie sat too.

'Don't look at me in that tone of voice, Charlie. I've said I'm sorry. Here, have a biscuit.' She gave him one. He ate it and looked at her expectantly.

'You want another one?'

He licked his lips.

'One more. You know you have to watch your weight.'

She bent down and stroked his smooth fur. He rolled onto his back, demanding a tummy rub. She'd been forgiven. But Iris was too stiff to bend all the way down to the floor to reach him, and so after a few moments, he jumped onto her lap.

'Good boy,' she said, giving him a hug. 'I've been thinking while I've been away, and there are some things I'm going to change around here.' She had been thinking, but she hadn't actually come up with any ideas. She'd said what she did to make herself feel better, but she knew they were empty words. The reality was, she didn't know what to do.

Charlie cocked his head as if he understood. They sat there at the Formica-topped table. The kettle boiled, but Iris didn't move. She had her dog, she was home, and for the time being, that was enough. She looked around her kitchen. Reg had built it years ago, made and fitted all the cupboards and painted them olive green on her orders. It looked shabby now, the paint peeling in places, faded in others. What had seemed so modern and chic twenty years ago was just old and tired now. Like her. She could afford to have it redone if she wanted. Reg and she had saved a bit, and she had her pension, but if she updated it, it wouldn't remind her of Reg and her family anymore, of their evening meals taken together, of Barry and Laura doing their homework or fighting over an afternoon treat at this very table. Every inch of the house held a memory – the step on which Barry had slipped and broken his arm, the marks on the wall by the fridge that followed the growth of her children, the scratch on the sideboard from when Laura came in drunk at sixteen and scraped her keys across its surface. Reg's clothes were still in the wardrobe. The very thought of tossing them out made her shudder. They were all she had left of him. The children's school reports were in the desk drawer along with wedding invitations, letters and the drawings Laura and Barry had given her when they were little. It was like a museum of memories, and it was all Iris had left. She'd read once about the aborigines in Australia who knew their land by songlines; they sang songs as they moved about, songs that named the features of the landscape so they were never lost. Well, she had her own songlines that traced not only the features of the house, but its history and that of her family. If she changed anything about it, there was a chance her memories would fade. And if she didn't have her memories, what would she have? She was too old to make many new ones, and she drew such comfort from the old.

Her stomach rumbled and she took a TV dinner out of the freezer. Crumbed fish with mashed potatoes and green beans. She zapped it in the microwave and set the table. She always set the table for a meal. It didn't do to get sloppy and eat on a tray. Charlie sat at her feet, waiting for a morsel to fall.

After she'd washed and dried her knife and fork and made herself another cup of tea, she sat in the living room. Monday afternoon was usually bowls, but Iris had expected to be in Milton Keynes with Laura until midweek, so Jean, her partner, had agreed to play with someone else. There were other people she could play with, but she decided to give it a miss. She'd go to bridge club tomorrow, though; Edna loved her cards and would be happy she was back early. With a mind as sharp as a tack she was a good partner too. Yes, tomorrow she'd go out, but today she'd rest. She let her eyes close, and was asleep within minutes.

Iris was woken by the glare from the street light coming on outside her window. She looked around, momentarily disorientated, and then recognised her sitting room with its faded furniture and its worn carpet. Her back ached from sleeping in her chair but the rest had revived her and she felt ready to listen to Laura's messages. Perhaps she had called to apologise.

She limped to the sideboard on feet that seemed to have cramped into hard knots while she was asleep, pressed the voicemail button and listened.

'Mother – where are you – and why?'

Iris was about to delete the message when she changed her mind, and carried on to the next one.

'Mother – how dare you leave and not tell me.'

And the next:

'This proves exactly what I was saying. You can't be trusted to live on your own any longer. You are a selfish, stupid old woman.

It's just this kind of childish behaviour that proves to me what I was saying was right.'

And the last:

'Mother – I'm getting worried now – just call me.'

Selfish, stupid, childish. Iris didn't believe she was any of those things but still it hurt to be accused of them. She sat again, leaning down to rub her aching feet. Was it selfish to refuse another's demands? Childish to leave without giving a reason? She sat straight and took a deep breath. She knew she wasn't stupid. She was resourceful and had done what she needed to do, that was all.

And Mother. When had Laura started calling her Mother, and in that tone? She used to call her Mummy, and when she was a little older, Mumsy, and when that became embarrassing in front of her school friends, Mum or Ma. But never Mother. It was so cold, so formal. No loving daughter called their mother Mother, surely.

She blinked away a tear. Charlie trotted over and licked her hand and then sat, his head cocked on one side looking for all the world like he understood what she was going through and was offering his sympathy. Iris realised with a jolt that he was her best friend these days; the one who was always there, who listened to her without judgement and who sat on her feet to warm them when she was cold. He was loyal and true. All she had to do in return was feed and walk him, give him a little treat once in a while. Their friendship was simple and straightforward, so unlike her relationships with her children, and yet she'd given them so much more than food and treats. Maybe she'd done too much for them and made them into the selfish people they were now. No, that wasn't fair. Barry wasn't selfish, or at least she didn't think he was; he'd just slipped out of her hands and away on the tide of his life, leaving her behind in the wake. Laura, though, she was selfish. It was always about her.

She sighed. Too late to change anything, and what would she change anyway? She'd enjoyed doing things for her family; cooking nice meals, making the house homely so they were proud to bring their friends back. She'd thought it a point of honour she never had to ask for their help in the house, that she could do it all herself. She had been expected to do chores from when she was quite small; at six she was cleaning out the grate in the mornings, and by the time she was ten she was cooking meals and doing the laundry. Children did in those days. If she'd given Barry and Laura jobs to do, would they have grown up differently? She had thought it an act of love to do everything, but maybe she'd been wrong. Perhaps she should have thought more about it all those years ago. She hadn't loved her parents any less because they expected her to help. In fact, now she thought about it, it had made her proud to be able to contribute. So maybe she hadn't been such a good mother after all. Perhaps she deserved all she got – or didn't get – from her children.

'Oh, Reg,' she said, looking at the photo of him on the table next to her. 'If only you were still here I'd be able to face anything. Anyway, Laura would never have done what she did if you'd been around, so I wouldn't be facing it in the first place.' She turned the picture away from her as she did when she was angry with him for dying and leaving her on her own, only to feel guilty a moment later and lift it to her lips for a kiss. 'Oh, Reg, you old bugger.' She sighed.

Her shoulders slumped and she leant back into her chair again. She sat for a few minutes, letting her body sink into the cushions as if she was trying to disappear from her own living room. Living room – what a funny name for a place, as if you didn't exist anywhere else, or you were more alive there than anywhere else. Well, here she was in her living room and she wasn't ready to give up.

'I'm just going to slip out for a while,' she said. Charlie wagged his tail at her, got to his feet and looked towards the kitchen.

'All right, I'll feed you first,' she said, and made her way to the pantry to get his food. He ran round in circles as if he was chasing his own tail the way he always did when she fed him. It always made her laugh.

'Anyone would think you'd never seen food the way you carry on,' she said as she put his bowl down and gave him a rub between the ears.

While he was eating, she went to her room and changed into a good dress, pulled a comb through her hair, powdered her nose and swiped a bit of lipstick at her lips. Then she called a cab for the second time that day.

Standing outside Barry's house half an hour later, she wondered if she'd done the right thing. The downstairs curtains were drawn but soft light leaked round the edges. She looked along the street. There was no one about. Many of the houses were dark, their occupants not home yet. It was that sort of street, Iris thought. Young people who worked long hours in the city to pay for the houses they didn't have time to live in.

She walked up Barry's front path, noting the neat flower beds, the small patch of cropped grass. A place for everything, and everything in its place, as Reg would have said.

She rang the bell and waited, hands in her pockets fiddling with her keys and an old packet of mints.

'Oh! Hello, Iris,' said Luke, opening the door. 'What a surprise – are you okay?' He looked over his shoulder and called to Barry. 'It's your mother.' Turning back to Iris, he ushered her in.

'Mother – what on earth are you doing here? Are you all

right?' He was wearing an apron and had a knife in his hand. Waving it around, he said, 'I was just making dinner.'

Iris looked from her son to Luke and back again. She thought what a handsome couple they made, her son and his boyfriend. Manfriend really, she supposed. And she noticed that he also called her Mother, and wondered what else he could call her – they were both too old for Mum, and Iris had never liked the way some grown-up children called their parents by their first names. Reg would have had a fit if ever Barry had called him by his given name. She hated the way Mother sounded coming from Laura's lips – somehow spiteful and angry – but from Barry there was a softness to it she could accept.

An ambulance sped past, siren blaring and lights flashing. The three of them stood frozen on the doorstep looking at each other until the noise had faded into the distance. She drew herself up to her full five feet, looked into her son's face and took a deep breath.

'I know you're gay,' she said. 'I've known it for a long time.'

They were still standing half in and half out of the house. Barry let his knife hand drop by his side. Luke bit his lip.

'It's fine. I don't mind. I've got gay friends.' She didn't, but it made her sound more modern and accepting. And, she reasoned to herself she could have gay friends, it was just that she hadn't met any.

She went on, speaking into the lengthening silence. 'I just feel hurt you didn't tell me. What did you think I'd do?'

Barry and Luke glanced at each other, and Iris saw such tenderness between them it made her heart stop for a beat. No one looked at her like that anymore. In fact, she often felt quite invisible. Even people on the street and shopkeepers didn't really look at old people, and they were often the only people she saw during the day.

'Come in and sit down, Mother,' said Barry, finding his voice.

He gave Luke the knife and he headed into the kitchen while Barry led her into the front room. He called it the lounge.

They sat together on the sofa. Barry held her hand, and Iris enjoyed the warmth of it. Touch was another thing she missed. It was the reason she'd got Charlie, but it wasn't the same.

'I'm sorry, Mother, I should have told you years ago but it never seemed to be the right time.'

Iris nodded.

'I'm glad you know now though.'

She smiled at her son. Her adult son who had thought she would be angry or disappointed in him and the way he lived his life. If only he knew how much she loved him.

'And I'm glad you know I know,' she said, and leant back into the sofa, suddenly drained. His love life wasn't the reason she'd come and she didn't really know why she'd said what she had, but she had, and it was okay. But now she didn't have the energy to say what had brought her here. It was enough, for now, to sit with her son feeling closer to him than she had for years. She felt as if the tapestry of her family had been unravelling all this time but now this part of it at least, was being woven back together. Laura was another matter entirely, but for this moment, she could enjoy being with Barry knowing that the biggest secret of his life was between them no more.

When Luke popped his head around the door and invited her to stay for dinner she could have kissed him.

Iris hadn't eaten so well in years. Both Luke and Barry loved cooking, they told her in their new-found easiness. She learned more about her son in one evening than she had in the previous twenty years. He told her they often went away for weekends and stayed in country houses or cosy cottages, and they knew a lot about wine. Several years ago they had tried to adopt a baby. Iris was rather glad they hadn't been successful – she was of the opinion that children needed a mother and a father, not two parents of the same sex. She knew she was old-fashioned, but that's the way she was. So she said nothing in response to Barry's revelation; tonight was not the time for discord.

It seemed there was no stopping Luke and her son from sharing memories now the secret was out. She felt safe and content in the web of their lives. They loved each other, that was evident. The knowledge made her feel both happy and lonely; she was glad Barry had found love in his life. She remembered what it was like to feel loved, but hadn't experienced it for a long time. She'd wanted to die when Reg went, hadn't thought she could carry on on her own. For months her life had been so many shades of grey with no flashes of colour to ease the crushing sadness. She had been angry with him for not warning her he was going to die so that she could have made plans too, but you just don't know when your heart's going to give out, do you? You don't wake in the morning and think, *I'm going to die today. My heart is going to beat its last.* So she'd forgiven him for his thoughtlessness and raised her chin a little higher, taken some deep breaths and carried on, because that's what you do.

Barry and Luke ushered her into the lounge and made her comfortable while they cleared the table and made tea. It was so unlike her living room – the furniture matched and was new. There was a rug on the floor that looked handmade and expensive. There were few knick-knacks and those on display were tasteful but impersonal, not the hotchpotch of photos and ornaments she had, all of which meant something to her. Theirs yelled 'designer'. Hers was a home.

'Tea, Mother.' Barry put a mug down beside her and took her hand, giving it a squeeze.

She looked at her handsome son, wondering when his hair

had started going grey, and how long he'd had the little paunch that pressed against his belt. He sat down next to her and looked at her expectantly but she didn't know how to go on.

'What is it, Mother. You're not yourself.'

Iris pulled a handkerchief out of her pocket and wiped her eyes. She was surprised, not by the fact that she was crying, but by the amount of tears. They cascaded down her face and into her hanky, making her nose run and no doubt carving a trough through her make-up. Barry waited, his comforting hand on her back.

'I'm sorry,' she said when, finally, she'd managed to stem the flow.

'Don't be, just tell me what it's all about.'

'You haven't heard anything from your sister recently?' she asked.

'No. I don't think I've seen her since that time at your house – Easter 2012, was it? In the last few years we've only exchanged Christmas cards. She doesn't like certain choices I've made in my life.'

Iris raised her eyebrows. 'She doesn't like Luke?'

'Doesn't like the fact I'm with Luke. If she'd met him without me and didn't know he was gay, I'm sure she would have liked him. Everyone does.' He smiled. 'But she's a bigot, you must know that.'

Iris nodded. She supposed she did although they never really spoke about things like homosexuality, religion or politics, except for when Laura wanted to give her a lecture about something. She wondered what they had talked about that mattered over the years. She also realised she'd stopped hosting family occasions, but couldn't remember when. She knew why though: it was because she'd got bored of always being the one trying get them all together when her children clearly didn't want to be in the same house. In the end she'd admitted defeat.

Perhaps if they'd had children it would have been different, the cousins would have had things in common, surely. But Barry was gay and she'd never expected him to produce grandchildren, and Laura's marriage had broken down and afterwards she'd never been in a relationship long enough to get round to having babies. If she had, Iris would have spoiled them. She would have had them to stay and let them do things they weren't allowed to do at home, like leaving sweets for them to find in the pantry for midnight feasts.

Barry cleared his throat, bringing her back to the present.

'You used to love each other,' she said sadly.

'Yes, we were close until we got into our teens, I suppose. But you're not here to talk about the past. Something's happened. What is it?'

Iris took a deep breath. Where to begin? She looked at the hanky clutched in her hand.

'She invited me to stay for a few days last week. I go every now and then, you know. I don't like leaving Charlie, but Doreen goes in and walks him and feeds him. As long as I don't go for too long, he's all right.'

'Mother–'

'Sorry. I'll try and get to the point.' She stroked the back of his hand. He had a couple of age spots. 'So, I went last Friday. Have you been to her house in Milton Keynes? It's terribly small and damp.'

'Mother!'

Iris shrugged and drew her lips in. 'I know I talk too much when I'm in company. I spend too much time on my own these days.'

'I'm sorry,' said Barry.

'No, no, it's all right. I wasn't getting at you. Anyway, Laura collected me from the station on her way home from work. She'd made an effort to make things nice – there were flowers by my bed and she'd got something nice in for dinner. I asked where John was and she said he was on a business trip. I wondered about it at the time, about why a fish and chip shop owner would be on a business trip – they don't do that sort of thing, do they?'

Barry shrugged. 'Sounds a bit fishy – no pun intended.'

Iris smiled.

'Go on, Mother, you were saying John was away and you were having dinner.'

'Yes, well it all started normally. She told me about her work at the pharmacy, I told her what I was doing – you know, my bridge club and bowls and so on. And how I always take Charlie for a good walk every day even when it's raining.'

Barry smiled and shook his head.

'Sorry. Your father always said I told a terrible story. Or a good story badly.' Iris laughed. 'Anyway, she didn't seem terribly interested in what I was up to, but she never has. After dinner, she sat me in the sitting room and took her position on the other side of the coffee table and she got out all these brochures.' Iris felt her eyes filling with tears again. 'Nursing home brochures.' She blew her nose.

'She told me she was worried about me living on my own so far away from her. She said you'd never lift a finger to help me so it was left to her. She wanted me to sell my house and move to a home near her. She'd even called an estate agent to give her an estimate of how much my house is worth.' Iris wiped her eyes.

'That's terrible. But you know, she can't force you out if you don't want to go – it's your house.' Barry frowned.

'She threatened to call social services and have me committed. She wants to take early retirement and was going on about all the things she'd do if only she could afford to.' Iris suddenly felt calm. Sitting here telling Barry about it, she felt that everything would be all right. She'd been silly to work herself into a lather about it.

'She'll do no such thing,' said Barry. 'But do you need anything – I mean help around the house, that sort of thing?'

Iris looked at him and a tremor started ascending her spine. It had been the same with Laura:

'Mother, you can't live on your own, you need help, what if you have a fall? What if you have a heart attack and nobody knows?'

That had been her reasoning. Malice dressed as concern. Cruelty masquerading as kindness. Iris straightened her spine and stared into her son's eyes.

'I need about as much help as you do. I can still cook for myself.' She thought of her TV dinners and decided not to mention them to Barry. 'I can clean my house.' Although she had started noticing that she missed places sometimes when she was dusting and couldn't be bothered going back over them. 'I can get myself up, dressed and washed, and out to my appointments. I'm fine.'

She didn't want help, she didn't want charity, she didn't want people feeling sorry for her and she certainly didn't want people telling her what to do. What she wanted was to stay in her house.

'Well,' said Barry, 'if you're sure, that's that. Perhaps you could come over for a meal with us more often – make it a regular family dinner. And if anything needs fixing, Luke and I are quite good at that sort of thing.'

Iris smiled at him. 'And maybe you could call me Mum rather than Mother. I like it better.'

Barry laughed. 'That's taking it a bit too far!'

He grew serious again. 'It's more than Laura wanting you out of your house, though, isn't it?'

He'd always been perceptive, Iris thought. As a child he'd

been the sort to watch and take things in. It had unnerved her on occasion when he was a youngster. One time when he was about seven or eight he'd asked her why her friend, June, had made a face at her and a rude sign with her fingers as soon as Iris turned away.

'I don't think she likes you, Mummy,' he'd said. 'I think she's just pretending.'

Iris had dismissed it as a fancy. She and June had known each other for years – they'd looked after each other's children and cried on each other's shoulders when their parents had died. But a week after Barry had made his comment, June and she had a fight, their first ever. June accused her of changing, of becoming selfish and hoity-toity because she'd said she couldn't look after June's twins for the night so June could go out dancing with her new fancy man. Iris had been so surprised she hadn't been able to say anything. June had left and they had never seen each other again; Iris's attempts to talk to her had gone unanswered. She'd read her obituary in the local newspaper a few years later and hadn't known how to sort out her feelings – she was sad but she was also angry, disappointed and confused.

'Are you going to tell me?'

'Oh sorry, dear. I was miles away thinking about June. Do you remember her?'

'We were talking about Laura.'

'Oh, yes. What was the question?'

'I asked what else happened.'

'Well, more of the same really. She said she couldn't let me go home, that I had to stay with her until everything was sorted out. I didn't know what to do so I said I'd think about it and went to bed but I couldn't sleep. I heard Laura come upstairs and I was terrified she was going to come in and keep at me, but she went into her room. Hours later I needed to use the bathroom. Her bedroom door was open and I heard funny chirpy noises –

you know how sound carries in those ticky-tacky houses – so I peeped in. She was sitting at her desk, a nearly empty bottle of wine next to her, playing a card game on the computer. That pokie game, I think.'

Barry took a deep breath. 'Poker. You think she's gambling?'

Iris nodded. 'That's what I said. And yes, she is gambling. She must have heard me and caught me watching her. You'd have thought I was the one doing something wrong the way she shouted at me. She said it was my fault she had to do it, that I'd always been mean with money and I'd never helped her when she'd asked for a loan in the past. Which isn't true, by the way – I've given her money and never been paid back. Anyway, she called me every name under the sun, threatened to call the police to have me committed and accused me of making her life a misery. She said John wasn't on a business trip but had left her because she never seemed to think he was good enough and she's up to her ears in debt and can't wait until I'm dead for her share of her inheritance.'

Barry raised his eyebrows. 'She actually said those words?'

Iris nodded. 'Exactly those words. Her share of the house. She said that if I transfer it to her now and live another seven years there'll be no death duty. She said she wouldn't want to waste money on that.'

Barry put his arm around his mother's shoulders and drew her close. 'That's awful. Sounds like Laura's the one who needs help, not you.'

Iris shuddered. 'I didn't know what to do so I set my alarm for six o'clock this morning, just in case I fell asleep, although there was no way I was going to after that. I knew she'd still be snoring away – your sister's always hated getting up early. She still leaves it as late as she can and rushes into work at the last minute. And she'd drunk all the wine – never even offered me a glass with my dinner.'

Barry raised his eyebrows and shook his head slightly.

'Anyway, I'd packed my bag last night and I crept down the stairs only to find she'd locked the front door! I had to climb out of the kitchen window. It was awful – my knickers got caught on one of the – you know, the whatsitsnames – taps and I thought I'd be stuck there when she came down for breakfast, but I managed to wrangle myself free and half fell into the flower bed.'

'Mother – Mum – that was dangerous. Did you hurt yourself?' Barry looked her over. 'Is that a bruise on your jaw? Did she do that?'

Iris thought she'd covered it with make-up. 'No, she didn't touch me. I bumped into the wall as I fell.' Her hand went to her jawline. It still felt tender.

Barry started to say something but she waved away his concern. 'It would have been more dangerous to stay. So I got myself to the station and onto a train.' She paused, remembering waiting at the bus stop hoping it wasn't too early for a bus to the station, the fear she'd felt that Laura would come after her. 'The train stopped somewhere between Milton Keynes and London, and for a moment I thought she'd found out I was on it and managed to get it stopped, but it was a suicide. I know it sounds awful but I was relieved – at first anyway. And I got talking to such a nice young girl, a socialist worker she was.'

'Do you mean social worker?'

'That's what I said.'

Barry smiled. 'Did you tell her what had happened to you – she might be able to help?'

'Oh, no. I didn't tell her. I didn't want to talk about it to anyone. Anyway, she had enough on her plate with her own parents.'

Barry sighed. 'Picking up lame ducks again?'

Iris chuckled. 'No, not this time. She was sad but she was

strong. She'll be all right. I think she put her number in my phone. She thought I was a Tyrannosaurus for using an old-fashioned address book. Maybe I should give her a call.'

'I think the term you're looking for is dinosaur.'

'That's what I said, isn't it? I think you need your hearing checked.'

Barry laughed. 'Okay, whatever you say. Perhaps I could talk to her. I don't know much about these things but I promise you, I won't let Laura sell your house out from under you. And perhaps we should get you some advice from a solicitor.'

Iris took his hand, gripping it hard, wanting him to know how relieved she was that she wasn't having to face all this on her own.

'Should we ask her about getting help for Laura too? She's obviously not happy.'

'She hardly deserves it but you're right, she does need help. I'll see what I can do – perhaps we can get your social worker on to her too.'

She started trying to tell him how grateful she was, but Luke came in and sat opposite them in the tasteful cream armchair. 'Am I missing something?'

'I was just telling Barry how like his father he is – kind and thoughtful. Good at solving life's problems. And how happy I am we're all here together.'

Barry raised his cup.

'I'll drink to that,' he said, and smiled at his mother.

8

LAWRENCE

The ear-piercing screech of brakes competed with a crackly voice over the loudspeaker, urging passengers to brace themselves and stay calm. The train was performing an emergency stop.

Lawrence, his feet already pressed firmly into the floor forcing his buttocks back into the seat, held on to the table with a grip that made his knuckles ache. If his jaw hadn't been so tightly clenched, he would have laughed at the redundancy of the message.

He had to admit to welcoming the delay, although he shuddered at the reason for it. Trains didn't stop like that for nothing. There must have been something on the line. Maybe young thugs chucking stuff onto the tracks. Possibly a suicide. Bloody selfish thing to do either way. Not only did it inconvenience a lot of people, it traumatised the driver. If it was hooligans, Lawrence hoped they were found, locked up and the key dropped down the nearest well. And suicide – which seemed more likely – Lawrence thought was a coward's way out. It showed lack of moral fibre. But he could also think of a few people he wished would swallow a bottle of pills and put everyone out of their misery. His mother-in-law came to mind. And several members of the Labour Party.

He looked around the first-class carriage briefly as the train came to a halt. The woman diagonally opposite him on the other side of the aisle had taken a shoe off and was rubbing her foot. Such a mundane act in the circumstances. But everything was mundane compared to a suicide he supposed. Someone taking their own life made every other act seem somehow insignificant, however important it had felt the moment before. Lawrence shuffled in his seat, straightened his tie and cleared his throat. He snuck a quick glance in the window to make sure his hair was still neat and tidy, glad he couldn't see the telltale silvering in his sideburns. He was proud of his hair – fifty-seven years old and he had a full head of hair only just beginning to go grey. Many of his colleagues had been dying their hair for years. Mainly the females, of course. He stared over at the woman for a moment, at the shoe in one hand, the other massaging her foot. They were nice hands, long-fingered. He wondered what they'd feel like round his cock. He sighed and got back to his perusal of the news. A minute later he saw the woman out of the corner of his eye as she slipped her shoe back on and looked around. Their eyes met, briefly, then she looked away.

He took a deep breath. He wasn't looking forward to the day. It wasn't just this awful case he was working on and the client meeting he had later; he felt burnt out and wanted to retire. What he really wanted to do was go off on his motorbike. Just him, a credit card and the open road. His wife had called it his mid-life crisis – a BMW R 1200 GS, a great roaring beast that throbbed under him. He'd got a hard-on when he took it out for a test drive. He bought it on a whim, and had barely ridden it, but he could ride from Alaska to Tierra del Fuego, or around the coast of Australia. Even Land's End to John O'Groats would do. Or he could buy a boat and sail solo round the world, no one expecting anything of him, no one relying on him. He could afford it but it just wasn't done, to go off and leave a wife at home like that. Especially now. Damn her and that bloody horse.

He closed his eyes for a moment. As if he didn't have enough to deal with already, today he had the added problem of Liam. He clenched his jaw and took his paper out, trying to shake off any thought of his son. He attempted to concentrate on the news but in the lead up to the referendum, he was bored with the whole thing. There was no way the UK was going to vote itself out of Europe, no one was that crazy even with the fool Farage whipping people into a frenzy with his xenophobia, and Boris Johnson standing there and saying we'd all be better off and the NHS would be saved. What rubbish.

He looked at his watch and at the police cars in the field, glad he wasn't in court today at least.

The carriage door opened and in came the guard. He was about the same age as Liam, and Lawrence felt the surge of anger that always accompanied thoughts of his son these days. Bloody young fool. Why couldn't he get a job and settle down – he'd had a far better education than this lad but he wouldn't even get a job on the trains the way he was going.

He got his season ticket out and flashed it.

'Suicide?' he asked.

The guard's lips tightened for a moment and he didn't make eye contact.

'I'm not at liberty to say anything at the moment, I'm afraid.'

Which, as far as Lawrence was concerned, meant, *Yes, suicide.* 'Is the driver all right?' he asked.

The conductor looked surprised.

'What I mean is, will he be looked after? My grandfather drove a train and it happened to him once. He never got into the driving cab again.'

'He'll have his sick leave and that,' said the conductor.

Lawrence drew a card out of his wallet. 'If he has any trouble, call me. I can put him on to the right lawyer if he needs one.'

When the young man had gone, Lawrence smiled to himself. He might be pissed off with his son, but he was still a decent sort. Giving the guard his card had been a magnanimous gesture. He was unlikely to use it.

He closed his eyes and thought about his grandfather. He remembered him as a humourless man who had made a fortune when he was still quite young and let it go to his head.

He'd been a train driver – steam trains, of course – before he'd invented the gadget that had made him rich. An addition to the braking system that made it more efficient, and had started him on the road to making his fortune. No one had been more surprised than him, but he'd had the foresight to patent his invention and was able to raise some capital. He left the railways to start an engineering company manufacturing his gadget and others and eventually settled into the life of the wealthy – 'hunting, shooting and fishing'. Although there was no fishing for him, he said it was too passive. He liked the thrill of the chase. He'd bought an estate near Northampton from a man whose gambling and womanising was running it into the ground. Lawrence smiled to himself. He loved the house and gardens, had wonderful memories of playing there with his cousin, Jeff, when they were children. Then there'd been the terrible falling out in the mid-seventies over his grandfather's will, in which he left the entire estate to Jeff's father, and not a penny to his own. Lawrence didn't know what it was all about, but his anal sphincter still clenched when he thought of it, the injustice of it all. His grandfather may have had an issue with Lawrence's father, but that was no reason to cut his grandchildren out of the will. If he'd been a lawyer then he'd have contested it, but he'd only been a powerless teenager. His father had refused to talk about it and had never spoken to his brother again. Lawrence was just glad he and Jeff hadn't allowed it to mar their relationship.

The thought of Jeff made his chest feel tight. Grief, he'd been told, could do things like that to a person. Fucking cancer. How many years had it been – three? He forced himself to relax, to lay his hands gently in his lap, to think of other things. He hadn't seen Jeff's kids for ages. He wondered what Elspeth was doing these days and why Russell wasn't married. Lawrence had thought Lucy was the one for him and suddenly it was all over.

He looked around. He was on his own again. Well, not exactly on his own, there were other people in the carriage, but they nodded to each other when they got on and didn't look at each other again for the duration of the journey. He could have been travelling to and from Euston with a serial killer for years and he wouldn't have been able to identify him – or her – in a line-up. Terrible admission really, for a barrister.

He picked up his paper again, opened it to the crossword and reached into his breast pocket for his pen. Another stab of loss hit him as he pulled out the Bic. He hadn't had a chance to replace his Montblanc and hadn't dared admit to his wife he'd lost it. She'd given it to him for their wedding anniversary a few years ago. It was likely an important one – silver or something. He'd probably asked his secretary to order the usual flowers and book a restaurant.

Feeling discombobulated, he stared at the first clue.

1A *Very sad unfinished story about rising smoke (8)*

He read it and read it again. He did the cryptic crossword every day and usually managed to finish it in under ten minutes. Today, however, it was as if his brain was frozen. The individual words all made sense but he couldn't pick them apart and delve into the meaning of the clue. He just kept imagining a ruined house with smoke rising from the rubble. After a few minutes he threw the paper onto the seat next to him in disgust and sat with his fists clenched in his lap.

He wanted a coffee. His throat felt parched. He wondered if the trolley girl would come through with the train stopped, or was there some protocol stating that no drinks be served in the event of a suicide? He looked at his watch and wondered where they were and how long it would take to get to Euston. He considered going to find the guard to ask him, and get himself a coffee at the same time but decided not to bother. It wouldn't make any difference.

His phone rang. Deidra. A wave of exhaustion passed over him. He didn't want to talk to his wife. She was probably just calling to remind him about the meeting with Liam and what to say and what not to say, as if he couldn't decide on his own. As if he had to be coached to say the appropriate words when his whole working life was about choosing the right words because someone's future might depend on him being precise and accurate. He knew she'd wanted to come to the meeting. She hated being 'out of the loop', as she called it in an awful American TV way. Truth be told, he wished she could take care of the whole thing too, but she'd broken her neck in a riding accident a couple of weeks ago and was still in a lot of pain. It was pure chance she hadn't ended up a paraplegic – the fracture to her vertebra was displaced and could have severed the nerve. He had rushed to the hospital dreading what he would find, wondering how he would cope if she was an invalid for the rest of her life. She was younger than him by a few years, he was already thirty when they'd married and she in her mid-twenties. She was the one who looked after people, not him. She'd been a stay-at-home mother to their children, she organised their social life, engaged gardeners and painters as necessary, cooked the meals and made sure all the household duties were seen to. Everything would fall apart if she were a vegetable.

He pressed 'decline' and the phone stopped ringing. Sitting with his head resting against the back of the seat he let himself drift off to thoughts of that boat and the places he'd go.

He'd nodded off by the time the train dragged itself from its inactivity and slowly worked up to its mechanical canter. He rubbed his eyes, dry from the train's air conditioning, hoped he hadn't snored, and once more looked at his paper. It was a matter of principle to finish the crossword. It was like a private competition between him and the compiler every day and he would not be outdone just because of some bloody fool throwing themselves in front of the train.

1A Very sad unfinished story about rising smoke.

Tragical. Of course. He couldn't believe he hadn't seen it first time. He frowned at the idea that perhaps he'd been blind to it because the word somehow seemed to encapsulate what he expected from his day, and then carried on with the crossword. He finished it in nine-and-a-half minutes. But the word tragical stuck in his head. Was it even a word? Surely it was tragic. Was it an American corruption? He hated the way they abused and changed the language. He pulled his phone out and looked it up before he worked himself into a lather about it. The definitions were all for tragic, but there were quotes from Shakespeare and Henry Fielding that used tragical. So it was old, falling out of use but proper English at least. That established, he slipped his phone back into his pocket.

By the time they pulled in to Euston he had read the paper, written himself a few notes for the meeting he had to attend and given some serious thought to what to do about Liam. There was nothing like a train journey to concentrate the mind.

When he got to the hospital Lawrence followed a Chinese woman into the room he'd been directed to for Liam's case conference. He stood while she took a seat and then made his way to the only chair left in the small, airless room that had certainly seen better days. He forced himself not to think about how the stains on the seat had been caused. Crossing his legs, he tried to look more relaxed than he felt. He was used to being in court, to standing in front of people and presenting a case or tearing the opposition's apart. This, however, was altogether new – a mental hospital and a meeting to talk about how his twenty-three-year-old son had gone mad.

'Right. Sorry I'm late, but now we're all here, shall we get started?' said the Chinese woman, looking around at everyone. 'I'm Mei-Ling, a social worker and Liam's case manager,' she said to Lawrence before turning to the others again. 'Why don't we all quickly go round and introduce ourselves.'

Lawrence realised this was for him. He sighed, turned his head. Surely he didn't really need to know who they all were? He would have preferred to talk directly to the doctor, the man in charge, but when he'd suggested it on the phone they'd invited him along to the case conference instead.

'It's how we do things here, as long as Liam doesn't mind you being there, that is,' the bumptious woman on the other end had said. Lawrence had bristled at the idea of his son having a say in anything but held his tongue. He'd be there whether Liam wanted him or not.

'I'm Sue, nurse in charge of the inpatient unit,' said a comely woman with full lips and clear eyes.

'I'm Diana, one of the OTs in the day hospital.'

Lawrence looked at the anorexic woman who had just spoken. 'OT?'

'Occupational therapist,' she said, blushing.

'Faiz Noor, senior registrar,' said a man of Middle-Eastern

appearance with a neatly clipped beard. 'I've been looking after Liam since his admission.'

'And the consultant psychiatrist, will he be here?'

'No, Sunita – Dr Sachdeva – is busy. She's presenting at a conference today.'

Lawrence huffed. *How very convenient*, he thought.

'And I'm Liam,' said Lawrence's son. He was sitting in a deep chair he'd pulled back slightly out of the circle. Half-hidden behind the door, Lawrence hadn't noticed him.

'What are you doing here?' asked Lawrence.

Liam shrugged. 'Funny, I could ask you the same question. I'm here because it's about me, and the staff thought I might like to make a contribution. But you? I don't know why you bothered.'

The young black girl sitting next to him took Liam's hand and squeezed it and turned back to the rest of the group.

Lawrence had been looking at his son, thinking he needed a good haircut and a shave, not to mention a kick up the arse and a lesson in manners.

'I'm Felice, Liam's girlfriend.'

Lawrence's narrowed eyes bolted themselves onto her. Girlfriend? He knew of no girlfriend. And a black one into the bargain. He wondered if Deidra knew.

He already felt the meeting slipping away from him. He had come to organise, to order, not to be palmed off with underling doctors and have his son being rude to him in front of all these people. Ungrateful little sod that he was.

'Well, let's get started, shall we?' said Mei-Ling. 'Thanks for coming, everyone. As you know, Liam's been an inpatient for three weeks. He was brought here by the police having been found on Kensington High Street shouting obscenities at passers-by and threatening to conjure the devil.' She turned to Liam, who looked as if he was trying to disappear into the chair.

'You still have no recall of the events leading to your admission?'

'No,' he said so quietly that Mei-Ling repeated his denial for everyone to hear.

'No. Okay.'

Lawrence hadn't known the details of his son's madness before, just that drugs were involved. If he'd been told more, and he probably had by Deidra on several occasions, he had let it skim over him. Now he wanted to slap his son for being so stupid.

'How's it been on the ward, Liam?' asked the woman whose name Lawrence had already forgotten.

'Fine,' said Liam.

Lawrence curled his hand into a fist. He hadn't sent his son to one of the most expensive schools in the country so he could speak in monosyllables. His left foot started jiggling involuntarily.

'That's great,' said the Chinese woman. 'Do you mind if I ask the others how they think you've been doing?'

Isn't that what we're fucking here for? thought Lawrence. Jesus Christ, the boy was a psychiatric patient and they were treating him like he was the king of England. Was this where political correctness had got them, a room full of professionals deferring to the lunatic?

Liam shrugged his bony shoulders again.

'Thank you. So, Sue, how's Liam been on the ward?'

'Well,' said Sue, addressing Liam, 'you've kept yourself to yourself pretty much, haven't you? But you have been taking your medication, and you're happy to engage with the staff. How do you feel about your time on the ward?'

'Okay,' said Liam.

'Great. How about in the day hospital?' The Chinese woman turned to Lawrence to explain. 'Liam has been attending groups in the day hospital for the past two weeks, ever since his acute symptoms subsided.' She turned back to the anorexic OT. 'What groups has he been attending?'

Diana cleared her throat. 'He's been in the daily community meeting, a small psychotherapy group, art therapy, assertiveness training and cooking and budgeting.'

Lawrence's eyebrows hit his hairline. What was this, a holiday camp? A bit of painting, a bleeding hearts group and cooking? Jesus Fucking H Christ.

Dr Noor nodded and turned to Liam. 'And how are you finding the groups?'

His son had always been facetious so Lawrence expected him to say, 'I go to the day hospital and there they are,' but he didn't. Once again, he just said, 'Okay.'

Lawrence's foot jiggled harder.

'Find it easy to join in?' asked Dr Noor.

'I suppose so.'

'And do you feel able to contribute in the groups?'

'A bit.'

Lawrence was in danger of losing his shoe, his leg was so busy. He interlocked his fingers round his knee in an attempt to still it, then uncrossed his legs and planted his feet firmly on the floor. He wanted to shout. This was a complete farce. Why were all these people talking to his son as if it mattered what he said or did? The little prick had been taking drugs for God's sake. He clearly didn't know how he felt or what he wanted. If they cared to ask Lawrence, he'd tell them exactly what he thought they should do with him.

The doctor droned on.

'...and reduce the dose over the next few weeks, but we can monitor that at the day hospital. I think discharge on Thursday with a couple of evening passes before that to see how you go. How does that sound, Liam?'

'Great.'

Lawrence cleared his throat. 'I'll tell your mother to get your room ready. She'll be pleased to see you.'

The Chinese woman held up a hand. 'Actually, Liam is going to stay with Felice, right?' She turned to the black girl who smiled, showing straight white teeth.

'Yes, that's right.' She looked at Liam. 'I'm so looking forward to you coming home.'

Liam, for the first time in the meeting, smiled.

Lawrence clamped his lips together; this really was too much. He looked at his son, the boy who had shown so much promise. He was bright, had played rugby in the school's First XV, captained the cricket First XI, was popular, outgoing, motivated. And now, here he was, sitting in a dingy room in a public hospital with a psychiatric label which may as well have been tattooed on his forehead, holding a black girl's hand and smiling like he had it all. Actually looking happy! Lawrence's jaw was clenched so tight he thought his teeth might shatter. When had his son started going off the rails? And why? It was probably because Deidra had always mollycoddled him and then he went off to university and got in with the wrong crowd. That must have been it. He'd come home less and less, much to Deidra's dismay, although she had gone to see him fairly regularly.

'Well,' said the Chinese woman, 'that all sounds good. You'll keep coming to the day hospital for a while and see Faiz for follow-up, okay?'

'Sure,' said Liam. 'If we're done, I'd like to show Felice something on the ward.' He rose and pulled his girlfriend to her feet. 'Come on,' he said, and they practically ran out.

'Hold on, Liam – we need to talk,' said Lawrence.

Liam didn't stop.

Lawrence realised that at no time during the meeting, apart

from the barbed comment at the beginning, had Liam acknowledged him. Little sod.

Faiz Noor got up to go.

'A word, doctor?' said Lawrence. He had, after all, come to get answers and had been given none as yet.

'Certainly,' said Faiz, looking at his watch.

Lawrence got straight to the point. 'My wife wants him home where she can keep an eye on him and make sure this doesn't happen again.'

The doctor looked the older man in the eye. 'Your son is over eighteen and can therefore go where he likes. He and Felice have a strong, stable relationship and she is very supportive. She's been in to see him every day.'

Lawrence felt the rebuke in the words. Before her accident Deidra had been to see her son, begging him to let them transfer him to a private hospital closer to home, but Liam had refused. Lawrence, in spite of working in London every day, hadn't been to see him once. He wished he had the doctor in the witness stand. He would tear him to shreds. Instead, he took a deep breath, counted to ten and changed tack.

'What is his actual diagnosis and do you expect there will be a recurrence?'

Dr Noor answered the question with one of his own.

'Is there any history of mental illness in the family?'

Lawrence stiffened. 'Of course not.'

'Hmm. Your wife mentioned there may have been an aunt with schizophrenia?'

Lawrence felt a shot of ice rip through his body. Surely this man wasn't implying that Liam was going to end up like Aunt Marjory, in and out of hospital as fast as she was in and out of reality. She'd died in an asylum, convinced the *Invaders* were coming, and making phone calls to politicians on her matchbox to warn them of the imminent danger.

'No, she must have been mistaken,' he said, as if in denying it he could protect his son from the same fate.

Dr Noor looked at him for a moment. 'Can you tell me anything about the family dynamics – how would you say you all get on?'

Lawrence puffed out his chest. He was a big man and knew how to use his size to intimidate. The doctor, however, remained relaxed, waiting for an answer.

'We all get on fine when we're all sane. And I fail to see what bearing this has on Liam's mental health,' Lawrence sneered.

Dr Noor nodded, doing his thoughtful look again.

'What's my son been saying?'

'Well, I obviously can't break confidentiality, but let's just say he doesn't quite agree with your perception of the family.'

He'd heard enough of this mumbo-jumbo. It was bad enough Liam was there at all but how dare they infer it was caused by an issue within the family? His son was a disappointment, a drug addict, no doubt. He needed stern words and a strict regime, not all this namby-pamby, touchy-feely stuff.

'Just answer my original question, if you'd be so kind,' said Lawrence from between clenched teeth.

'We're keeping our fingers crossed this was a one-off but, of course, no one can say for sure.'

'So what you're saying is, if he takes drugs in the future, he could go mad again?'

Faiz looked at him thoughtfully. 'We don't use the word "mad" anymore, but he may have another psychotic episode, yes.'

What an arrogant little prick the doctor was. 'Right. Thank you. I need to speak to my son. Where's the ward?'

Faiz pointed to the right. 'Just down that way.'

As Lawrence approached the ward he saw Liam and Felice hugging in the corridor.

'See you later, babe,' said the girl as they pulled apart.

Liam smiled at her. 'Love you.'

'Love you more.' She blew him a kiss and walked off towards the main door.

'Just a moment – Felice, isn't it?'

She swung round, nodded, and took a few steps towards him. Lawrence cleared his throat, looked from one to the other, and said, 'You must both know this can't be allowed. This relationship has to end.' He turned to Felice who was standing next to Liam again, as if shielding him from his father. 'Liam needs to be with his family at this time, as I'm sure you understand.'

'Felice is my family,' said Liam simply.

'Liam and I have made plans, Mr Kelly. You needn't worry about him. Now, sorry, but I must go – my dad's waiting for me.' She kissed Liam on the cheek, said goodbye to Lawrence, and left.

Standing in the corridor, fists clenched, Lawrence for a moment was unsure what to do. Making a decision, he said, 'Liam, I need to talk to you. Stay here, I'll be right back,' and ran off after the girl.

As he went, he heard Liam say, 'Can't wait.' Lawrence heard the sarcasm in his son's voice and considered going back to tackle him, but he actually could wait. Or he could go and talk about his feelings to one of the staff, fill their ears with more rubbish or smear a bit of paint around and call it therapy. Lawrence would talk to him about that but right now he needed to talk to the girl.

Lawrence marched back to the hospital, fists clenched. He couldn't believe that black man and his daughter had been so rude to him and that he'd let them put words in his mouth. He, a Queen's Counsel, had been bettered by a bloody nigger. He smirked at his own use of the word. He secretly loved it, it was so un-PC, and yet, perfect for what it described. So he was racist. So what? At least he admitted it unlike all the politicians who wrapped themselves in knots to say the right thing, even though he knew they felt exactly the same way he did.

There'd been a black boy at school; Pious Kawande had been the son of a minor chief in some ex-colonial African shitpile from which anyone who could afford it still sent their children to boarding school in the old country. He'd been quiet, spoke English with the same accent as Prince Philip, played cricket as well as any other boy and joined the army cadets. Lawrence had made friends with him in their first week, both small for their age, new, scared and lonely. It didn't take long before Greenwood and Beauchamp started putting the pressure on – taking the tuck his mother sent him, calling him a nigger lover, scratching under their arms like a chimpanzee every time they walked past. Over the first term Lawrence and Pious were ostracised, never asked to dorm parties, not picked for teams in games classes. After the Christmas holidays Lawrence went back to school and ignored Pious. He was, after all, the reason Lawrence wasn't making other friends, wasn't included in things, and he so desperately wanted to be included. He had a father who hardly seemed to know his name and a mother who was more interested in golf than she was in her son. He had always hoped at boarding school he would be able to make a niche for himself, that it would be a place where he felt important and liked. Lawrence grew in popularity and Pious shrank into the corners. But he never said anything to Lawrence, never questioned his change of heart, showed anger or upset at his friend deserting him. And Lawrence hated him for his weakness in the way that only shame can make you hate someone.

If he had his way immigration would be slashed. Mind you, he thought Farage and his gang were going too far. There was private opinion and there was political beat-up. It didn't do anyone any good to incite violence and that was what concerned Lawrence about this whole Brexit circus. Britain had once been Great when it could rely on its own empire, but these days one had to be pragmatic – they needed Europe and the Europeans. If that meant having to take their share of refugees and immigrants, it was the price they had to pay. And he had to admit most of them were okay. Intelligent, hard-working, tax-paying individuals had a place in British society. Small 's' society only, of course. Everyone needed a Paki shop nearby, and who else would clean the hospitals?

Taking the steps two at a time, he entered the building again, looking for Liam. He wasn't where he had left him, where he had told him to wait. Typical. He went into the ward and approached the nurses' station.

'My son – where is he?' he asked, interrupting a conversation between the two staff members there. At least, he assumed they were staff. No one wore uniforms so it was hard to tell.

'Your son?' said a pimply man turning to him.

'Liam Kelly.' Lawrence drummed his fingers on the counter.

'Oh, Liam. I think he's playing table tennis in the games room.'

A fucking games room? What was this place, a resort or a hospital? Lawrence raised an eyebrow.

'Just through there.' The man pointed across the room. A door was open and when he glanced over Lawrence could see a couple of people moving in and out of view. He left the nurses' station without a thank you and approached the games room.

'Liam,' he said, standing at the door.

'Wait.' His son didn't even glance over at him.

Lawrence felt his blood pressure rise. He looked at his watch. Damn. This *would* have to wait. He needed to get to his chambers.

'Don't think you're getting away with this. I'll talk to you later.'

'Promises, promises.' Liam hit a winning shot, wide down the backhand side.

Lawrence wished his son was ten again and he could take him over his knee and give him the thrashing he needed.

In the taxi on his way across London he decided to refer the matter of Liam back to Deidra. It was her fault he was so unruly, after all. And he would cut off his allowance so he had to move back home under their supervision. Only then could they be sure he wouldn't do anything stupid again. And it would get Deidra off his back having her son at home again. She needed a project. Satisfied he'd worked it all out, he turned his thoughts to the afternoon ahead.

Dyson, the clerk, greeted him as he walked into the chambers.

'Mr Beauchamp was asking when you'd be in. He wanted your opinion on the Dawson case, I believe.'

Lawrence nodded to him but didn't stop to talk. He closed the door of his office behind him, put his briefcase next to his desk and took a deep breath. George Beauchamp had become his best friend at school, after which they'd gone to university together and were now in the same chambers. And he'd married his sister. Greenwood, their other school friend, had become an accountant. They still got together regularly for a drink. He sighed and looked around his office. He loved this room with its oak panelling and thick carpet, the mahogany desk polished daily by a cleaner whose name he should remember but didn't, till it gleamed with a dark sheen. The latticed window looked out over the inner courtyard with its ancient oak tree, stone birdbath in the centre and the neatly-trimmed grass no one ever walked on. Here he was at home. Here he was treated with respect. Here no one told him to wait and muttered under their breath when he spoke.

He'd talk to Beauchamp later, but now he sat and turned on his computer. After staring at the screen for a while he realised he couldn't concentrate on work. The morning had unsettled him more than he had thought. Not only Liam. The suicide.

He hadn't told the guard quite the whole story earlier. It was true his grandfather had driven a train and that a man had thrown himself in front of it. What he hadn't added was that it had been his grandfather's own brother. The two had been close, brothers who had grown up on an isolated croft on the west coast of Ireland and had left home together in the 1920s to seek a better life in England. Lawrence's grandfather, Conor, had found himself a job on the trains, and Sean had become a clerk in an insurance company, being better at his letters than his older brother. They'd lived together in a rooming house, looked after by the fearsome Mrs Deakin. All went well until the brothers met Dora Fairweather, and both took a shine to her. When she made it clear she favoured Sean, Conor became so jealous he wouldn't talk to his brother anymore. He moved to another rooming house and ignored Sean's overtures. When he heard through a mutual acquaintance that Sean had broken off with Dora in order to make peace with him, Conor went straight round to Dora's to offer what he could in the way of solace. Four months later Dora died on the table of a backstreet abortionist, and Sean was thrown into despair. He'd given up the girl he loved to make peace with his brother and had been betrayed by both. The only way he could think of getting back at Conor was to make his brother the agent of his death since he had nothing left to live for.

What must it have been like, Lawrence wondered, to have been driving that train? Seeing the man on the tracks and applying the brakes. And as the train began to slow down, recognising his brother. Pulling harder on the brake, the wheels locking and even in the engine room he would have smelled the metal wheels overheating, would have seen the sparks flying. The noise would have been deafening. How would it have felt to look into his brother's eyes at the final moment before contact? Lawrence shuddered. He couldn't imagine. Didn't want to imagine.

Conor never drove a locomotive again but went back to the railway as an apprentice engineer, vowing to find a way to make the brakes more effective. Too late to save Sean. Too late to save himself. A few years later he invented the gadget that started him on the road to fortune. He'd become very wealthy but he'd been driven by his grief and anger. Too many nights he was carried to bed so drunk he couldn't get there himself, too many days he spent alone, wandering his estate, shouting at the trees, the sky, the universe, shooting wildly at noises in the woods, riding his horses into the ground. Lawrence had been terrified of him as a child, and scornful of him as an adolescent. By the time he died, he hadn't seen him for over a year.

He shook his head to rid himself of the thoughts. Enough was enough. It was old news, and nothing could be done about it anymore.

He buzzed Dyson.

'I need to see Paula. Do you know where she is?'

'Yes, Mr Kelly. She was in court this morning, but she should be back soon. I'll send her in directly when she returns.'

Lawrence spent the time until Paula arrived looking out the window. A sparrow played in the birdbath, pecking at the water and shaking its head, spreading its feathers and puffing out its chest to ward off the starling that approached. The bigger bird wasn't intimidated, though, and the sparrow flew off and perched on the branch of the oak tree. Lawrence could almost hear it muttering to itself about the injustice.

A knock at the door brought him back. He never daydreamed. He was concerned about himself. What a waste of time.

'Ah, Paula,' he greeted his pupil. 'Come in.'

Paula was tall, dark-haired, olive-skinned. She had an armful of files which she put on the desk and stood waiting for Lawrence to tell her what he wanted.

Lawrence was struck by her beauty, as he always was when he saw her. By the sheer elegance of her. She'd danced as a child, she'd told him when he commented on her poise but told him nothing more about herself. She was a mystery he often found himself puzzling over. She spoke well, but her CV told him she'd been to a state school. She'd topped her year at university but taken a year out to work in an orphanage in Africa somewhere. He would have thought she would have gone in for humanitarian law after something like that but here she was, a pupil of criminal law under his supervision.

'Sit.' He gestured to the sofa against the back wall of his office, away from the window.

Paula sat with her knees together, hands clasped in her lap. She couldn't know what a turn-on Lawrence found the demure maiden posture. He felt his cock stir.

'How was court this morning?' he asked.

Paula gave him a detailed rundown of the case they were working on. It was at a stage of the proceedings where he wasn't required to be there – Alasdair, one of his juniors, was well enough equipped to deal with the mundane stuff and Paula, as a pupil, was lucky to be able to shadow him in court. Still, he thought, he would have preferred to be there next to her than in that bloody case conference.

Paula shifted her position and Lawrence realised he'd been staring at her.

'Sorry,' he said. 'Lot on my mind today.'

'Anything I can help with?'

Lawrence turned the question over in his mind. If only his son would choose a girl like her – not that she'd give him a second look, of course. But if Liam aimed higher perhaps he'd start making something of himself. But then he wouldn't be able to have her himself. And he wanted her.

'What are your ambitions?' he asked.

Paula looked taken aback at the abrupt change of topic.

'I want to take silk, eventually.'

Lawrence nodded, rubbed his chin. 'Takes a long time, a few showcase trials and a lot of help from your superiors.' He shook his head as if he was sad to have to impart this information to her. As if, if he had his way, things would be different.

'I'm prepared to work hard, you know that.' Paula looked him in the eye.

'Oh, I have no doubt about that but it takes more than just hard work. I don't admit this to many people, but there is an element of luck in it too.' He held his hands up in front of him to stop her from interrupting. 'I know what you're going to say – it should be based purely on merit and I agree, it should. It really should. But that's not how it is.'

He glanced at his pupil who was looking at him from her place on the sofa. He unbuttoned his jacket and sat beside her.

'I can help you, Paula. I'm willing to help you.'

She edged away from him so she was sitting right against the arm of the sofa. 'Thank you.' She smoothed her skirt over her knees. 'I should get on – unless you wanted to go through the court documents I brought?' She indicated the pile of files on the desk.

Lawrence didn't even look at them. 'Another time.' He placed his hand on her thigh. 'I want to help you, Paula.'

She stood abruptly. 'Thank you, but I'm not going to have sex with you to get ahead. If that's the kind of help you're offering, I'm not interested.'

Lawrence also stood, facing her, too close. 'No, you've got the wrong end of the stick.' He stroked her arm, looked into her eyes. 'I just want to give you every opportunity, that's all.'

'I'm going now. I propose we forget this conversation ever happened.' She took her files and left.

Fuck, thought Lawrence. Fuck her. None of his pupils had turned him down before. What made her think she was so bloody special? Trashy little bitch. And now what was he going to do? He hated to admit it, but being rejected by her had given him a massive hard-on. He sat behind his desk and buzzed Dyson again. 'Send Margot in, would you?'

'Of course.'

Margot didn't have the intelligence of Paula, nor the looks, but she was savvy. She knew how to get on in the world. She'd practically launched herself at him from the first day she arrived in his chambers.

She smiled as she entered. 'What can I do for you, Lawrence?'

'I've had a bloody awful morning and I need to take my mind off it somehow.'

She walked round behind him and started massaging his shoulders. He closed his eyes and breathed deeply. She wore a heavy, musky scent that sent him into a fantasy about a voluptuous whore lying amongst silk cushions, legs spread wide, begging him to fuck her. He turned and lifted her skirt. Margot tensed but didn't stop him as he pulled her tights and knickers down, still with his eyes closed, still enjoying the image of the whore. He slid a hand between her thighs. She gasped and moved round to straddle him but he took her arm and stopped her. Nodding towards the couch on the other side of the room, he said, 'On your knees. Please.'

She looked momentarily surprised and then did as he said, her forearms resting on the sofa. He knelt behind her, stroking her buttocks, enjoying the smooth roundness of them, then unzipped himself.

He thought of Paula as he reached round and under her shirt to fondle her breasts, as he kissed her neck, as he thrust deep inside her. She braced herself against the sofa as he plunged deeper and deeper and then she started rolling her hips and moaning. With a grunt, he came and eased back onto his heels, pulling her with him, so she was sitting on him. He was still inside her but he'd lost interest already. Margot leant back against him momentarily, but it felt too intimate a gesture and Lawrence pushed her upright again.

'How's the case?' he asked.

'Going well, I think. We weren't in court today, but we're getting ready for the summing up at the moment. The defence was exactly what we expected, so we had it all covered.'

'Good. Better get back to it.' He lifted her off him and she pulled her knickers up, pulled her skirt down, looked at her reflection in the window, smoothed her hair down and left.

Lawrence took his laundered handkerchief out of his pocket, wiped himself, zipped his trousers, and went to his computer. He'd decide what to do about Paula later but one thing was for sure – she wouldn't get admitted to the Bar if he had anything to do with it, let alone make silk.

Lawrence was in a foul mood. Nothing had gone his way all day, through no fault of his own. He'd considered staying in town at his flat in Camden but decided he couldn't face a solitary dinner and the call to Deidra to tell her he wouldn't be home. She didn't like him staying in town at the best of times and hated it now she was incapacitated. She expected him to come home every night to bring the world to her since she couldn't go out to embrace its wonders.

And then, having made the effort to go home some bloody woman mutters something under her breath when he accidentally bumps into her at the station. *Well, sorry, love – you asked for it, standing there like a stuffed rabbit in the middle of a busy concourse.*

He fished his keys out of his pocket as he headed for the car park. He'd had to park further away than usual because Deidra had been talking at him as he was leaving that morning and delayed his departure by a critical two or three minutes. He peeled off his coat and threw it and his briefcase onto the passenger seat of the Merc and got in.

He loved his car. The white-leather interior, the polished-wood trim, the way the safety belt hugged him into the seat before releasing a little. And the purr when he started the engine, the thrum of power under the bonnet as he pressed his foot on the accelerator. His only regret was that he couldn't drive it as it deserved to be driven, not in England with its bloody stupid speed limits. He sat in the driver's seat stroking the steering wheel, the smoothness of it reminding him of Paula's taut skin – not that he'd been allowed to touch it. She'd made a grave mistake rebuffing his offer of help. Who did she think she was? She may be all Queen's English in chambers, but he knew where she came from. He bet she was all glottal stops and dropped h's as soon as she got home to Peckham or whatever dreary little suburb she lived in. He smiled to himself and drove out of the car park toward home.

Pulling onto the A5 he turned the music up and surrounded

himself with the 'Ride of the Valkyries'. It was stirring stuff. As he listened, he wondered what they would have chosen for him with their power over life and death: to live or to die? Not usually one to let chance decide anything for him, tonight he thought it might be a relief for someone else to take charge. He was tired of having to deal with family dramas, of Deidra being out of action, of having to take up the slack. A buxom Valkyrie, perhaps with Paula's full sensuous lips and Margot's smooth, round buttocks, could escort him to Valhalla where he would never have to do anything except eat and drink and shag nubile young women. He might have made the last bit up but it made the whole package sound quite appealing.

He went past his normal turn-off at Monks Way, preferring to stay on the A5 where he could keep his foot on the accelerator. It was a longer route to go through Old Stratford and back along Watling Street but he wasn't in a hurry to get home. He briefly considered keeping going until the A5 joined the M1 and beyond, driving until he ran out of road and had to get a ferry to the islands off Scotland where he would rent a small cottage under a false name. Live a simple life fishing, walking, having a pint in the local pub in the evening.

He sighed and turned off towards home. Fishing, walking, making friends with the locals – none of it was him. It was too parochial. He was a man of the city. He may live in the country but he was alive in the city. No passive fisherman, he was a hunter, like his grandfather.

As he pulled into his drive and parked the car his phone rang. He glanced at the screen and declined the call. The last thing he needed was to talk to his daughter. As if it wasn't bad enough having Liam a drug-addicted dropout, his daughter was a self-absorbed financial black hole. She never spoke to him unless it was to ask for money. He had no idea how a seventeen-year-old could spend so much when she was at boarding school all week and riding her bloody horse all weekend. How many pairs of shoes or new dresses did a girl need?

The rich smell of roast meat hit him as he opened the front door. Deidra came into the hall to greet him. He looked at his wife in her expensive clothes, well-groomed and coiffed as always, the only differences being the collar she had round her neck, the flat heels instead of her usual court shoes and the stick she'd been using since her accident. Lawrence hung his coat in the cloakroom and walked past her into the lounge.

'Scotch?' He waved the decanter at her.

She limped in and sat on the sofa. 'Lovely,' she said in her refined Home Counties voice. Not a glottal stop within miles. 'How did the case conference go?' she asked. Not, 'How are you, did you have a good day?' She didn't care about him anymore, it was all about Liam.

Lawrence dropped two ice cubes into each glass and poured the drinks. He gave Deidra one and stood looking out the French doors into the darkening garden. He was aware of his wife's impatience in spite of her stillness, her need to hear the details of their son's mental health and immediate future. Not one to fidget. His wife was the epitome of good manners and forbearance.

'Almost didn't make it there in time. There was a suicide on the line this morning.'

Deidra's hand went to her throat. 'I heard. Nancy rang to tell me. Such a tragedy. We knew her – you met her once, too, although you probably don't remember her. It was Judith Strasser, the woman who organised that fundraising dinner we went to towards the end of last year. You know, for the animal sanctuary. I used to meet her in town for coffee every so often.'

Lawrence's hand shook as he lifted his glass to his mouth and downed his drink in one. He continued to look out into the garden. Judith Strasser. He wondered vaguely if ending their affair had anything to do with her decision to kill herself but put the idea out of his mind again quickly. They'd had a bit of fun but they were both grown-ups – she'd always known it was just a fling.

'Poor woman,' he said and turned to the table to refill his glass.

'And what about Liam?' Deidra asked.

'He's not coming home, if that's what you were hoping to hear.'

Deidra let out a quiet sigh. 'But is he well? Will they let him out of hospital soon?'

Lawrence turned to her, eyes hard. She wasn't surprised. She must know about the girlfriend and hadn't told him. She'd let him look a fool in front of the hospital staff. Well, what did it matter? What did they matter? He'd never see them again. Jaw clenched, he looked towards the garden again, watching the last of the day's birds flying home to roost in the tall trees separating their house from the farm next door.

He heard her getting up and going into the kitchen, the smell of meat intensifying as she opened the door of the Aga. Usually he would offer to help. She never let him but it was one of the set pieces of their marriage – he offered to help, she said no, but thank you. Tonight he stayed quiet and poured himself another Scotch.

Over dinner she tried again. 'Did he look well – physically, I mean?'

Lawrence wiped his mouth on his serviette, folded it and put it down next to his plate. 'He looks like a dropout. Which is what he is. I'm going to suspend his allowance. Let him find a job and support himself, the ungrateful little prick.'

Deidra gasped. 'That's rather harsh, isn't it? He needs us now more than ever.'

Lawrence looked at her and spoke in a hard voice. 'As the

doctor pointed out, he's over eighteen. It's time he was made to live with the consequences of his own choices. He's on his own as far as I'm concerned.'

He rose and left the dining room but out in the hall he hesitated. He wasn't interested in sitting in front of the television, he didn't want to talk to his wife, he wasn't ready for bed.

'I'm going out,' he called as he grabbed a jacket out of the cloakroom and banged the door behind him.

The A5 was almost empty. Most people were having their dinner, at home in their boxy, boring houses. He opened the throttle allowing the bike to accelerate slowly. Seventy, eighty, ninety. So smooth, so powerful.

He knew Deidra had only asked what any mother would and that he'd behaved badly. He thought about turning back and apologising to her but then he remembered she'd known about the girlfriend and had withheld the information from him. He gritted his teeth. What was wrong with her? She had everything she could want – he left her to make all the decisions about the family so she felt she had a useful role in life and she responded by keeping secrets. His whole family seemed to think of him as a bottomless wallet and nothing else. He nudged the bike up to a hundred.

The scenery flashed by in a dark blur. Out in the country now, no street lamps piercing the dark, only the headlights of a car occasionally causing him to narrow his eyes against the glare. But this was England and too soon he was slowing down on the approach to Towcester. He knew he should go back, but instead took the A43 towards Northampton and sped up again.

He didn't want to think. He was tired of thinking. Tired of making decisions. Tired of working to make money for a family who showed no appreciation for his efforts. Let Liam starve, it would probably do him good. At least he wouldn't be able to buy drugs if he didn't have any money. His daughter already had more clothes than she could wear in a lifetime. And Deidra – what did she have? A beautiful home, swimming pool, tennis court, horses, charity work. When did the wife he loved turn into a boring woman like his mother, going to town occasionally for an exhibition or a show but otherwise burying herself in the country like a mole? When had their marriage become empty of the passion and excitement that had been its hallmark in the early years? When had they last even laughed together?

The lights of Northampton rose before him. He slowed and turned off the main road, driving between high hedges where the approach of a car in the opposite direction was heralded by ghostly beams of light sweeping around the bends. The BMW surged beneath him like a living thing, straining to go faster but Lawrence kept now to a steady thirty miles per hour, the road familiar to him from the visits they'd made to the 'big house' when he was a child. And coming to the brow of a low hill, there it was before him. The house, the drive winding through trees and rhododendrons. He'd been so afraid of those bushes as a child, sure that bad men lurked in them ready to carry off small boys. He had no idea where the notion had come from but it had persisted in various forms and places. Fear. And shame because he wasn't brave.

He stopped at the gates and stared up the drive, breathing heavily as if he'd run there rather than driven. He turned off the engine and sat looking at the house, remembering happy times as well as the childhood fears. His grandfather, the inventor, had been a scary old man, but when he was younger he'd been all right, and he'd liked his grandchildren when they were small. He would set treasure hunts for them in the grounds. The prize would be a cake or money. Once it was a stamp. Lawrence had won that time and been disappointed until his father told him it was a rare first edition and would one day be worth a lot of money. He still had it in the safe at home, although he had no idea if it really had any monetary value.

Thinking of his grandfather brought his thoughts once again to the suicide that morning. Judith. He'd liked her for a while. Longer than many of the women he had affairs with. She was uncomplicated, undemanding. What a waste of a life. And yet, what was he doing with his time on this earth? Working like a bloody Trojan. And what for? Was he happy? He closed his eyes and tried to relax as he straddled the bike.

Am I happy? It wasn't something he ever thought about. What constituted happiness anyway – the fleeting glow after sex? No, it never lasted long enough and was often replaced by a profound sense of loneliness. It wasn't love, it was just a physical need. He hadn't felt close to Deidra for years, ever since the children came along; she was so focused on them there was no room for him anymore. So, winning a difficult case, being well regarded by one's colleagues – was that what it was all about? He had always endeavoured to be top of his game, but did it make him happy? Were the endless hours of work and the energy required to stay at the top worth it? And what about the desperate fear he could lose it all? Suddenly everything he had based his life on felt hollow. Aware of his heart beating faster in his chest he forced himself to stay with the question. What gave a life meaning – success, status, love?

His eyes widened. Fear gripped him like a knife being driven into his guts. A piteous cry escaped his lips and he pulled his helmet off as he slumped forward over the handlebars. He held on to them for grim death – or was it dear life – tears now coursing down his cheeks unchecked. He was alone. That wasn't new. But he was lonely, and that was. His life had become a long, narrow, empty path. He had loved his children when they were little, had at times resented the career that demanded so much of his time. As they got older he knew them less and when they were young teenagers and still at home, he would hear their gay chatter, their laughter, but when he entered the room it would cease, the conversation becoming stilted, formal, only to resume its lightness when he left. He hadn't allowed it to bother him then but now it made him ache to turn back the clock and make it different. To be at home more, to listen to his children, to understand what made them tick.

And Deidra. When had they become so distant? When had they stopped taking delight in each other, calling during the day just to hear the other's voice?

Slowly he wiped his eyes, sat up straighter, kicked the bike back into life and turned for home. He took the shorter route, by the A508, and felt the miles speed away.

Twenty minutes later he arrived home. The lights in the kitchen and lounge were out but Deidra had left the hall light on for him. Without taking off his jacket he took the stairs two at a time.

His wife was getting ready for bed, sitting in her negligée at her dressing table, taking off her jewellery. She turned when she heard him come in. Lawrence watched her looking at him out of the same blue eyes he'd fallen in love with. Her skin was still smooth and unblemished. Her red hair, thick and natural, fell in soft waves to her shoulders.

'Deidra– I–'

'What's the matter, Lawrence? You look like you've seen a ghost.'

Lawrence couldn't find the words to express what he wanted to say. He was struck by a feeling. Several feelings. Fear that he was too late. Gratitude she was there at all. Love. Most of all, love.

'An awful thing happened today and it's made me realise a few things. Let's go away somewhere,' he said.

Deidra laughed. 'What are you talking about? Aren't we going to the house in France in a few weeks?'

'I mean away away. Not France. Somewhere we've never been. For a long time. I want to see and do things I haven't done before. I could retire and we could go off for a year – or more. The children are old enough now – they can have this house while we're gone. We could swim with dolphins, or learn to paint, eat local food, drink terrible wine. Escape the drudgery. Live!'

Deidra was looking at him in quizzically as if assessing his mental capacity. 'What's brought this on?'

Lawrence sank onto the bed, letting out a sigh. Deidra wasn't excited at the prospect. He felt a weight settling on him and anger starting to coil round his insides. Damn her.

He paused and reminded himself to use the technique he'd learned for dealing with bolshy witnesses. Unclenching his fists he pictured sending the anger back to the place it came from – a well of childhood shame and disappointments.

He looked at her again, tried to think of it from her perspective. Of course she wasn't excited – this was all so new for her. He needed to convince her.

He smiled, looked her in the eye and blinked slowly. 'I want to live before I die and I want you to be my companion. I've realised I haven't always been the most attentive husband, but I do love you. I want things to be different from now on. *I* want to be different.'

She smiled. He loved her smile, the way it lit her up. She smiled with her whole face, not like some people whose smile didn't reach their eyes.

'So?' he asked, holding out a hand to her, hope fluttering in his stomach making him feel as anxious as a teenager asking a girl out on a first date.

She took his hand in both of hers and Lawrence felt his

heart lift and stretch to encompass long days and nights together, free of the past. He envisioned the light of southern France, the vibrant colours of India, the endless desert of Morocco. The feel of Deidra's skin under his fingertips, the heady sweetness of her perfume, the way they used to give each other such pleasure.

He raised his eyebrows. 'Well?'

'Oh, Lawrence.' She stopped. The smile faded and was replaced by a thoughtful look, her eyebrows drawing together, her lower lip slightly pouting.

'Lawrence what?' he asked.

'We can't just leave. Liam needs us. Charlotte's doing her A levels next year. And anyway, I'm sorry, but I think we both know it's too late for that, don't we?'

Her response winded him like a punch in the stomach. The physical pain followed quickly by anger and shame. She was meant to be there for him, wasn't that what their wedding vows had stated? For better, for worse, till death do us part? He had allowed himself to be vulnerable and it had ended the way it always did; rejection, ridicule.

Deidra sighed and turned back to the mirror, started brushing her hair. He wanted to yank the hairbrush from her hand and thrash her with it, leave her begging for mercy.

Instead, he got up and left the bedroom without a word.

9

TREVOR

It felt like his constant companion these days, the sensation in the pit of his stomach telling Trevor all was not well. He felt it now, on the train on the way to see his daughter, Felice. He couldn't put a finger on it, but the last time they'd spoken he'd got that heavy feeling like something was being dragged through his guts that shouldn't be there. It was a physical feeling but the cause, he knew, was not physical.

He loosened his collar and rubbed his sweaty palms together. The air conditioning had stopped working soon after the train stopped, adding to his anguish.

The woman sitting opposite him looked about as uncomfortable as he felt. She couldn't settle to anything. Got out her Kindle. Put it away. Got out a notebook, wrote furiously for a while. Put it away. Fiddled in her pocket, pulled out a tube of lip balm and swiped it across her mouth, then proceeded to chew on her bottom lip like it was her last meal.

He lost himself in his thoughts again, trying to put a name to this feeling he had. Dread? Fear? Both of those but also something else. He felt threatened. He knew without a doubt his life was about to change, and not for the better. If he was honest with his daughter, he ran the risk of losing her. If not, he'd lose himself.

A gasp from the woman opposite drew him from his thoughts. She didn't look well. She'd gone pale, even for a white person. He looked around but no one else seemed to have noticed so he did the only thing he could think of – he got his hanky out and tapped her on the hand, offering it to her when she opened her eyes. She took it, wiped her face and clasped it to her mouth. No way he wanted it back after that, so he told her to keep it. She seemed grateful but Trevor was even more thankful when she gathered herself and her belongings and left the carriage. He watched as she swayed along the aisle, relieved she'd gone. Probably a nice enough woman, but stakki.

Having made his assessment, he closed his eyes again. Stakki: mad. The word had prompted the dragging feeling in his guts again. He had no idea how to tackle Felice, what to say to her without making her explode at him. He just wanted a chance to tell her how he felt, what he thought. But he knew with the certainty of night following day, she wouldn't want to hear it.

He looked at his newspaper. Not his usual newspaper. He had no idea why he'd grabbed *The Sun* today instead of *The Guardian*. Perhaps his state of mind. His hands acting without the benefit of his head. The headline screamed out against the EU and Trevor shook his head. How could anyone truly believe that leaving Europe was a good idea. Or that the likes of Farage and Johnson knew how to tell the truth. He was comforted by the fact that the sane, thinking people of the UK would never vote to leave the Union.

Closing his eyes again, he thought about the meeting he was going to before he took Felice out for lunch. He wasn't sure what his wife's parents wanted this time but he knew they didn't like him and that always put him at a disadvantage. It was another old feeling, being treated like muck. He knew the role of the underdog, the outsider. And he knew very well where it came from – not only being black in England, but being small and bookish, he hadn't fitted in at his South London comprehensive school, nor in his own family. He had learned to behave like the other children at school, swaggering, full of bravado to avoid bullying, and rushed home at the end of the day to shut himself in his room with his books. His brothers were both over six foot tall and half as wide and he'd had trouble getting to five foot eight. He had childhood asthma and had never been allowed to play sport. Gavin, the eldest in the family still called him Lilly Bud, Little Bird, and not in a nice way. Gavin intermittently drove a forklift. Samson was a sometime bouncer. Trevor was the only one in the family to go to university despite his school's best attempts to quash his ambitions and persuade him to lower his expectations. He'd gone to Leeds to study English, and afterwards done a teaching diploma. He was proud to be a teacher and encouraged his pupils to aim high and believe in themselves. He loved everything about teaching, even marking assignments. Sure, there were kids who were unmotivated and didn't hand work in, but he even loved the creativity they showed in their excuses for not having done it. Like young Peter the other day who told him he hadn't been able to do the work set over the weekend because his parents had taken him to a nudist colony in Wales for the weekend and he wasn't allowed to take anything with him. Trevor had laughed long and hard over that one. Wales, indeed!

He smiled to himself and forced his thoughts back to Veronica's parents. They had requested that he meet them in their solicitor's office but gave him no more information than that. Fortunately, it was half term but they would have expected him to take a day off anyway. They always treated him as if he was a man to be ordered about. Even when they finally gave their blessing for him to marry Veronica, his beloved Frostie, it had felt like it was given under duress, unwillingly, as if they viewed him as unworthy. Yet they were not racist, or so they said. And it was true, they also treated many white people the way they treated him – with a certain disdain, a distance, as if they were wearing gloves so as not to taint themselves. When he'd commented on it to Frostie after he'd known them for a while, she'd suggested that perhaps they were protecting others from themselves rather than the other way around. It made no sense to Trevor but when he pressed her, a pained expression crossed her face and she would say no more. It remained one of those mysteries he thought about in the early hours of the morning before even the rubbish collectors were about and the only sound was the occasional bark of a fox in the fields behind the house. And now Frostie wasn't around to ask.

His grief hit him like a punch in the solar plexus, winding him and making him hunch forward, clasping his chest, panting. Not wanting to draw attention to himself, he coughed and opened the newspaper, holding it up in front of his face. Once upon a time he would have been mortified if anyone thought he was a *Sun* reader but right now he didn't care. He needed something to hide his tears.

It had been three years since his wife had died. Three years of loneliness. Three years of anxiety that he wasn't doing enough for Felice. Three years of walking the tightrope between loving his daughter and letting her go. There were days he was so grief-stricken all he wanted to do was hug her and keep her close, but she was almost twenty when her mum died, taking her first steps out into the world on her own. His job was to help her leave the nest not tie her to it. He sighed at the memory of how exhausting it had been to pretend to be coping better than he was, of not letting on to her that he cried himself to sleep at night and sometimes at school had to excuse himself from class to press his emotions back down into the dark, churning place they had to stay so he could function in the world.

The train still hadn't moved. He would be late for the in-laws so he texted with apologies. He didn't tell them the reason. Let them think he'd overslept and missed the earlier train, he no longer cared what they thought of him. He knew they loved Felice, and that was all that mattered.

He overheard one of the other passengers tell her neighbour there'd been a suicide on the line. Trevor shuddered. What a violent way to go. Any way was a bad way to go but some were worse than others. When they were younger Frostie and he had sworn to each other that if the need arose, they'd help each other along, whatever the consequences. When the time came and his wife asked him to get her the medication required to end her life, he couldn't do it. He agreed wholeheartedly with assisted dying, understood Frostie's desire to be free of the pain and degradation her life had become but he couldn't be part of ending it. Every day she'd asked, and every day he had a different excuse. Felice was coming home soon, the doctor had mentioned a new medication, it was nearly Christmas, nearly her birthday, almost his. In the end, she stopped asking, and Trevor felt guilty about that, knowing he'd let her down. He simply couldn't imagine life without her. It was selfish but that was how it was. He made sure she had adequate pain medication. He looked after her with care and devotion and still she slipped away.

He sighed and wondered if it took everybody so long to mourn for their wife. He still felt as if it had happened a week ago rather than years. A colleague at school who found him sobbing in the staff toilet suggested that maybe he should see someone but he didn't want to do that. A counsellor might encourage him to get over it and in many ways he didn't want to.

Grief gave shape to his life now, where once his wife and daughter had.

He sat straighter in his seat. The passengers were restless, raising eyebrows, looking at watches, texting work. No one was reading the paper like they normally would. Some were even talking to each other. He wondered if the food shop was open, or did they close for a suicide? He needed a cup of tea – two teabags, a good dollop of milk, three sugars. And having thought about it, he had to go and see if he could get one.

Half the train had had the same idea and the food shop was packed. He shuffled through, excusing himself and trying to make himself smaller to fit between overweight men in suits and made-up women in high heels. Eventually he got to the counter and ordered his tea.

'Like it strong, then,' said the woman who served him. Her name badge said Sandra. 'Just like our Tim, the conductor on this train. That's how he likes his tea too. Put hairs on your chest it will!'

Trevor smiled at the thought. He'd always been somewhat lacking in the bodily hair department. Plenty on his head, it just hadn't ever stretched to anywhere else. Sandra certainly had plenty of hair, plaited in thick, neat cornrows, the dark skin of her scalp showing between them. Trevor smiled, remembering Felice fidgeting and muttering under her breath when her mother tried to do them for her once. In the end, Frostie had given up, and Felice had run round to a friend's house and come home later with her hair burnt from the straightening iron.

People were jostling him to get to the counter. It was a shame it was so busy. He would quite like to have stayed talking to Sandra and hear more of her theories about hair growth and tea. She had a word or a joke with everyone and they all ended up laughing or smiling. Funny how sometimes a stranger made you feel better, just by being there. He squeezed along to the end of the serving area and drank his tea, occasionally making a comment to Sandra who seemed to like the attention. Maybe he made her feel a bit better too. After he'd finished the first one, he ordered a second cup, and Sandra remembered how he liked it. It was a small thing, but it made him feel happy.

When he went back to his seat he was smiling and instead of dreading his lunch with Felice, he was looking forward to it. He'd got himself all worked up about it, but it would be all right.

Trevor leant against a letterbox and waited for Felice to come out of the building opposite. He had been rehearsing what he wanted to say all week, but now he was here, and she was about to join him, he couldn't remember any of the arguments that had sounded so persuasive when he was on his own, practising in the bathroom mirror. Yet after the meeting with her grandparents he was even more determined to say his piece.

She'd said one and it was now one twenty. He hoped he hadn't missed her, but surely she would have waited if they'd finished early? He checked his phone again. No missed calls. Nothing. He shifted to the other foot and turned his face to the weak May sun for a few moments.

'Dad – there you are. Sorry I'm late. The meeting went over time.'

They hugged and then Trevor held her away from him. His fingers itched to pinch her cheeks like he used to when she was younger. She'd always pretend she didn't like it but she never stopped him. She'd grown up so fast – twenty-two now, and in a real job but she'd always be his little girl.

He loved looking at his daughter, had stared at her for hours when she was little, wondering how something so perfect could have anything to do with him. She still had the same smooth, brown skin, the pert little nose, straight white teeth. But her hair was short now instead of braided and her eyes more knowing. Or guarded. Yes, that was it – she was ready to defend herself from him as if she knew what he was going to say. Trevor felt the dragging feeling in his abdomen again, accompanied this time by tightness around his heart. He didn't want his daughter to feel she had to defend herself from him. They'd always been so open with each other. Theirs had been such a tight, happy family until Frostie got sick. He winced inwardly at the memory of his wife. He'd called her Frostie the first time they met because she was so pale, even for a white woman, and it had stuck. Frostie by name, but certainly not by nature. She was as warm and loving as the Jamaican sun.

'Where do you want to go, Dad?'

He drew his thoughts away from his dead wife and looked at his daughter again. His adult daughter. 'I don't mind. You choose.'

Truth was, it had been so long since he had lived in London he didn't know it anymore. It was Felice's city now, her playground. Funny how you move away from a place to give your family better opportunities – good schools, less pollution, the country life, bigger house – and they end up back at the very place you left.

'Okay. This way.' She hooked her arm through his. Trevor's heart felt full and he walked tall with his daughter by his side.

'Felice!'

They turned and saw a man waving at them from the step of the building Felice had exited. Felice tightened her grip on her father's arm. He took in the well-cut suit and the tie and raised his eyebrows.

'The doctor?' Trevor asked.

'No, Liam's dad.' She rolled her eyes and sighed.

Before Trevor had a chance to ask more, Liam's father had crossed the road at a trot.

'Lawrence Kelly,' he said, putting out a hand and then seeming to think better of it and retracting it again. 'You must be this young... lady's father.'

'Yes. Trevor Jackson.'

'I wonder if we might have a word.'

'It'll have to be another time, Mr Kelly.' Felice tugged on her father's arm. 'Dad and I have to be somewhere.'

Trevor looked at his daughter and saw a glint of anger in her eyes but her body said resignation. Then he looked at Lawrence Kelly. By the sneer in the arch of his eyebrows and the curl of his lip, Trevor thought he knew what this Kelly wanted to say. He'd heard it so many times before. Not about his daughter but directed at himself. He drew himself up to his full five feet eight and rolled his shoulders back to make himself look a bit broader.

'Say what you want to say.'

'Dad–' Felice pulled at him again.

'Shall we go to a café and have a chat?' asked Lawrence.

'No,' said Trevor. 'You can say what you have to say right here.'

Lawrence Kelly looked around, ran a hand down his tie, moistened his lips with his tongue. 'Very well.' He paused, looked about again which gave him a shifty air. 'I don't want my son seeing Felice anymore. I've said the same to your daughter already, and to my son, but they don't seem to be able to see reason. So I'm asking for your help. You look like a sensible man, Trevor. You must see that this relationship of theirs can't continue.' He smiled the smile of a man used to getting his way. It made him look rather like a toad, Trevor thought.

He glanced at his daughter who now had the begging look in her eyes she got when she wanted her father to come quietly, to not get involved in whatever issue she was dealing with. But he couldn't back down. He'd never been able to when he sensed an injustice against his little girl. He looked back to Kelly.

'Because your son is a mental patient?'

Lawrence Kelly's eyes widened and he drew a sharp breath. 'Now look here–' he started.

'Or would it be because Felice is black and you're a racist bigot? Which one is it?'

'Dad, please–'

Trevor turned to his daughter. 'Just a moment, Sweetpea. One minute.'

She shook her head slowly, crossed her arms and turned away.

When Trevor looked back at Kelly, he noticed the other man's jaw was clenched, his eyes cold.

'Well, if you want to be so blunt, it is about your daughter. Not because of her colour, but because she... she... she just isn't the right girl for my son.'

Trevor kept his gaze steady. 'Not right in what way?'

Kelly looked up at the sky as if hoping for divine intervention.

'Is it her education? The clothes she wears? The food she eats? Her choice in music perhaps? What, Mr Kelly, is the reason you believe my daughter is not right for your son?'

'Now you're being ridiculous – of course it's none of those things, it's just that she's...'

'The wrong colour.'

'All right. Yes. It is. There you have it. I will not have my son going out with a black girl.'

Trevor took Felice's hand and held it firmly. She didn't look at him but she didn't pull away either. He took a deep breath, working hard to keep his anger at bay. One of the reasons he'd taken his daughter's hand was to stop himself from punching this Kelly on his bigoted nose.

'Well, Mr Kelly,' he said evenly, 'I came here today to convince my daughter to break off this relationship because I do not want her going out with a drug-addicted lunatic.'

Lawrence Kelly gasped. 'My son is a highly educated young man with his whole life before him. He may have taken a wrong turn but he's paying the consequences. I will not have him held back by an association that is not–' He stopped mid-sentence and smiled, a look of triumph spreading across his features. 'So we're in agreement.'

'But,' continued Trevor as if he hadn't heard Kelly, 'Felice is over eighteen and so is your son, so it is of little consequence what we want. They are old enough to make up their own minds.' He turned to Felice.

'Do you love this stakki boy?' Felice laughed, nodded and squeezed his hand. Trevor smiled. He knew she loved it when he used Jamaican words in front of people who didn't know what they meant. It had been like a secret code when she was little. Their private language.

'This can't work. You know it can't.' Lawrence had his hands on his hips.

'The only thing I'm worried about is my daughter's happiness. If she really believes your son can make her happy, I will not stand in their way. Goodbye, Mr Kelly.' Trevor turned on his heel and walked away. He heard an expletive but didn't grace it with a response.

'Thanks, Dad.' They walked for a minute or two in silence, then Felice said, 'Did you mean what you said about wanting me and Liam to break up – is that really why you came?'

Trevor slowed down. Here it was, the moment he'd been dreading. The words he'd rehearsed had fled, and he stood in front of his daughter, the most precious thing in his life, knowing if he was honest she might hate him, and if he wasn't he would hate himself. He swallowed hard.

'Do you remember what your mother used to say?' he asked.

Felice looked at him, eyes narrowed. 'She used to say a lot of things, which one are you thinking of in particular?'

Trevor smiled at the reminder of his wife's pontifications. She did have an opinion about most things, it was true, and she wasn't scared to voice them. He used to call her his soap-box queen. *Oh, Frostie.*

'I was thinking about what she said about honesty always being the best policy, even, or perhaps, especially when it is hard.' He glanced at Felice who was looking off into the distance, as if hearing her mother's voice. He went on. 'But if two people love and respect each other they have to be truthful with each other.'

Felice nodded. 'Yeah, I remember. Sometimes it hurt. Like when she told me I was a fool for thinking Tony Riley really wanted to marry me. We were eight and so in love. We held hands in the back row of form two.'

'I didn't know that. I'd've been round to his house with a cricket bat if I had!'

Felice laughed. 'Yes, Dad, you probably would. That's why we didn't tell you! You've always been overprotective.' She looked at him as the laughter faded between them. 'You're at it again, aren't you?'

Trevor looked at his shoes. 'Let's go find some lunch,' he said, knowing he wouldn't be able to eat. The dragging sensation had returned.

In one of the few establishments in the area that hadn't reinvented itself as a gastropub serving expensive organic food art, Trevor watched Felice tuck into a ploughman's lunch. She'd always had a hearty appetite. She was the person he knew best in the entire world and yet, he realised, there were parts of her life he knew nothing about and while he knew this was normal and natural, it made him ache. He had held her moments after her birth, fed her, changed her nappies, been there to witness her first steps, had marvelled at her first words. He'd encouraged her first attempts at reading and writing, praised her stories. He and Frostie agreed they had been sent the most beautiful, talented, perfect child on whom to lavish their affection and it was their job to nurture and guide her to independence. They'd done a good job. Too good, maybe. They'd looked forward to the time when Felice gave them grandchildren, lived nearby and asked them to babysit, to be involved in her life and that of her family. But her mother was gone and here she was living in London, working in her chosen career and not needing him anymore.

Trevor sighed, ran a hand over his eyes, realising he was lonely.

'You're not eating, Dad,' said Felice, glancing up, and then looking closely at her father. 'Are you okay?'

Smile, say yes, Trevor told himself. 'I don't know.' He took her hand. There was a sticky spot where she'd spilt a bit of pickle on her skin and hadn't licked it off. He had to stop himself from moistening the edge of a napkin and rubbing it away.

Felice stopped chewing. A crease appeared between her eyebrows. It hadn't been there before her mum died, Trevor noted.

'Do you think of your mother much?' he asked.

The crease deepened. *I'm upsetting her*, thought Trevor and wanted to cradle her in his arms and take all her pain away like he had when she fell down as a little girl, or quarrelled with a friend.

'I think about her a lot. I talk to her every day.'

Trevor smiled. 'She'd like that. I do too. It must be pretty busy for her up there, both of us chatting away to her.'

'You're lonely, Dad. You need to get out more. You're still an attractive man, you should meet someone.'

Trevor's hands flew to his face. How could his own daughter say something like that? He'd thought they knew each other, but obviously his daughter didn't know him at all. He wondered, fleetingly, if in loving her as devotedly as they had, he and Frostie had allowed their daughter to become somewhat self-absorbed – unable, or unwilling – to look beyond herself. He pushed the thought away quickly. That wasn't it. She'd spoken out of concern for him. If she thought about it she'd know he would never find another woman like his wife.

They fell into an awkward silence. Felice started eating again.

Watching her, Trevor wondered if, perhaps, this was his daughter's way of telling him she would never be moving back to Milton Keynes, that her life was now in London with friends he didn't know and work he didn't understand. She couldn't be his little girl forever, nor his companion. His throat tightened at the thought but he knew it was right. He had to let her go, had to take what scraps of her life and her time she offered and be proud she was resilient and strong. If only it didn't hurt so much. He carried her around with him day in, day out, tucked away in his heart but she carried other things, other people with her. It was what he'd wanted and he hated it.

'So,' he said, 'tell me about this boy.'

He saw Felice's face soften and knew she'd been waiting for him to ask. 'What do you want to know?'

What he really wanted to know was how she could let herself fall for someone so obviously unsuitable. A young man with a mental illness.

'How did you meet?' he asked.

'At a party. I was with my girlfriends and one of them knew him from school.'

'And what does he do?' *When he's not mentally ill,* Trevor added to himself.

'He's back at university. He's already got a degree, but it wasn't what he wanted to do, so he's studying again.'

Of course, thought Trevor, *a dissolute.* The son of a wealthy family who never set any limits, who gave him to understand he need never do anything because there would always be money for him to indulge his little whims.

'What is he studying?'

'Photography. He's very talented. You should see some of his work.'

'I'd love to.' Trevor smiled tightly. 'What does he plan to do when he finishes?'

Felice put her knife down, wiped her mouth and smiled. 'What is this, the Spanish Inquisition? Don't you trust me to choose my own boyfriend?'

Trevor wanted to say, *No, no one will ever be good enough for you, especially this one.* He wanted to whisk her away to a place where all the young men were healthy and worked hard and knew the value of his little girl.

'I just want to know you're happy, that's all.'

'I am. I really am.'

'So... what's the nature, I mean, how is he... what's he got?'

Felice sat back in her chair, arms folded. 'Why does it matter so much?'

The ache in Trevor's belly intensified.

'I only want to know he can make you happy, that you're not going to be held back by his...' It was all coming out wrong. He'd put Felice on the defensive, the very thing he had wanted to avoid. 'I'm sorry. Look, I'm your father, I only want what's best for you.'

'Attacking my boyfriend isn't exactly helping, is it?'

Trevor shrugged and shook his head. He was fighting a losing battle. If he didn't concede defeat he might lose more than this argument.

'I'm sorry, Sweetpea. When can I meet him?' The words felt false in his mouth but they had the right effect. Felice smiled.

'Tonight – you can stay, can't you? He's coming round later.'

'I thought he was in hospital?'

'He's going to be discharged soon and he's allowed out a bit before then. He goes to a day programme now.'

'So what was the meeting this morning about?'

'His future. We were talking about his support network and stuff.'

So that's what she was – one of a support network. The boy was so damaged he needed a web of people around him to depend on so he didn't go mad again. It was even worse than he'd thought. He swallowed, ran a finger round the inside of his collar which suddenly felt too tight, and said he would love to stay to meet him.

After lunch Trevor occupied himself by going to the National Gallery while Felice went back to work. He found looking at paintings soothing and went straight to the Impressionists. He loved Monet's Giverny paintings; the colours made him feel so tranquil. He also liked his snow scenes. Another favourite was Goenuette's *Boulevard de Clichy Under Snow*. There was something about snow, the way it made a place look clean and sharp. He had memories of taking Felice tobogganing on the rare occasions it snowed enough to do so – the flush of her face, the shrieks of excitement, the exhaustion at the end of the day as he trudged through the slush pulling his shivering little daughter home and the tingling of fingers as they warmed again near the fire. Maybe it was also that the scenes in the paintings were so different to the country he remembered as the place of his birth; Jamaica, with its lush tropicality, its verdant hills, its vibrancy. He had become so English that he was discomfited by the fecundity of the place, the overt sensuality.

He sighed, moved into the next room and took a seat on one of the comfy leather sofas in front of the Constables. *The Hay Wain* evoked fond memories of the cycling holiday he and Frostie had taken in Suffolk. They'd gone to Willy Lott's cottage specially to see the place where it was painted. They'd gazed at the cottage and walked in the fields along the River Stour, chatting about how different it must be now to how it was when Constable sat there painting. His favourite painting, though, was *Stratford Mill* which hung next to *The Hay Wain*. A group of young boys fishing, a little girl watching and the sky reflected in the wide, slow river. He sat for over an hour, his eyes on the pictures but most of the time his mind elsewhere.

Did he really have any right to interfere in his daughter's life anymore? She was twenty-two after all, had a good degree and a job she enjoyed and which paid enough for her to live in London.

What he couldn't convince himself of was that she really knew what she was getting herself into with Liam; life with a man who would never earn a regular income in his chosen profession. Trevor stopped himself. Income didn't matter, as well he knew. He and Frostie had never been well off, with him a teacher and her managing a dress shop but they had been happy. And anyway, he reminded himself of the meeting with his in-laws that morning. They were odd people. They'd never accepted their daughter marrying a black man but they preferred to talk to him about their granddaughter's inheritance rather than directly to her. They'd said it was because they wanted his assurance he would guide her in how to invest the money, but he thought it was more about rubbing his nose in the fact that Felice would be getting no money from his family – there was none to be had. He thought how little they knew their granddaughter if they thought she needed help in that department. She was far more financially savvy than him.

She'd be comfortably off with what they'd put in trust for her and for that he was grateful. And even though he believed most difficulties could be overcome if two people loved each other, he couldn't convince himself that was the case with mental illness. Felice clearly didn't understand the magnitude of the problem. The revolving door they called it. In and out of hospital, getting a little worse each time. And what if he became violent when he was psychotic, if his voices told him to kill Felice? It had happened before – he'd read about it in the news. The very idea made him shake with anxiety.

He dragged his attention back to the painting, tried to imagine himself holding a fishing rod, sitting on the bank or the flat barge, listening to the twittering of birds and the buzzing of insects. His heart rate slowed and a smile lifted the corners of his mouth. How beautiful, how uncomplicated a life like that would be.

He turned to an elderly man who had sat beside him.

'Beautiful, isn't it?'

The old man said nothing, and Trevor noticed he had his eyes closed. He nodded to himself; a gallery was a good place to take a rest but he felt slightly let down, cheated out of a bit of human interaction. His nod turned to a shake of the head. What had things come to when he needed to talk to strangers to make the time pass?

At half past four he left the fields and rivers of the Suffolk countryside in the art gallery and plunged into the chaos of

Trafalgar Square. Tourists climbed onto the lions to take photos, pigeons plucked at the ground feeding off the scraps of fast food and its wrappers, suited men and women rushed by carrying briefcases and furled umbrellas. A mother screamed at her toddler who was teetering on the edge of the fountain. *Ah, London*, he thought, and realised he missed it now. He never had before. He'd had everything he wanted in Milton Keynes – a loving wife, a gifted daughter, a job he never grew tired of, his garden, his bicycle. It all seemed meaningless without Frostie and Felice to share it with. He went through the motions, but his heart wasn't in it anymore.

He took a deep breath and squared his shoulders. *No use getting maudlin*, he told himself and launched into the stream of humanity that was London foot traffic.

An hour later, bearing a bunch of roses and an M&S cake as peace offerings, he approached Felice's flat. She lived in a tiny one-bedroom apartment in a large house in Lewisham that had been divided into seven flats, some of them, she'd told him, even smaller than hers. It was the first time he'd visited her in London – she usually came home to see him. If Frostie was still alive they would have been down before now – she was the organiser, the one who made arrangements for both of them. He would need to start making more of an effort. He sighed at the weight of the realisation.

Standing before her door in the brightly lit hall he became aware of a feeling of awkwardness, as if the easy camaraderie of their relationship would be tested by this change, by her being the hostess and him the visitor. By the fact she was familiar with this place and he wasn't. When he rang the bell she opened the door almost immediately.

'Did you check the spyhole?' asked Trevor. He had wanted her to live in a more secure block, one with video security and an entry phone. Felice had told him he was being ridiculous, that London wasn't an unsafe place to live. Anyway, she liked this flat and even if she didn't, she couldn't afford anything else.

'Da-ad,' she said, drawing the word into two long syllables like she did when she thought he was being overprotective.

He shrugged. 'I can't help it. There were riots here, you know.'

'Yes, I know, but I wasn't living here then and it's all been quite calm since I moved in. Anyway, there were riots in Brixton when you lived there.'

'Indeed, and they were one of the reasons we decided to move out of London. We didn't want to raise a family in an environment like that.' Trevor looked at his daughter sternly, but he knew nothing he said would sway her. She'd always had her own mind and there was no good trying to change it now. He'd learned over the years which battles were worth fighting and which weren't and this one was a lost cause. He had to start trusting her judgement.

Inside, the flat was tastefully decorated. Felice had a flair for colour and lighting. Trevor was taken by how different her taste was from her mother's. Frostie went for three-piece suites in floral fabrics, muted colours, a clutter of ornaments and photos on every surface. Felice tended towards the minimalist – a few bright, textured cushions on the navy sofa, pictures on the walls, lamps rather than a central light, no clutter. Just the one photo on the mantelpiece of her and her parents, taken the day she'd received her university offer, their faces full of joy and pride and anticipation. Trevor picked it up, ran a finger along his wife's face and put it down again with a sigh. He hoped Felice hadn't seen; he didn't want his daughter to know how lonely he was.

'Drink?' she asked.

'I'd walk to India and back for a decent cup of tea.' He rubbed his hands together.

Felice laughed. 'You and your tea, Dad. I meant a glass of wine or a gin and tonic. But tea it shall be.'

Gin and tonic. His daughter was so sophisticated these days. That's probably what working in an advertising agency did to you. He felt the tug of another apron string releasing. Those strings did that one by one he'd found, as Felice grew up and needed him less and less, made her own way in the world, started living a life that wasn't the mirror of his.

While Felice made the tea in the tiny kitchen, Trevor looked at the pictures on the wall. One in particular drew him. It was a black-and-white photograph of an old man, his face wrinkled and weathered by a life lived outdoors. There was a faraway look in his eyes as if he was thinking not of the photographer, or even the present moment. There was a shadow over half his face making him look wistful, not quite sad. His jacket was worn, threadbare round the collar, his jumper frayed. In the background were fishing boats. What made Trevor linger over it was the sense of calm he felt, as if the old man was reaching out to him and reminding him that life was all right. Next to the portrait was another photograph, also in black and white, of a pair of hands, the gnarled, weather-cracked fingers interlinked, resting on a stained wooden table.

'They're amazing, aren't they?' Felice nodded at the pictures as she came in with two mugs of tea. 'Liam took them in Portugal when we were there last year. They're of a fisherman we met in this tiny village in the north.'

Trevor raised his eyebrows. 'I didn't know he went to Portugal with you.'

Felice settled herself on the sofa and motioned to her father to take the chair. 'We weren't an item then, just friends. Six of us went.'

'I knew you went with friends, I just didn't know he was one of them.' He sat, the mug of tea burning his hands. 'So, how long have you been "an item"?' *And why haven't you told me about him*, he wanted to ask. When had she started shutting him out?

'Since that trip. We've known each other since first year at university, but that trip changed everything.'

'I thought you said you met him at a party.'

'I did, in Oxford. He was at Keble, I was down the road at Wadham. There were always parties.'

Trevor considered that for a moment. The boy had been at Oxford. He must have been okay then, not suffering from a mental illness or taking too many drugs. He wasn't naïve enough to believe that any teenager these days was entirely straight.

'What did he study?'

'Politics, philosophy and economics. He got a first. He's very bright.'

'So what happened?'

'What do you mean, what happened? He finished his degree, realised he didn't want to do any job available to someone with those skills and decided to do what he loves. He's at LCC now.'

Trevor realised he must have looked blank because Felice went on, 'The London College of Communication. Doing photography. Or did you mean, what happened to make him end up in hospital?'

Trevor looked down at his feet, the scuffed shoes, mismatched socks he only now noticed. He didn't know what he meant by the question. He wanted to know everything and nothing about this boy, Liam; why she loved him and whether he deserved her love in return, why he felt so jealous. Trevor knew his relationship with his daughter would never be the same again, that the special place he had held in her heart now belonged to another. He took a deep breath to let the pain of that realisation pass. When he looked up, Felice was staring at him with such softness his throat constricted and his eyes stung with unshed tears.

'Are you okay, Dad?'

He suddenly felt very tired. All he wanted was to lie down and sleep, and wake up five years ago, before Felice had left to go to university, before Frostie had become ill.

'Your grandparents have made a will. You are to receive everything when they die, being the only grandchild. I had a meeting with them this morning. They wanted you to know. I don't know why they didn't tell you themselves.' It was easier to talk about trusts and wills than it was to think about the loss of his daughter.

Felice had sat straighter and looked shocked. Whether it was because of the abrupt change of topic or what Trevor had actually said, he didn't know.

'Wow, I always thought I might get something in their will, but I imagined they'd leave most of it to charity or the church.'

'Apparently not. You will be an heiress. I don't think there's much cash, but the house must be worth quite a bit. What does Liam do for money?'

'He doesn't live off me, if that's what you're thinking, and he won't want to fritter away my inheritance. He gets a bit from his parents and he works in a photography shop a couple of days a week, photographs the occasional wedding. He lives in a dive with four others, so the rent is low. He gets by.'

Trevor imagined a dope den. Five young men spending their time getting stoned day in, day out.

'Look, Dad, I know what you're thinking, but give him a chance, please. For me. I think you'll like him when you get to know him.'

Trevor didn't know anything anymore. He'd been so proud when Felice had been offered her place at Oxford. His main worry was that she'd meet a toffee-nosed type who looked down on her family. He couldn't have imagined that not only would the boy she fell in love with be from a wealthy family but he would also be mad. No one expected such a thing, surely.

'Just tell me what happened.' He had to know. He didn't want to like this boy. He didn't want anything bad to happen to him, he just wanted him gone from his daughter's life.

'He wants to tell you himself, and it'll be better coming from him.'

A silence lengthened into the shadows of the room. Trevor considered leaving, running back to Milton Keynes, but he couldn't outrun the future.

He drank his tea slowly, as if by doing so he could slow time down. Felice talked to him as she prepared dinner in her tiny kitchen. He was perching on the edge of the sofa, watching her through the open door, trying to remember every detail of their time together, just the two of them.

He imagined himself at home later, thinking back to this time, calling it The Time Before. He had always divided his life into eras.

There wasn't much he wanted to remember from his childhood. His brothers were bullies and although he knew his mother loved him she was ineffectual, unable to intervene in what she must have known was happening. Perhaps she had been as scared of his brothers as he was. Or maybe she thought he should toughen up and deal with it himself. Well, he had dealt with it. He'd left.

At university there had been little fun and lots of hard work; as the first person in his family to finish school let alone go on to do a degree, he had something to prove. And his brothers were left behind, underemployed and feckless.

Teaching followed, and weekend bike rides. Drinking. Not too much usually, but sometimes a lot, to dull the ache of loneliness. His university friends had marched into jobs all over the British Isles and he had ended up a token black teacher in a white neighbourhood and no one asked him to dinner.

Then he'd met Frostie. He thought of meeting her as the beginning of his real life, the life he'd been preparing for. His mother had recently died of a brain tumour and he had volunteered to help at a fundraising event for a cancer charity. He'd been selling raffle tickets at the door and Frostie – she introduced herself as Veronica – had been taking coats. He knew as soon as he heard her voice and looked into her eyes that she was the one for him.

Theirs was true love. He'd rush home to spend long evenings with Frostie cooking, eating, talking, going to movies, seeing friends, having picnics, bike rides. All the things that matter so much more when there are two people instead of one. And they made love, oh, how they made love. Black and white and white and black in the kitchen, on the sofa, in the bath, behind the shed where the hydrangeas offered privacy from nosy neighbours, in their bed, beside their bed, and, when Frostie was heavy with their soon-to-be-born daughter, in the nursery.

With Felice's birth he felt a sense of completion. Now he had his own family to love and protect. The joy he felt was marred only by the anxiety he wasn't equal to the task.

When Frostie became ill he couldn't shake the belief that somehow he had failed her. If he'd been a better husband she wouldn't have got sick, wouldn't have died.

After his wife's death there was Felice. Only Felice. His one joy, his one success. He loved her fiercely but she was already away at university. He still taught at the local high school but with Frostie and Felice gone he had nothing left in his heart for the children nor his subject. He knew he was letting the students down, they deserved more, and yet he had no reserves to draw on; he was barely managing to get out of bed each day.

So what should he do now she was living her own life, a life of her choosing, a life and a partner he may not approve of? Yes, tonight was the cusp and he couldn't see what lay beyond.

'Dad – did you hear me?'

He lifted his head. 'Sorry, what did you say?'

His daughter smiled at him. 'Honestly, Dad, you live too much in your head. You ought to get out more. I asked you to open the wine.'

'Open the wine? But he's not here yet.'

Felice handed him a bottle and a corkscrew. 'It's red, needs to breathe.'

Since when had she known red wine needed to breathe? And when had she been able to afford a wine to which breathing made enough difference to notice? He shrugged and did as he was told. 'You are so sophisticated these days,' he said, and smiled. She winked and blew him a Hollywood kiss, then turned her back on him to attend to something in the kitchen.

'Felice, are you sure this is the boy for you?' He knew it was wrong to ask again but the question was out of his mouth before he could stop it. She looked at him with eyebrows raised, took a deep breath and was about to speak when the doorbell rang.

'Be nice,' she said to him as she took her apron off and ran her hands through her hair. As she passed him, Trevor noticed her face had softened. And he realised that if he wanted her to include him in her life with this boy, he had to make an effort.

Trevor stood as a tall, blond man came in, kissed Felice on the cheek and then turned towards him. His first impression was that he looked nothing like his father, the angular man with the abrasive manner. A point in his favour, as far as Trevor was concerned. He also noticed how Felice looked; like Frostie had when they fell in love – more alive, somehow, as if all the cells of her body were suddenly infused with the elixir of life and were straining to reach out to him, to this man, this Liam, whose cells were behaving in the same way. It was a moment so intimate

Trevor had to look away. His daughter and this man, they brightened each other.

He felt a small, sharp pain in his side and recognised it as envy. He'd had what they had and he wanted it again. The sense that the day was worth living because at the end of it you'd see the one you loved, that there was someone else out there in the world who thought you into existence during the day and was pleased to see the flesh-and-blood you when they got home.

He plastered a smile over his pain and shook Liam's hand. It felt like a damp fish in his firm grasp. Trevor put a cross in his ledger of Liam. A strong handshake was the mark of a decisive person and this Liam had produced a limp offering.

'Sit down, you two, I'll get the wine,' said Felice. Trevor noticed her voice was strained through her anxiety and wondered if Liam knew her well enough to notice.

'Not for me, thanks, Felice.' In his mouth her name sounded like Fliss. Was it an endearment or an attempt to make it sound more English? Either way, Trevor didn't like it. He'd always loved her name. He and Frostie had taken almost the whole six weeks they were allowed before registering her birth, just to make sure it was exactly right for her. They sang it to her, said it to each other, wrote it down with fancy embellishments and in square capital letters. And they agreed it was the most beautiful name in the world for the most beautiful girl in the universe. Fliss sounded like a waitress or something you cleaned your teeth with. Another cross.

'So, Liam,' said Trevor, and stopped. He couldn't ask the thing he most wanted to know: *How did you get sick and are you going to go in and out of madness all your life?* Which shorthand for *Will you weigh my daughter down, or lift her up?*

'Mr Jackson, it's so good to meet you at last. I'm sorry about my father earlier – Fliss phoned and told me what happened.'

He spoke like he couldn't move his tongue very well, so his

vowels were flat and his consonants too soft. Trevor wondered if it was the drugs or if he always sounded like that. He didn't like this boy apologising for his father either. Mr Lawrence Kelly was, undoubtedly, racist, but he had only been doing what Trevor himself wanted to do – keep these two apart. They were allies, of a sort. He decided to ignore the comment.

'Tell me, Liam, what it is you do?'

'I'm studying photography and working in a photographic shop. I hope to be a freelance nature photographer but I'll do weddings and other things too – the bread-and-butter stuff.'

'I already told you that, Dad,' said Felice from the kitchen.

'So you did, Sweetpea, so you did.' Trevor wondered if Liam ever called her Sweetpea or Starlight, or any of the other names he had for her. He drummed his fingers on the table, unable to think of anything else to say.

'Ta-da!' said Felice, setting a casserole dish down on the table and going back to the kitchen to collect a salad. 'Let's eat.' She looked at him and then at Liam. Trevor suddenly had no appetite and no energy for this dinner. It didn't matter whether he liked this boy or not, or if he was sane or mad, rich or poor. His daughter had made her choice, just as he and Frostie had done all those years ago and there were plenty of people telling them they were making a mistake. He loved his daughter and had to try and trust she knew what she was doing. *What goes around comes around*, he thought, and almost laughed.

'It smells good.' He managed a smile.

Liam nodded and took a deep breath. 'Fliss is a great cook.'

Trevor knew that. He didn't need this stakki boy to tell him. He bit his lip to stop himself from saying anything. This Liam was a hard boy to like. Or was it that his own prejudice was too great an obstacle to see past?

Liam looked at him. 'I'm sure you want to know why I'm in hospital and what will happen in the future. I would, I suspect, if

I were in your shoes.' He looked into Felice's eyes as if for support.

'Yes.' Trevor didn't trust himself to say anything more.

'I am ashamed to say it was all my own fault. After university I was rather rudderless. I'd done a course I loved but it led to nothing I wanted to do. My father was pressuring me into making decisions about a career. He wanted me to go into law, like him, and I suppose I rebelled. I drank too much and smoked too much weed – marijuana–'

'I know what weed is.'

'Of course.' Liam nodded but didn't look Trevor in the eye. 'It went on for a few weeks. When Fliss' – he looked at her and took her hand in a gesture that was reassurance and apology – 'and my friends tried to stop me I felt they didn't understand, that they were against me somehow, so I smoked more. I had a psychotic episode and was sectioned. I realise now how stupid I was and my doctor reckons that as long as I stay off the weed, it'll never happen again.'

'And can you – stay off the weed, I mean?' asked Trevor.

Felice gasped and he realised he had sounded aggressive but he had to know.

'Yes, sir,' said Liam. 'I wouldn't want to go through it all again, for my sake or Fliss's.' He looked at her and smiled.

Trevor felt angry. This Liam had been a self-indulgent fool. If it was only his life he was messing up, fine, but Trevor knew that even if he never smoked again, there were no guarantees he would stay well – his cousin back in Jamaica had never been the same after his first ganja-induced episode.

The evening didn't go well. Trevor would start to say something and hear the accusation in his voice – *you are not good enough for her* – and stop. Liam feigned interest in his half-statements but was defensive and didn't offer anything more of himself. Felice tried to introduce non-controversial topics but the air was so heavy with the things none of them were saying that the conversation fell between them and settled into a congealed mass that, in the end, none of them could find the energy to wade through.

Trevor made his excuses and left soon after nine, seeing the accusation in his daughter's eyes: *You didn't try.*

He shook Liam's wet-fish hand, tried to hug Felice, who stiffened in his arms, and went out into the night. Two young boys who should have been tucked up in bed were lighting cigarettes, shading the match with their hands, heads together. Trevor wanted to tell them to stop now, to go home and stay safe. But home wasn't always safe as well he knew, and anyway, who was he to tell anyone else what to do with their life?

He walked slowly towards the station, hands in his pockets, trying to breathe past the tightness in his throat and chest.

At Bank Station he changed from the Docklands Light Railway to the Tube and sat staring at the adverts without seeing them until he got off at Euston. He'd just missed the ten o'clock train, and now they were all slow, stopping at every station. He sighed. Nothing was going his way.

He heard himself, thinking the thoughts of a man defeated by life, and took a deep breath. That wasn't who he was. He had survived the bullying of his brothers, the death of his wife, the departure of his daughter. He was still alive, still healthy, still able to make choices. But he had behaved badly at Felice's and was ashamed. He would have to do better in future.

He pulled his phone out to text her and saw a notification from the *MK Citizen*, the local online news. He opened the app and scrolled down the list of headlines. And there it was.

Local woman dies in tragic circumstances.

He read on, intrigued to know more.

Judith Strasser, 43, of Stoke Hammond, took her own life today. Estate Agent and tireless fundraiser for an animal sanctuary in the local area, she will be missed by family, friends and colleagues.

Trevor bit his lips. Here she was, the woman who killed herself in front of the train. It had to be her, he knew the name – she had briefly joined the cycling club a few years back. Quiet woman. Frostie had thought she was lonely and made an effort to get to know her but she was very shy, didn't mix much and soon she stopped coming.

He took some deep, steadying breaths. He hadn't known Judith Strasser more than to nod a greeting to, or make small talk about the weather or the route they were cycling but he felt a sense of loss nonetheless. She had been a living person who had been sad or desperate enough to end her own life. What a terrible thing.

Walking towards the platform, he wondered what had prompted her to throw herself in front of the train that morning. Had she had a big heart that had broken? Life was so precious, and yet for some, so precarious. He wondered how her parents were coping. How did anyone cope with news like that? One minute you have a daughter, the next, she's gone, and in such a terrible way. No time to say goodbye, I'm sorry, I love you. No chance to put back the clock and make things right.

And he thought about his own daughter who was alive and happy. He loved her and was going do whatever was necessary to stay in her life. He wouldn't let his feelings about this Liam boy get in the way of his relationship with his daughter and any possible children they might have. He wanted to be the kind of granddad who had his grandkids for the weekend and took them on adventures, taught them to ride a bike, catch tadpoles, eat fish and chips in front of the telly. Because Frostie's parents had never really accepted him they'd never had the closeness with Felice they would have enjoyed. It saddened him to think of it now, the wasted opportunity for all of them. And Trevor's family hadn't been involved in Felice's life either, but for different reasons. They didn't care that he had married a white woman, they just didn't care, full stop.

He sat on a bench, pulled out his phone and wrote a text.

So sorry for appalling behaviour this evening. Blame it on your old dad being jealous. Liam seems a nice boy. I'm sure we'll get on fine. I love you xxx

He hit send and sat watching the screen, willing it to light up with a response from his daughter.

With his spirits sinking, he boarded the train and found a seat in the surprisingly full carriage. Who'd have thought so many people were still out after ten on a weeknight?

Trevor set himself a goal: by the time the train reached Milton Keynes he would have a plan for the rest of his life. Or if not the rest of his life, because that was quite a big task, at least the first step on the way. Felice was right; he couldn't sit around waiting for life to happen to him, he had to do things to invite opportunities.

He stared out the window as London slipped by, lit by street lamps, car headlights, shop signs.

Number one, he was going to rejoin the cycle club. He hadn't been since Frostie got ill – time with her was too precious to go cycling, even though she encouraged him to continue. And after she'd died, he didn't want to have to talk to anyone about it so he'd avoided everyone who knew her.

Number two, he would go to the staff drinks on Fridays after school.

Number three, he'd sort out the allotment. He and Frostie used to love spending time there, growing vegetables, pottering about in the shed, 'Frostie's Castle' as he called it. Since she'd been gone he'd neglected it but perhaps it was time to go back. He'd been putting it off for far too long.

Number four –

He knew Felice wanted him to find a nice woman to go out with. She'd suggested online dating but Trevor knew he wouldn't do that. Was he ready to meet someone else? He remembered the feeling he'd had earlier when he saw Felice and Liam looking at each other. He wanted that. Frostie had made him promise he would find someone else. Until now, the idea had made him immeasurably sad because if he fell in love with another woman it would mean he had finally accepted she had gone. But perhaps it was time to let go, or try at least.

He sighed and looked up. A Chinese woman was sitting across the aisle, looking out the window, chin in her hand. She looked sad but not as sad as the man sitting opposite him who he now noticed had tears running down his cheeks from beneath the heavy frames of his glasses. Trevor felt in his pocket for his handkerchief but his hand came out empty.

'I was going to offer you a hanky, except I gave mine to a woman on the train this morning. Terrible thing it was – a suicide on the line and the lady was badly affected by it.'

The man looked at him. 'Sorry?'

Trevor indicated the tears on his face. 'Bad day?'

The man reddened and tugged a tissue out of his pocket. 'Bad day – yes,' he said quietly. He blew his nose and looked up. 'I was on the same train – awful thing to happen. Poor bloke.'

'It was a woman. A fairly young woman.'

The man shook his head sadly. 'It makes one's own problems seem insignificant, doesn't it – someone taking their own life?'

'Puts things into perspective, that's for sure. I'm Trevor, by the way.' He extended his hand.

The man shook it. 'Ray.'

'Well,' said Trevor, 'I can tell you the events of today have made me rethink my life and what I want out of it. A death can do that, can't it?' He wasn't just thinking of the woman who had suicided.

'I suppose you're right,' said Ray, then he looked down. Trevor took the hint.

The Chinese woman glanced over. 'I was on that train too. It's made me realise I have to embrace each day. Tell my parents I love them, fully commit to my girlfriend. Take pleasure in the little things.' She smiled, dropped her chin into her hand again and went back to looking out the window.

Sitting in his seat, he thought about what the woman had said. What were the things that made his life worth living? Grief was his companion these days, the loneliness, the aching sense that part of you has been amputated, the silence in the once laughter-filled house. Even the fact he referred to it as a house rather than a home was a telling fact. His daughter was what mattered now. He looked at his phone to see if she'd texted.

Nothing. He sucked in his bottom lip and clamped his teeth down on it, took a deep breath. Should he call her or send another text? No, he had to give her time to respond, to calm down, to forgive him for his rudeness.

With difficulty he turned his thoughts away from his daughter and spent the rest of the journey going over his plan for the future. The Time After.

When they got to Milton Keynes he said goodbye to Ray and Mei-Ling who were also getting off the train and walked with more of a purpose to his step than he'd felt for a long time.

He opened the front door and was about to call out he was home as he always had but this time he caught himself and said nothing as he hung his jacket on its hook next to his wife's and went into the kitchen for a glass of water. Sitting at the table, he took a long drink and wiped his mouth with the back of his hand. He wanted to tell his wife about his day and about the lady who killed herself, but he had a growing sense that if he continued speaking to his wife as if she was still there he'd never have room in his life for new friends. He didn't have to forget her, but he did have to let her go, as he was learning to let Felice go.

I feel so small and helpless in this world sometimes, he thought, and looked out the window at the dark shapes of the trees in the starlit garden. *But life is what you make it and I've got a few more years on this earth. If I don't want to be a sad old grump and a burden on my beautiful daughter, I'd better do something about it. If that woman's death has taught me anything, it's that life is precious.*

He jumped when his phone rang. Pulling it out of his pocket he saw Felice's picture on the screen and was about to hit accept when he paused. What if she was calling to tell him she had chosen Liam over him, that his behaviour had been so out of line she wanted nothing more to do with him? He took a deep breath and answered. He had to know one way or the other.

'Dad – it's me.'

'Starlight – sorry.' He felt his eyes water and held his breath.

'I just noticed your message. Did you get home okay?'

'Yes. I'm here now, safe and sound.'

'That's good. Come again soon, Dad, okay?'

Trevor let out a long, slow breath. 'Yes, Starlight, I will. Thank you.'

The Milton Keynes Bugle

Obituary of Judith Strasser

A well-known and highly regarded Milton Keynes businesswoman, Ms Judith Strasser, sadly took her own life last week. She had lived here for many years having been born and raised in Birmingham and attending Nottingham University from 1994 to 1997. She studied Psychology but made her career in property, becoming a successful estate agent in the area.

Ms Strasser never married and had no children but is survived by her mother, who still lives in Birmingham. Her colleagues were devastated at the news of her death, many saying they had enjoyed warm friendships with her over the years. None of them knew she was unhappy, let alone thinking of ending her life.

'She hid it well,' said Sharon Blyton who worked with Ms Strasser. 'She was always so good at finding people their dream home.'

Deidra Kelly, close friend of the deceased, says she is in shock. 'I saw her last week and she seemed fine. Just the same as usual. I can't believe it.'

Ms Strasser had volunteered at the local animal sanctuary since it opened in 2001. David Heath, a co-worker there, says she will be missed.

Her funeral will be held in the chapel at Crownhill Crematorium on Thursday, 11th May at 3pm.

No flowers. Donations to the Animal Sanctuary.

THE END

ACKNOWLEDGEMENTS

Novels take a long time to write and even longer to revise. When you spend so much time with a project, many other people become involved in the process!

I'd like to thank my husband, Neil, for being a willing ear and an honest critic, my writers group for keeping me on the straight and narrow, and my beta readers for providing food for thought in the revisions.

I also offer thanks to New Authors Collective, in particular Michael Cybulski and Sue Anderson for helping me on the path to publication.

Ian Skewis was a thoughtful and encouraging editor, and all the team at Bloodhound Books have been fantastic and made the journey a smooth and joyful experience.

A NOTE FROM THE PUBLISHER

Thank you for reading this book. If you enjoyed it please do consider leaving a review on Amazon to help others find it too.

We hate typos. All of our books have been rigorously edited and proofread, but sometimes mistakes do slip through. If you have spotted a typo, please do let us know and we can get it amended.

info@bloodhoundbooks.com

Made in the USA
Middletown, DE
20 September 2021

48662435R00170